THE INVISIBLE
BULLET

The Bond Street Poisoning Bureau

Magnum—Scientific Consultant.

THE INVISIBLE
BULLET

& OTHER STRANGE CASES OF
MAGNUM, SCIENTIFIC CONSULTANT

Max Rittenberg

COACHWHIP PUBLICATIONS

Greenville, Ohio

The Invisible Bullet & Other Strange Cases of Magnum,
Scientific Consultant, by Max Rittenberg
© 2016 Coachwhip Publications
Introduction © 2016 Mike Ashley

ISBN 1-61646-340-6
ISBN-13 978-1-61646-340-3

CoachwhipBooks.com

CONTENTS

MAX RITTENBERG:
THE FORGOTTEN PIONEER
OF THE SCIENTIFIC DETECTIVE

MIKE ASHLEY

TV programmes today such as *CSI* and *Silent Witness* place a huge emphasis on the use of forensic and scientific techniques and knowledge in the interpretation of a crime scene and its victims and how that data helps identify the perpetrator. These programmes have proved highly popular since the mid-1990s but the original scientific detective became a highly popular figure in fiction over a hundred years ago, in the first two decades of the twentieth century. This was undoubtedly prompted by the scientific experiments and observations of Sherlock Holmes—after all, he and Watson first meet in the laboratory of a hospital where Holmes is delighted at discovering a re-agent that will test for bloodstains. Several of the stories refer to Holmes's frequent "weird and often malodorous scientific experiments" and, in one story, "The Adventure of the Devil's Foot" (*The Strand Magazine*, December 1910—the date of this story is rather relevant), Holmes conducts the experiment on himself and Watson. Yet through the full canon Holmes does not use the results of his experimentations quite as much as you'd expect.

It was not until R. Austin Freeman brought Dr. John Thorndyke centre stage in *The Red Thumb Mark*, published at the end of November 1907, that the scientific detective really took off. Dr. Thorndyke never goes anywhere without his bag of forensic tools.

The emphasis on scientific analysis was made all the more prominent when Freeman produced a string of short stories featuring
Thorndyke starting with "The Blue Sequin" in *Pearson's Magazine*
for December 1908. The magazine illustrated the stories with
photographs of the evidence encouraging readers to spot the clues
themselves.

The Dr. Thorndyke stories were serialised in the United States
in *McClure's Magazine* starting in the May 1910 issue which means
that whilst he was the first scientific detective in Britain he already
had rivals in the United States. Luther Trant, a laboratory assistant with big ideas, had first appeared in "The Man in the Room"
in the May 1909 issue of the prestigious *Hampton's Magazine*. He
was the creation of Edwin Balmer and William B. MacHarg. Where
Trant differed from Thorndyke was that he was called a "psychological detective", though he was not in himself a psychologist. He
used scientific instruments to measure the reactions of people to a
series of set questions and from that deduced the guilty party. Nine
of the Trant stories were collected as *The Achievements of Luther
Trant* in April 1910, and were all variations on a theme with little
development.

From the same starting point, Arthur B. Reeve introduced Craig
Kennedy in "The Case of Helen Bond" in the December 1910 *Cosmopolitan*. This story is almost a rerun of "The Man in the Room",
but Reeve could see the potential of Kennedy, who was dubbed "the
Scientific Detective", and he rapidly developed the character,
using a wide variety of scientific tests to try and solve the crimes.
The first collection of Kennedy stories appeared as *The Silent Bullet* in February 1912.

Within a little over three years, and with a particular focus in
1910 (hence the relevance of "The Devil's Foot" experiment), the
British and American reading public became acquainted with the
full gamut of scientific and forensic analysis through Dr. Thorndyke, Luther Trant and Craig Kennedy. All three are well remem-
bered amongst aficionados of crime fiction. But, right in their midst
stepped an author who created both a true psychological detec-

tive—Dr. Xavier Wycherley—and an ingenious scientific detective—Magnum—and yet that author has unforgivably been all but forgotten. That author was Max Rittenberg.

* * *

"The Strange Cases of Dr. Xavier Wycherley, Mental Healer" began in Britain in *The London Magazine* for February 1911 and in America in *Blue Book Magazine* for June 1911. Unlike Trant and Kennedy, Wycherley uses no scientific apparatus to resolve his cases. He is revealed as a "mental healer", a specialist not on any register, but with sufficient wherewithal to travel the world either in research or treating exceptional cases. He has a London clinic, but is seldom there. In one story he states clearly, "I am not a detective, but a psychologist." In another he remarks that detective work was "distasteful to him unless it were to open out fresh experiences in the realm of the human mind." Thus, in "The Errand of Death", he uses his abilities to help a man convicted of murder to relive the events through hypnosis and identify the real killer. In "The Giant Sloth" the English police employ him to identify a murderer and his motive from a number of suspects. This is the closest he comes in the series to being a forensic psychologist. In "The Betrayer of Secrets" a leading London banker employs him to discover how confidential information is being leaked from the business and by whom.

Although none of the stories is supernatural, his investigations sometimes come close in his ability to apply a sixth sense or detect a mental aura. In the very first episode, "The Man Who Lived Again", Wycherley encounters a man called Chenieston who appears soulless. Somewhat in the manner of Sherlock Holmes, Wycherley is able to judge Chenieston's thoughts simply from his demeanour. He unveils Chenieston's boredom with the world, of chances missed, and of a wish to live his life again. Through progressive hypnotism Wycherley provides Chenieston with just that opportunity. In "The Sorcerer of Arjuzanx", Wycherley investigates a girl who appears to be possessed, leading to a battle of minds between Wycherley and his adversary. This is the closest Wycherley comes to being a *psychic* detective, though not an *occult* one.

In all of the stories, some but not all of which were reworked as *The Mind-Reader*, published by Appleton's in America in April 1913, Wycherley takes great pains to explain his methods and as a consequence some later newspaper printings of the stories referred to him as a "scientific detective".

Rittenberg would soon turn to a real scientific detective, Professor Magnum, a scientist who is consulted from time to time by various parties to resolve complicated crimes or unusual circumstances. In appearance and temperament, Magnum is not unlike Conan Doyle's Professor Challenger, with bushy red eyebrows, an unkempt beard, an explosive temper, and exuding self importance. He is assisted in his cases by the shy young Ivor Meredith, a superb chemical analyst who does most of the detailed work, leaving Magnum to use his mighty brain to resolve the cases.

As with the Dr. Wycherley series, the Magnum stories ran complete in America in *Blue Book* magazine whereas in Britain they started in *The London Magazine* but after only four stories switched first to *Pearson's Magazine* and then occasional appearances in *The Novel Magazine* and *Short Stories Illustrated*.

The first in *The London*, for October 1913, was "The Mystery of the Sevenoaks Tunnel" in which a man, recently heavily insured, is found dead having fallen from a railway carriage and been run over by a passing train. Mysteriously he had a phial in his pocket containing the antidote to sleeping sickness. The first story in *Blue Book*, also in the October 1913 issue, was "The Cyanogen Affair" in which a family believe they are being poisoned because they wake each day dizzy and nauseous. In the third tale, "The Bond Street Poisoning Bureau", Magnum's adversary is not unlike Dr Wycherley, a veritable mind-reader who claims to be a clairvoyant. "The Mystery of the Vanishing Gold", the fourth story in *The London*, but the fifth in *Blue Book*, was an impossible-crime story, where six large ingots of gold, conveyed across the capital, reach their destination considerably lighter than when they started.

There are a few other impossible crime stories in the series. "The Invisible Bullet" is the best in which a man is shot dead with two bullets in a gymnasium, with a policeman on the scene within seconds, but no perpetrator visible, no means of escape and no sign of the second bullet. "The Empty Flask" has a man killed by something evidently toxic but of which there is no evidence either following an autopsy or after an analysis of how it must have been administered. "Red Herrings" explains how a man can be kidnapped in broad daylight on a busy London street without anyone noticing. Perhaps most intriguing of all is "The Three Henry Clarks" in which three people with the same name die within hours of each other, apparently poisoned and yet their deaths are witnessed and there was no poison present.

Other stories have cryptic plots. In "The Secret Analysis" Meredith is kidnapped and Magnum has to deduce from minimal information where he is. Similarly, "The Message of the Tide" has a message in a bottle from a kidnapped man from which Magnum must trace his whereabouts.

None of the Magnum stories was collected in book-form, perhaps because Rittenberg did not have the time to rework them into an apparent novel-like format as he had with the Wycherley stories. As a consequence the series has all but been forgotten, as has its author. After the last story in the series, "The Message of the Tide", Rittenberg wrote only a few more stories and turned his attention to other matters. Even his two children were unaware of this series and of all of the many stories he wrote for the British and American popular fiction magazines.

* * *

So, who was Max Rittenberg?

He was born Max Mark Lion Rittenberg in Sydney, Australia, on 18 April 1880. His father, Benjamin (1848-1905), a merchant, was a Russian Jew who had been born in Walkowski, Lithuania, at that time part of the Russian Empire, and had emigrated to Australia in 1869, taking on Australian citizenship in 1878. The following year he married Lily Moss (1860-1934), an Australian by birth, of German-Jewish ancestry. The family moved to England when Max was about 7 or 8 and his father became a commercial agent in London.

The father was not especially successful and his wife took to travelling around Europe, supported, in all likelihood by her father who had made his fortune during the Australian Gold Rush at Ballarat. As a result young Max had a cosmopolitan upbringing which is reflected in his fiction. He wanted to be a doctor and had studied science and medicine at Caius College, Cambridge, but finances dictated otherwise and for a few years he served as a teacher at Swansea Grammar School. He enjoyed cycling holidays in the Alps, and was a good bridge and chess player, later setting chess puzzles for *Punch*.

Max's father died in March 1905 of tuberculosis. He had been in a sanatorium for five years and the cost had drained their dwindling resources. Max secured a teaching post in South Africa and he and his mother moved there, returning to Britain by late 1906. Despite his upbringing, perhaps even in reaction to it, Max had an ordered mind and an efficient approach to life and he was quick to comment upon the shortcomings of others. In February 1908 he had criticized the General Manager of the Central London Railway (known today as the Central Line on the Underground) for not taking full account of the temperature and humidity on the existing underground railway and the planned extensions and he provided details on how this could be overcome.

In January 1907 Rittenberg had launched the magazine *The Organizer* aimed at advising businesses how to operate more efficiently, which included not just reorganization but market surveys, public relations and developing a mail-order business. This was to be his primary work for the rest of his life. Many of his early books deal with business efficiency, such as *How to Compose Business Letters* (1909), *Everyone Has Something to Sell* (1910) and *Office Organisation. Buying, Selling & the Wholesale House* (1911). This last title was published by Harmsworth's, the publishing enterprise of Lord Northcliffe and it may have been this that brought

Rittenberg to the attention of Northcliffe. Certainly for the period up to and during the War, Northcliffe took an interest in the business organizer. Rittenberg found that, in order to remain peripatetic, writing and journalism were the most efficient way to operate and he became the science reporter for Northcliffe's *Daily Mail*.

I'm not sure exactly when he turned to writing fiction. There was a small spoof, "Suffragistes in Evidence", in the London newspaper *The Express* (29 October 1906), where he proposed the idea of granting female emancipists a separate Parliament and speculated on the consequences. He became astonishingly prolific. Between January 1911 and October 1915 barely a month passed when he did not have a story in at least one issue of the popular fiction magazines. He also became the editor of one, *The Lady's Realm*, though his role was anonymous and I am not entirely sure how long he served. This role, which I believe started in July 1911, may well have been on the strength of his recent book *What Editors Want: a reference book for every Free-Lance Writer*, published in 1910. I am not sure how long he remained as editor, but it was probably curtailed soon after the start of the First World War.

Rittenberg had poor eyesight so was unfit for service. He became involved with the Overseas League which had been founded by Sir Evelyn Wrench in 1910 to foster international friendship and understanding. It was while working for the League that he met his future wife, Daisy Minter, who worked as his secretary. In October 1916, with the support of Northcliffe, Rittenberg went to the United States for the League, partly to avoid the anti-German prejudice in Britain—at that time he had no intention of changing his name. Daisy followed about a year later and they were married in Baltimore in 1918.

After the War Rittenberg wanted to travel to Hollywood, but Daisy wished to return to Britain where Rittenberg settled into business life. In 1920 he established his own Advertising and Public Relations company, Max Rittenberg & Partners, and became highly respected in the business.

He continued to produce reference books for businesses: *Effective Postal Publicity* (1923), *How To Finance a Business*

(1923), and others, but there seemed to be no desire to write any more fiction. He had a family to raise, as well as a business to run. His daughter, Linda, was born in September 1920, and son David in November 1924. It was when warning signs of a second world war loomed in the 1930s that he gave thought to changing his name. He changed David's first, by deed-poll, in 1937 to Ritson, and then followed course in June 1940. He was known as Max Ritson ever after and it seemed that by then his crime-fiction career as Max Rittenberg had been completely eclipsed. He died on 15 January 1963, at Haverstock Hill in London, aged 82.

* * *

Coachwhip Publications has already reprinted *Dr. Xavier Wycherley, the Mind-Reader* as part of a "2 Detectives" double in 2011. At last, after over a century in the wilderness, it now presents the exploits of Magnum, the Scientific Consultant.

ACKNOWLEDGEMENTS

I would like to thank the help of Gene Christie and Richard Fidczuk in obtaining the texts of several of these stories, and I would also like to acknowledge the help of Max Rittenberg's daughter, Linda René-Martin, in providing much treasured memories of her father.

PUBLICATION DETAILS FOR THE STORIES

This lists in chronological order the first US and UK publication of each story reprinted here.

"The Mystery of the Sevenoaks Tunnel", *The London Magazine*, October 1913; *Blue Book*, November 1913 as "The Seven-Oaks Tunnel Enigma".

"The Cyanogen Affair", *Blue Book*, October 1913; *The London Magazine*, November 1913 as "The Queer Case of the Cyanogen Poisoning".

"The Bond Street Poisoning Bureau", *The London Magazine*, December 1913; *Blue Book*, December 1913 as "The Society Murder Bureau".

"The Secret of the Radium Maker", *Blue Book*, January 1914.

"The Mystery of the Vanishing Gold", *The London Magazine*, January 1914; *Blue Book*, February 1914 as "The Vanishing Gold".

"The Invisible Bullet", *Blue Book*, March 1914; *Pearson's Magazine*, April 1914.

"The Rough Fist of Reason", *Blue Book*, April 1914;
The Novel Magazine, April 1914.

"The Three Ends of a Thread", *Blue Book*, May 1914;
Short Stories Illustrated, July 25, 1914.

"The Empty Flask", *Blue Book*, June 1914 (reprinted
February 1944).

"The Secret Analysis", *Blue Book*, July 1914; *Short
Stories Illustrated*, July 11, 1914

"The Mystery of Box 218", *Blue Book*, August 1914;
Short Stories Illustrated, July 18, 1914 as "The Virgin Vault".

"The Secret of the Tower House", *Blue Book*, September 1914; *The Novel Magazine*, September 1914
as "The Hidden Menace".

"Dead Leaves", *Blue Book*, November 1914; *The
Novel Magazine*, April 1915.

"The Three Henry Clarks", *Blue Book*, December
1914.

"Red Herrings", *The Novel Magazine*, January 1915;
Blue Book, January 1915 as "The Disappearance of
Mr. Holsworthy".

"Cleansing Fire", *Blue Book*, February 1915.

"The Message of the Tide", *Blue Book*, March 1915.

THE MYSTERY OF THE SEVENOAKS TUNNEL

"What does it matter whether it were accident or suicide?" said Magnum into the telephone with decided irritation, because he was being interrupted in the midst of a highly complex calculation of a formula based on crystallographic angles and axes, requiring quaternions and perfect quiet.

"It matters fifty thousand pounds," replied the legal voice at the other end of the wire. "That's the value of his insurance policy. The company contend it was a case of suicide, and therefore the policy is null and void."

"At the present moment," snapped Magnum, "I don't care if he were insured for the National Debt! Find a detective, and don't bother *me!*"

Leaving the receiver off the hook, so that he could not be rung up further, Magnum plunged again into the world of $\sin \alpha$ and $\cos \beta$.

The interrupter was the junior partner in East, East, and Stacey, a young man of some pertinacity as well as legal ability. He happened to have a very special interest in the case of the deceased, because the next-of-kin was a particularly charming young lady; at least, particularly charming to himself. So he jumped into a taxi and drove from Clifford's Inn to Upper Thames Street, where the scientific consultant had his office and laboratories.

"The deuce!" was Magnum's welcome for him.

"Awfully sorry to interrupt. How long will you take to finish?" was the soft answer designed to turn away wrath.

"Till midnight!" snapped Magnum, hunching his bushy reddish eyebrows, and thrusting out his straggly reddish beard belligerently.

"I'll wait," decided Stacey. "I'll go and talk scandal with Meredith."

Ivor Meredith was a young Welshman, an analytical genius and Magnum's right-hand man. He was the very essence of shyness and modesty. Stacey went into the laboratories and began to chaff him in order to kill time.

"What's this I hear about you and a certain fascinating widow?" was his opening gambit.

Young Meredith, blushing furiously, protested that he didn't know any fascinating widow. Which was perfectly true, as he was mortally afraid of all the feminine sex.

In an hour's time Magnum appeared from his office. His crystallographic analysis had borne out his personal guess exactly, and the thundercloud temper had vanished from his skies. He found that his young Welsh protégé had scored off Stacey by challenging him to blow a glass bulb, which looks delightfully simple and in reality requires months of practice. Stacey, perspiring over the blow-lamp, was surrounded by a score of horrible bulbous monstrosities.

"Better stick to the law," smiled Magnum. "You can make a successful lawyer even if you have ten thumbs to your hands. Now what's this trouble about the insurance policy?"

Stacey answered him seriously with a résumé of the case. Abel Jonasson, a somewhat eccentric recluse, a man of fifty-four and a bachelor, had insured his life for fifty thousand pounds with the Empire Assurance Company six months previously. On a railway journey through the Sevenoaks tunnel, he had been alone in a second-class compartment. In some way he had fallen out of the moving train; had been killed possibly by the fall; and had certainly been run over by a train passing on the other line of metals. A coroner's jury had returned an open verdict. On the advice of their doctors and counsel, the Empire Company, a firm of first-class reputation, had decided to fight the claim up to the House of Lords if necessary.

They contended that, for a man of his limited income, a fifty thousand pound policy was far too heavy, unless he deliberately intended to take his life in order to secure a large sum of money for his relatives. Such cases had cropped up before.

"Then they shouldn't have insured for such a heavy amount," interrupted Magnum.

"Well, they did," answered Stacey. "They took his premium, and now they fight the claim. Miss Gerard, his niece and next-of-kin, has very slender means, and so—"

Something in Stacey's tone gave Magnum the clue to this unusual interest in a client of slender means.

"Another wedding-present to buy!" he interjected cynically.

Stacey took the remark on the half-volley, and flicked it neatly over the net:

"Help us, and we'll consider it as the wedding-present."

"I don't see that the case lies in my province. Try Scotland Yard."

"I have. No satisfaction. A scientist is wanted. Scotland Yard can't tell me why the dead man carried in his pocket a phial of atoxyl."

"Specific against sleeping sickness."

"A Central African disease. It's unknown in England. Why should he carry the antidote about with him?"

"Have his serum examined."

"That's been done. No trace of the disease has been found. But the Empire doctor claims that Jonasson must have *thought* he had the disease, and therefore committed suicide. A book on the subject was found at his country cottage. Our side will have to prove some other reason for his carrying that phial of atoxyl. That's one point on which I want your help."

Magnum pulled out a disgracefully malodorous pipe from his baggy, shapeless working-jacket, and proceeded to stuff it with a smoking mixture of his own blending, strong to the point of rankness.

Meredith hastened to their library above the office, and returned with one of the twenty bulky volumes of Watts's Dictionary of Chemistry. His chief took it, and turned thoughtfully to the half-column description of the chemical properties of the drug, one of the arsenic derivatives. Presently he remarked:

"Have you considered the possibility of foul play?"

"That was one of our first thoughts," returned Stacey. "But Jonasson was seen alone in the compartment at Tonbridge Junction, only five miles from the tunnel, and there were no traces on the footboard of anyone clambering along from one compartment to another."

"Windows?"

"All shut."

"A man under the seat?"

"No traces."

"When was the discovery made?"

"As soon as the train came out of the tunnel into Sevenoaks Station. The door of Jonasson's compartment was open, and banging to and fro . . . All the evidence goes to show that he was entirely alone in the compartment; that he opened the door himself—finger-prints on the handle—and fell out. We claim that he must have become suddenly frightened—he was a nervous old man—and that he lost his head, opened the door to call for help, and was thrown out by the rush of wind against the open door."

"Sounds very probable."

"The Empire Company say that if he wanted help he could have pulled the alarm-cord. There was no one else in the compartment—that's certain from the footprints in the dust. He had nothing to be afraid of, they claim."

"Equally plausible."

"Can you tell me why he carried that atoxyl with him?"

Magnum was not a man to confess openly to ignorance. He replied curtly:

"I'm not a theorist. Ask me *practical* questions."

For reply, Stacey produced from his pocket a blank manuscript-size envelope, and from the envelope a much-creased sheet of folded paper—blank.

"I found this in Jonasson's study while hunting for his will. I have a strong feeling that it contains a message written in invisible ink. Miss Gerard tells me that he was the kind of eccentric who would do that. Will you try to get the message out?"

"Suppose," asked Magnum shrewdly, "it were to say that he intended to commit suicide?"

"In that case," laughed the lawyer, "I shouldn't call you as a witness."

"You young scoundrel!"

"But it won't do that," answered Stacey, returning to seriousness. "Miss Gerard knew him well—he was very fond of her in his queer, angular way—and she is perfectly certain that he had no intention of committing suicide."

"If you prove wrong," warned Magnum, "don't count on me to keep silent in a case of fraud."

He passed the sheet of paper to Meredith, who examined it eagerly, his eyes alight at the thought of pitting his chemical knowledge against the secret of the apparently blank paper.

Meredith's first move was to cut the sheet into four quarters, so as to avoid the risk of spoiling the whole of it in the course of experimenting.

The heat test gave no result, nor did the iodide test, nor the sulphuretted hydrogen test.

Magnum, suspecting that they were in for a long session, looked at his watch, found it marking seven o'clock and sent out for three porterhouse steaks, a Stilton cheese and bread, and lager beer.

"I should prefer oysters, a fried sole, and a bottle of claret," suggested Stacey.

"You'll have what's good for you," retorted Magnum, who had unaesthetic views on food.

It was close on nine o'clock before Meredith at length triumphed. Fitting together three-quarters of the sheet of paper—the other quarter had become spoilt in the course of testing—the following wording stood out in roughly written capital letters:

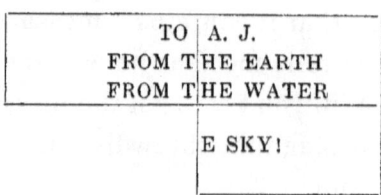

Magnum turned to Stacey.

"There's your wedding-present," said he grimly.

All Stacey's pose of flippancy had dropped from him. Staring at the paper, he asked, in a hushed voice:

"What does it mean?"

"A warning," returned Magnum. "A warning that must have put Jonasson's nerves on edge. In that railway compartment, alone, passing through the long Sevenoaks tunnel, something happened to terrify him into trying to escape."

"If we could prove it! But what exactly happened?"

"The last words of the warning were, judging on the first two lines, 'FROM THE SKY!'"

"Yes, yes!" cried Stacey eagerly.

"That railway-carriage—of course it's been sealed and shunted into a siding?"

"Naturally."

"To-morrow morning we'll go and examine it."

"Yes, but what's your theory?"

Magnum's temperament included a strong dash of human vanity. He liked to have his achievements bulk large. He liked to display his results against an effective background. Having arrived at a simple explanation of a puzzling mystery, he preferred to keep silent about it until the morning should bring the glowing moment for the revelation.

Stacey had to be content to wait.

The railway-carriage—possible evidence in a fifty thousand pound law-case—had been shunted into a goods yard of the Chatham and

South-Eastern, and housed in a shed under lock and key at the instigation of the insurance company.

A legal representative of the company, as well as a district goods manager of the Chatham and South-Eastern, accompanied Stacey and Magnum to the fresh inspection of it. The insurance lawyer—dry, thin-lipped, pince-nezed, cynically critical, abundantly sure of himself allowed a ghost of an acidulated smile to flicker around his eyes as he viewed Magnum's air of expectant triumph. The goods manager preserved an attitude of strict neutrality. Stacey was on a hair-trigger of expectation, masked under a pose of legal dignity and self-restraint.

The railway official broke the seals on the door of the compartment, and threw it open for Magnum's inspection. The latter's shrewd eyes darted about the interior, taking in every detail.

To all appearances, it was an entirely ordinary, humdrum, commonplace, second-class compartment, carrying no hint of tragedy. The dead man's ulster, umbrella, and traveling-bag, replaced on the rack in the position where they had first been found, merely suggested that some traveler had left them there while he went out to buy a journal at a bookstall. A small volume of Lamb's Essays, lying on a corner seat, might have been put there to secure his place.

Then Magnum asked to see the two adjoining compartments—one a smoker, one a general compartment. They were bare of extraneous objects and entirely unsuggestive.

"Well?" challenged the opposing lawyer, with his thin and acid smile. "Have you discovered some point we all have been dense enough to miss?"

"There are always two sides to every question," returned Magnum.

"Your side and my side?"

"The inside and the outside," amended Magnum, with a cutting edge to his words.

"And the application of that very sound maxim?"

"The application is that to view the outside one needs a ladder."

"And why a ladder, may I ask?"

"I am not a 'Child's Guide to Knowledge,' but if you are seriously anxious for an answer to your question, it is in order to climb." Having delivered this snub, Magnum turned, and addressed himself to the goods manager: "Please send for a short ladder, so that I can examine the roof."

When it arrived, Magnum mounted briskly to the roof of the carriage, and looked for the footprints or traces of a man having crawled over the roof, which he confidently expected to find. A grievous disappointment awaited him. The roof was streaked with raindrops trickling over soot, now dried into the semblance of a map of some fantastic mountain range. There were no footprints.

"Did it rain on the day of the accident?" he asked sharply.

Stacey, after a moment's thought, replied in the affirmative.

"Unfortunate," commented Magnum. "Rain would have obliterated footprints. Come up here."

At last Stacey understood what Magnum was driving at. "*From the sky!*" had been the concluding words of the warning to the dead man. Someone had crawled on the roof, pulled up the lamp over the compartment in which Jonasson was traveling, and then— In a flash he pictured the old man alone in the compartment, through the long tunnel, where a cry for help would be drowned in the roar of the rushing train, looking upwards to see a menacing face staring at him from the aperture of the lamp, a revolver at cock, and ready to shoot him down in any corner of the compartment. Trapped, helpless, terrified, Jonasson had tried to escape by the door, and had been thrown on to the line.

Magnum, moving forward over the roof, in plain view of the others, went to pull up the lamp and demonstrate his point, but a sentence from the railway official checked him in mid-action.

"You are thinking of the old type of lamp, sir. These ones are not removable. They're fixtures."

Magnum, incredulous, went on; found the lamp screwed in tight, and the screws rusted in firmly.

The insurance lawyer permitted himself a dry laugh of cynical amusement.

"Facts," said he, "have an unfortunate habit of contradicting the most ingenious and elegant theories."

When the ladder arrived Magnum mounted briskly to the roof of the carriage.

Magnum was now thoroughly roused by the mocking mystery of the railway compartment. He had, in plain words, made a fool of himself in front of the insurance lawyer. That was unbearable. The only way to get back his self-respect was to wrest out the secret, and flourish it in the lawyer's face.

Before, Magnum had been only half-heartedly interested in a problem which was somewhat outside his professional line; now, he was resolutely determined to work at it with a red-hot concentration of energies.

Hurrying to New Cross Station with Stacey, he took ticket to Paddock Wood, beyond Tonbridge, where Jonasson had lived his recluse life in a country cottage a couple of miles away from the railway line, alone save for a housekeeper-servant. On the way, Magnum plied Stacey with question after question regarding the life-history, the habits and eccentricities of the dead man. Stacey's information was limited; the housekeeper could tell much more.

On their arrival, they found the cottage bolted and barred. A hedger and ditcher, working in a neighboring lane, expressed the thoughtful opinion that the housekeeper must have locked up and gone away. Where? demanded Magnum, assisting his cerebrations with a couple of half-crowns. He didn't rightly know. Could he find out by asking neighbors? That struck the hedger as an idea of great brilliance, and, dropping his tools, he set off to make inquiries.

Meanwhile, Magnum, impatient of obstacles, broke a window in the cottage, and secured unconventional entrance. With Stacey's guidance, he went through the dead man's books and papers and personal possessions in search of a fresh light on the mystery.

Both were now firmly convinced that Jonasson had come to his death by foul play, or, more exactly, that he had been terrified out of the closed railway compartment by some human agency. Both were equally of the opinion that it was a matter of long-standing revenge, reaching back into the obscurities of Jonasson's past life.

But mere opinions would be poor weapons for a big law-case. They must have *facts*. They must find out whom, why, how. They must be prepared to prove in court how a man, indisputably alone in a railway-compartment, with closed doors, closed windows, and no aperture for human entrance, could be so terrified as to be driven out. In case of danger the first thought of any man would be to pull the alarm-chain running through from compartment to compartment. Why had Jonasson not done so?

A long search through books, papers, and clothes proved annoyingly inconclusive. Jonasson's tastes were evidently cultured and leisured. Whatever he might have been in his youth, in the immediate past he had been a trifler with books, garden, and fishing. That gave them no help.

In the bedroom of the dead man, Magnum on a sudden impulse threw up the window. Outside it, he was surprised to find a screen of fine-meshed wire netting.

"Why this?" he asked of Stacey.

"To keep out summer insects, I should imagine."

Magnum suddenly became very thoughtful, hunching his bushy eyebrows and twisting at his straggly beard.

The hedger and ditcher, beaming with pride at the success of his detective work, came to announce that the housekeeper had gone to visit a married daughter living at Tonbridge.

"We'll go there at once," said Magnum; "and the first question to ask her is why Jonasson put up that wire netting."

Stacey looked at him questioningly.

"The loaded revolver he kept in his bedroom," pursued Magnum, "is nothing out of the ordinary for a nervous man living in a lonely country cottage. But the wire screen is highly unusual. The unusual is worth analysis."

An hour later, they were at Tonbridge. Mrs. Pritchett was readily found in the parlour above her daughter's confectionery shop in the High Street—a time-worn, grey-haired, grey-minded woman, resigned to the arrows of misfortune, dull of speech, with that love for irrelevant, side-track detail which goes so often with one of limited interests and narrow outlook. Magnum, with his impatience of slowness, found his temper distinctly tried during his endeavors to get relevant answers to his pointed questions. In essence, her information amounted to this:

Jonasson had had the wire screen fixed up six months previ-ously. He was a very reserved man, liking to give orders without giving reasons. It was in wintertime, so that there was no reason to guard against wasps, gnats, or mosquitoes. No; she had no idea why he wanted it, but he was very concerned about having it put up at once.

"At once?" questioned Magnum, seizing on the suggestiveness of the phrase.

It was directly after he received a visit from the dark gentle-man with the gold-rimmed spectacles. High words had passed be-tween them. No; she had no idea who he was. Mr. Jonasson was very reserved, keeping his affairs entirely to himself. The dark gentleman was a foreigner—he looked like a half-caste. He was seen in the neighborhood of Paddock Wood three months later. She believed that this man must have tried to murder Mr. Jonasson in the train. She was convinced that he was hiding under the seat of the compartment.

"That has been proved impossible," put in Stacey.

Mrs. Pritchett was of the opinion that nothing was impossible to a foreigner.

Regarding the past life of the dead man, her information was mostly conjecture, embroidered fantastically after the fashion of country gossip. The only definite fact was that he had gone to Africa as a young man. The name "Uganda" persisted in her memory. At one time he had kept souvenirs of Africa in his study, but some years back he had made a clean sweep of them, burning them in a bonfire at the end of the garden.

Letters? When Mr. Jonasson received letters, he usually burnt them. No, indeed, she never pried into his private papers! She hoped she knew her place! No; she didn't listen to the conversa-tion between Mr. Jonasson and the foreigner. She couldn't help hearing that they were angry with one another, but to suggest that she would stoop to listen at a keyhole—

"If you had," retorted Magnum impatiently, "Mr. Jonasson might be alive to-day."

Mrs. Pritchett relapsed into the easy tears of old age, and it took all Stacey's efforts to comfort her.

"You'll be saying next as it was me as murdered him!" she cried accusingly at Magnum.

He offered a sovereign as consolation for wounded feelings, and the interview proceeded. But no further information of importance resulted.

Magnum and Stacey returned to town. The scientist chose an empty second-class compartment of the same type as the mystery carriage, and asked Stacey to leave him there alone during the journey.

At Cannon Street, when Stacey went to rejoin his friend, he found Magnum glowing with excitement.

"I think we've got it!" he cried, slapping Stacey on the shoulder with a lusty thump. "First set your detectives on the hunt for that half-caste with the gold-rimmed spectacles."

"Yes, I'd settled to do that," returned the young lawyer; "but even if we find him, it doesn't help much for our side of the case. Assume that he threatened to murder Jonasson—assume that Jonasson was in deadly terror of him—assume that he travelled in the next compartment to Jonasson. Even then the Empire Company would claim that the deceased threw himself out of the train—suicide while temporarily insane, but still *suicide*. The fifty thousand pound policy money will never come to Miss Gerard unless we can show the court *how* Jonasson was terrified out of an empty compartment."

"I believe I can do it," returned Magnum emphatically. "The phial of atoxyl carried in his pocket, the book on sleeping sickness, the wire screen to his bedroom window, Uganda the home of the tsetse fly—they fit together like the pieces of a jig-saw puzzle. One more piece in place, and the whole pattern would stand out. To-morrow we'll search that sealed compartment once again."

"In the presence of the Empire's lawyer?"

"Naturally. Arrange it for the afternoon. And if I can show him that Magnum is not quite the fool he imagines—"

As mentioned before, Magnum was not without a dash of very human vanity.

On the following afternoon, the same four were back in the shed where the mystery carriage stood mutely waiting to deliver up its secret. The insurance lawyer's acidulated smile was now fattened out to a mellow tolerance. He was no longer afraid of any of Magnum's theories. The goods manager, while still outwardly neutral, had transferred his sympathies to the side of the Empire Company.

Although it was summer, Magnum wore a pair of thick gloves. In his side-pocket a packet bulged out noticeably.

"I want every inch of the compartment swept out," he said to the railway official. "Will you do it yourself, so as to avoid any suspicion that might arise if I were to do so?"

Tolerantly, the goods manager called for a carriage-cleaner's broom, and proceeded to the task, sweeping around the cornices, behind the cushions, and underneath the seats, and gathering the sweepings into a small pile, while the other three watched intently from outside.

"Stop!" called Magnum suddenly, his eyes alight with unsuppressed triumph. From the sweepings he picked up a large insect, dead, and displayed it emphatically in his gloved hand in front of the insurance lawyer.

"A tsetse fly!" he stated.

"Well; and what if it is?"

"The carrier of the sleeping sickness. Deadly. One sting from it, and a man would stand a poor chance."

"I don't follow your argument," objected the lawyer, with chilly impassiveness.

"That's what drove Jonasson to his death. That one, and perhaps a dozen others. The rest probably flew out of the open door in the Sevenoaks tunnel. This one was killed by him."

"Still, I don't follow you. How could your dozen tsetse flies enter a closed compartment?"

"Get inside, and I'll demonstrate!" snapped Magnum.

The lawyer, with a gesture of disbelief, entered the compartment, and the door was closed on him. Magnum immediately, proceeded to the smoking compartment alongside, lit himself a cigar, and then produced from his pocket the box which was causing the bulge. It contained a dozen live wasps, angry at their long imprisonment.

Magnum, standing on a seat, took out one of the buzzing insects with his heavily gloved fingers, and placed it in the tube of the alarm-chain passing from compartment to compartment. A few puffs from his cigar drove the insect to find escape through the further end of the tube. The other wasps quickly followed.

What then took place in the insurance lawyer's compartment would have been highly comic had it not been in demonstration of a tragedy.

Fighting with the furious insects, ruffled, disheveled, and wiped clear of cynical smiles, the lawyer made a hurried and undignified escape to the outside.

"And that," clinched Magnum, "was how Jonasson was sent to his death."

The murderer was never captured, and so the inner history of the tragic feud never came to light. But it became abundantly clear that the dead man had been fearing an attack by the tsetse fly; it was for that reason that he screened his bedroom window and carried in his pocket the drug which might counteract the terrible effects of the sting. No doubt the unknown murderer had threatened him with that particular form of revenge. Jonasson had insured his life heavily, either in the superstitious hope that it might avert death, or in order to leave his niece well provided for, or for both reasons.

The fact of importance which Magnum had demonstrated was the *method* by which Jonasson had been driven out of the railway-carriage. On that, the Empire Company compromised out of court for forty thousand pounds.

Magnum, who did not believe in hiding his light under a bushel, sent to Stacey's wedding-present table a neatly framed sheet of writing-paper with the wording: "To Mr. and Mrs. Stacey, forty thousand pounds, from Magnum."

THE QUEER CASE OF THE CYANOGEN POISONING

"Cost you five thousand!" snapped Magnum brusquely.

"Five thousand pounds for a consulting fee!" exclaimed his visitor in horror.

"No, not pounds—guineas."

"But that's preposterous!"

Magnum pointedly turned his back and called loudly through an open door into his range of private laboratories:

"Got that combustion analysis finished?"

From twenty yards away a diffident, almost inaudible voice murmured something about "only the weighing of the CO_2 bulbs."

"Hurry!" shouted Magnum, and then turned again to his prospective client with rather the air of a schoolmaster about to demonstrate an elementary proposition in geometry for the fifteenth time to a particularly dense dunderhead.

Magnum knew his own value as a scientific consultant, and had none of the usual scientist's modesty about him. His manner was brusque and rough-edged to the point of boorishness, and no one would have put up with such incivility had it not been for his infernal cleverness in his specialized field. In the City of London he stood as the undisputed head of his profession.

In age he was anywhere from forty-five to fifty; in appearance lean and wiry, and as hard as nails, with a straggling moustache and short beard of a sandy red, and a shock head of hair of the same tint. He acknowledged no front name—called and signed himself Magnum, *tout court*, like a peer or prince.

He was a bachelor, with a dwelling-place somewhere on the Plumstead Marshes, and he was possibly the only man in the City of London who went to and from business by way of the Thames, using a high-powered motor-launch, which he drove himself at a reckless rate amongst the crowded shipping of the lower river.

Turning to his visitor, Sir Julian Boyd, he sketched out the situation with a series of taps on the table from the horn spatula he held in his hand.

"You and your family are suffering from a mysterious form of poisoning. You've consulted doctors, and they can't place it. You've had the water analysed, the milk analysed, the whole of your food analysed. Nothing found wrong with them. Meanwhile, you're all tied up with these gastric pains—"

Sir Julian did at that moment wince and pass his hand feelingly over his ample lower waistcoat.

"And if you don't trace the source of the trouble, you'll soon be ordering your coffins. If it's not worth five thousand guineas to you to have the problem cleared up, you put a cheap value on your own and your family's life."

"But would you guarantee to solve the mystery?"

"If the problem's solvable, I solve it. If I take up your case, my *reputation's* at stake. What better guarantee could you have?" demanded Magnum truculently.

Sir Julian caved in before this brusque authoritativeness.

"Very well," said he. "I put the case in your hands."

Magnum passed him pen and ink.

"Cross the cheque to my bank—Coutts's," he replied, making it a business rule to get his fees in advance.

Sir Julian Boyd's town house occupied a most desirable position facing Hyde Park. It was one of the very few houses in Park Lane which are detached and surrounded by a garden. In the buying of it, he had had a spirited auction duel with a Cardiff colliery-owner, who also wanted the site for his town residence. Boyd, bringing up financial guns from the Kimberley diamond-field, had beaten him down, and erected a splendid mansion replete with every modern comfort (as the estate agents phrase it), including automatic electric lifts and the service arrangements of an ultra-modern hotel.

Magnum drove there in the evening with the young fellow whose diffident voice had answered something about "CO_2 bulbs." This young Welshman—Ivor Meredith, by name—was his chief's right hand. Magnum himself was the organizing brain and the commercial acumen of the firm, but he was too hasty of temperament to be fitted for the detailed work of scientific analysis, which requires the manual technique of a virtuoso pianist and the patience of a lace-worker. Magnum could think and originate and apply the world's scientific research to his own particular field in boldly new ways, but he would have been crippled without the help of a man such as Meredith, who was a genius at the analytical end.

The young fellow was very shy, very modest, very diffident—stammering and stuttering if he had to speak to a client, and blushing horribly if he had to make conversation with a woman. He looked up to Magnum as a master, a protector, and a being of immeasurable powers. Magnum would bully him for a whole day, and then wind up with a few words of shrewd praise which would completely outweigh the bullying. In his brusque, rough-edged way, Magnum loved the young fellow as an only son, and in his will had made over his whole possessions to him.

The taxi conveying them arrived at Sir Julian's house when the family—husband, wife, two grown-up daughters, and a nearly grown-up son—were at dinner.

"Ask Mr. Magnum to wait in the library for a quarter of an hour," said Boyd to his butler. "Give him the evening papers."

"Tell Sir Julian that I must see him *at once!*" said Magnum to the butler.

Boyd came to the library, dusting some breadcrumbs off his ample waistcoat, decidedly on his dignity at this ill-mannered interruption.

"What is this important matter?" he demanded.

"I want you and your family to leave the house now," returned Magnum authoritatively.

"We're in the middle of dinner!"

"I know. So much the better. Leave the meal as it is, and go off to some hotel."

"Unheard of!"

"But not impossible."

"You presume, sir!"

"When I take up a case, I expect a free hand. I want an empty house, left just as it is. The servants are to parade before me, and then go off at once. Your family are to follow, after they've made suitable packing arrangements."

"Leave the house empty?"

"Yes. You're insured against burglary, I suppose?"

"Of course."

"Then where's the difficulty?"

"It's unheard of."

"So is your poisoning problem. An unheard-of case requires unheard-of methods."

Sir Julian was impressed, in spite of his annoyance at being interrupted in the middle of a sacred meal.

"Leave for how long?" he asked.

"Say, a week. I may be able to solve the problem in a day, but it'll be safer to say a week."

"I'll consult with my wife," conceded Boyd; and presently returned with his wife and family, like a shepherd with his flock.

Young Boyd, tailing mutinously behind, eyed Magnum with considerable hostility, found the return gaze disconcerting, and switched his look of displeasure on to Meredith, who wilted under it.

Sir Julian made a cursory introduction of visitors to family, and Lady Boyd took the word, explaining symptoms and suspicions at great length. She was a thin, colorless little woman, with a thin, colorless voice that went tailing on interminably like a lump of insipid sweetstuff pulled out by a butter-cream machine. An ounce of fact served with her to make a whole soup-tureen of conversation. Distilling out the ounce of fact, it amounted to this:

Gastric pains, dizziness, and sick headache on awakening in the morning. Varied most erratically, being sometimes very severe and necessitating a day or two in bed, and at other times slight

Boyd came in, dusting some breadcrumbs off his ample waistcoat, decidedly on his dignity at this ill-mannered interruption. "What is this important matter?" he demanded.

and transitory. At the present time there was a lull. Next week it might be virulent again. Attacked all the members of the family, but none of the servants, with the one exception of the housekeeper. Applied only to the house; when they went elsewhere the trouble vanished.

"Then why not give up the house?" Magnum had interjected.

Young Boyd perked up at this suggestion, but indignation depicted itself on the countenances of Sir Julian and Lady Boyd. She explained lengthily that the idea was unthinkable. Continuing with the facts:

Analysts had given a clean bill of health to the water, the milk, and all the food examined. She had tried changing the milkman, the grocer, the greengrocer, and the baker. She had dismissed several of the servants. Still the disturbing symptoms continued.

"The wine?" queried Magnum.

It was all of well-known brands. Similarly with the liqueurs.

"Tea and coffee?"

Had also been analysed.

The two Misses Boyd began to eye the shy young Meredith. Seeing him blushing, they continued the ocular attack with minx-like maliciousness. He edged around behind Magnum, his pillar of protection.

The butler knocked and entered, to announce that the servants were now ready to depart. Magnum strode out to the hall, where they were lined up in strict order of precedence, beginning with the prim housekeeper and ending with the tweeny and the boot-boy. Each had his or her bag or package of clothes to take away. Magnum, impervious to hostile looks, went through every package, to make sure that nothing suspicious was being carried away from the house. Then he dismissed them, with the exception of the prim housekeeper, whom he wished to cross-examine.

Her symptoms, as she described them, corresponded closely to the family symptoms. She suspected that someone had a grudge against the family, and wanted to poison them all.

"Who?" demanded Magnum.

She would rather not say, sir.

"Speak out!" thundered Magnum.

Well, sir, the second housemaid had had a follower, a soldier, whom Lady Boyd disapproved of. She thought perhaps—

"Rubbish!" said Magnum contemptuously, and dismissed her.

The family went to make their own packing arrangements, and Sir Julian telephoned to a Piccadilly hotel to engage rooms and have a commissionaire sent to see to their trunks.

Meanwhile, Magnum's waiting taxi had been ticking up two-pences, with great satisfaction to the chauffeur. Magnum, who never bothered himself with details of that kind, now sent young Meredith with a handful of loose silver to settle the bill and bring in their own portmanteaus. He had prepared for their spending a week in the Park Lane house.

By eleven o'clock the mansion was empty save for Magnum and his assistant, left with a full set of keys.

They examined the house from cellar to roof, Magnum striding ahead and jingling the bunch of housekeeper's keys, Meredith following with eyes fixed more on his chief than on the articles examined. He was content to leave the thinking end of the work to Magnum, and let his own mind lie fallow until some definite analytical task was assigned to him.

They investigated pantries and cellars, gas supply, water supply, electric light and electric power arrangements. Magnum was naturally gifted with an inordinately keen sense of smell. In his early days, before he had started out as a scientific consultant, and was merely a university post-graduate student, he had written a monograph on odors. It roused no stir, because extremely few men could sense his minute distinctions, and the elaborate classification and terminology of smells which he had invented were of no general application.

It was no use explaining to the scientific world that tartrates and citrates and malates when burnt in a narrow glass tube gave out odors to be described and recognized respectively as paraligneous, acriligneous, and sesqui-sacchriligneous, because not one man in a thousand could appreciate the smell-meaning of those terms. As well ask a colour-blind person to appreciate the distinctions between purple and violet and lavender and mauve and heliotrope and wistaria and cornflower.

Nowadays, Magnum kept his specialized knowledge to himself, and used it for the purposes of his profession.

He employed his sense of smell on every food-substance in the house, including the remnants of the Boyd meal, which by his orders had been allowed to remain *in statu quo*. Meredith watched him with implicit faith in his powers of deduction, but Magnum frowned disgustedly as test after test gave him no clue to the mystery.

He had hoped to earn his five thousand guineas by a couple of hours' work, and then to spend a lazy week in the Boyd mansion for the sake of appearances, and to make Sir Julian feel that he was getting his money's worth.

Now the mystery seemed by no means simple. They might have to analyse hundreds of foods and drinks.

Magnum adjourned to the library, where he threw coals on to the dying fire, worked it up to a cheerful blaze, and drew up an armchair to the hearth in order to discuss the problem in comfort. Seeing Sir Julian's cigar-cabinet near, he helped himself to a brace of fat and moneyed-looking cigars. Meredith did not smoke; it made him ill.

"These analysts' certificates"—Magnum flourished a sheaf of papers given him by Sir Julian—"they look very pretty with the results taken out to seven significant figures. But what are they worth?"

The young Welshman studied them closely.

"I don't think I should like to trust to them altogether," was his diffident conclusion. "They seem to be routine work."

"They are. The usual humbug. Look at this item on the milk certificate: Other solids in solution, nought nought nought point nought nought four seven gramme.' *Other solids!*" His voice rang out contemptuously. "They might be the poisons of the Borgias, for all this fellow knows!"

"But wouldn't the servants be drinking the same milk as the family?"

"We have to eliminate everything that the servants eat and drink, because they don't get the symptoms. But that doesn't affect my point. Some poison might be dropped into the milk for the family table. We can't trust blindly to a humbug certificate."

"It seems to me that there may be months of work ahead of us," said Meredith mildly.

"We must find short cuts. That's my part of the work."

He began to pull furiously at the cigar, burying himself deep in thought.

An hour later he roused himself suddenly, found the patient Meredith dozing, and shook him awake.

"What did you make of the housekeeper?" demanded Magnum.

"I didn't notice her much," confessed the young fellow, who was afraid of all women.

"Booby!" growled Magnum, poked savagely at the fire, and returned to his thinking.

At three in the morning he gave up work, roused the again-dozing boy, and the two went up to their bedrooms.

Magnum woke out of a deep sleep in broad daylight. Usually he woke fresh as a country meadow, no matter what late hours he had been keeping. But now his head was buzzing, and he was feeling decidedly sick. Down below, sharp pains were gnawing at him.

"Splendid!" cried Magnum aloud.

They were the Boyd symptoms. He was right on the track of the mystery. No need to go through the tedious analysis of foods and drinks, because he had neither eaten nor drunk in the house. That eliminated a possible couple of months' work.

He had smoked two of Sir Julian's cigars. Was that the solution?

He rushed to Meredith's room and roused the sleeping boy.

"How are you feeling?" he demanded.

Meredith rubbed the sleep from his eyes.

"I feel very sick," he confessed.

"Excellent!"

"Why?"

"So do I. Head buzzing, and pains shooting about the interior. We've both got the symptoms. I was smoking Sir Julian's cigars last night. You were near me. You got my smoke. See it now?"

"I'm feeling very bad," said the young fellow dismally.

"Doesn't matter. Rouse yourself. Take a cold shower-bath. We must analyse those cigars. Hurry!" replied the relentless taskmaster.

They took a bundle of cigars to Magnum's private laboratories in the City, and started to work on the difficult analysis of the complex combustion products of tobacco. The case seemed clear now. Sir Julian smoked; so would young Boyd. Lady Boyd and the daughters would get the fumes.

But the housekeeper? Why was she attacked by the symptoms? That was the only fly in the deductional ointment. Was it possible that the prim housekeeper smoked her master's cigars on the sly?

For a whole day and the greater part of a night Magnum superintended impatiently the meticulously careful and painstaking work of his subordinate, lending a practical hand now and again, but leaving all delicate operations to the young Welshman. The result was perfect from the technical aspect. The higher alkaloids were neatly distilled off, separated and identified. But they revealed nothing unusual in the cigars.

By now the dizziness and internal pains had gradually worn off. Magnum, angry at the negative result of the analysis, took a couple of cigars of the same brand as before, smoked them furiously, and lay down to rest on an improvised couch in the laboratories.

When he awoke in the morning he swore vehemently. His head was quite clear. There were no internal pains. The cigars were innocent.

But if food, drink, and smokes could be eliminated from the mystery of the Boyd mansion, what in thunder was the cause of the sickness and pains?

The atmosphere of the library or bedrooms. That must be it. Something poisonous in the air of the house.

"Bring along globes for air samples!" he called to Meredith. And the latter obediently vacuumized a dozen large glass globes with air-tight taps, and packed them carefully in cotton-wool for transport to Park Lane.

Back at the Boyd house, deserted and looking horribly neglected with its litter in the dining-room and kitchen, its burnt-down fires, its unmade beds, and its still curtained windows, Magnum began to sniff atmospheres with a ferocious intensity of purpose, like a wolf scenting the wind. Nothing peculiar tanged his keen sense of smell. He then ordered Meredith to expose a couple of globes in the library, another in the dining-room, two others in the bedrooms they had occupied, and the rest in the bedrooms belonging to the family and to the housekeeper. They returned with their atmospheric booty to the laboratories in Upper Thames Street.

Magnum kept a show-office in Queen Victoria Street, near to the Mansion House, for the benefit of clients. When they entered it, they were invariably told by a solitary clerk that Mr. Magnum was away at his laboratories, or elsewhere. Then the client would be handed a card with a neat printed map, showing him how to get to the uninviting wilds of Upper Thames Street.

A very high, spiked wall, grimy from a hundred years of accumulated soot, enclosed on three sides the ground on which the laboratories had been built. The fourth side, fronting the street, was composed of some rough-and-ready offices in a chronic state of disorder; a huge, double-storeyed library of scientific literature, and garrets packed with reserves of experimental apparatus. In the back wall was a locked door leading to the waterside, where Magnum kept *Fifi*, his motor-launch.

Air analysis is a particularly tedious and trying procedure, and in this case there were twelve different samples to investigate. Magnum could barely keep his temper under control as, for three days on end, the young Welshman worked on them, one after another, with his meticulous carefulness, and in each case could only report: "Normal indoor air; no sign of anything unusual."

"Must be!" retorted Magnum. "Too small in quantity to trace this way. Get fresh samples and analyse on the J. J. Thomson method."

This is a highly delicate game, which involves the playing of cushion cannons with atoms far smaller than any microscope can detect. Meredith was one of the very few men who have mastered the technique of the game.

But the J. J. Thomson method yielded no result beyond what would happen with normal air.

Magnum was now thoroughly roused. Six days of trying work
had been wasted. If he did not solve the mystery inside the seven
days he had stipulated for, his reputation would be seriously damaged. Food and drink had been put out of court; cigars had been
proved innocent; air was found "not proven." Then what the blazes
could have produced the symptoms from which he and Meredith,
as well as the Boyd family, had so unmistakably suffered?

The two investigators went back to Park Lane.

"We must reconstruct that first night in the house," said Magnum, after he had examined the library and bedrooms, and been
exasperated by their mocking stare at his puzzlement. "We sat there
in armchairs, each side of the fire. We—I smoked two cigars. The
windows were exactly as they are now. The door—yes, the door was
closed."

He went to make up the fire, found the coal-box empty, and,
with Meredith by him, proceeded to the cellars in search of fresh
coal and kindling-wood. The coal-cellar was divided into three compartments.

"Low-grade stuff! That would be kitchen coal," said Magnum
decisively, pointing to the first compartment. "Now, why these
other two divisions? Ah, I see! Lady Boyd makes a rich woman's
economy by burning the best coal in her own living-rooms and
bedrooms, and giving an inferior grade for her servants' use."

Suddenly he wheeled round and slapped Meredith on the back
with startling force. "Got it!" he cried exultantly.

The young fellow rubbed his narrow shoulder feelingly as he
answered:

"I don't see what you mean."

"The coal! Something poisonous in the coal. We sat over the
fire for hours. So do the Boyds."

"But the housekeeper?" objected Meredith.

Magnum snatched up a lump from the third bin—a high-grade
Welsh anthracite coal—and hurried upstairs with it to the housekeeper's sitting-room. It was as he expected. The housekeeper, by
virtue of her exalted position in the hierarchy of servants, was
allowed to share the family's special coal.

"Now to collect samples, and take them to the laboratories for analysis!"

Magnum, having telephoned the following day to Sir Julian Boyd, received the family in the hall of the Park Lane mansion with the air of one to whom no secret of Nature is hidden. He had changed for the occasion into a respectably tidy suit of clothes, and carried no traces of his week's feverish day and night work.

"You have really and truly found out the mystery?" asked Lady Boyd.

"Yes, and the remedy."

"What is it?"

"Change your coal-dealer."

"Why?"

"The special coal you burn has been impregnated with a solution that gives off cyanogen gas when the coal's alight."

"Cyanide! You mean prussic acid?" ejaculated the startled Sir Julian.

"No; not cyanide—*cyanogen*," returned Magnum, with the impatience of the expert at a layman's ignorance.

"It's poisonous?"

"Yes, in sufficient quantity. Under the actual conditions of burning, only minute traces come out from the grate. The bulk of it goes up the chimney. When you sit close to the fire, you inhale those minute traces. Even air analysis wouldn't show the presence of cyanogen unless a sample were taken from in front of the burning fire. Even *I* couldn't smell it."

"But I've never heard of coal being poisonous!"

"Nor have I. This coal has been doctored by someone."

"Whose coal is it?" asked Sir Julian of his wife.

"It comes from the Pen-y-Clyd Colliery Company," answered Lady Boyd. "We have always dealt with them in London."

"But that's Llewellyn's colliery!" blazed out Sir Julian.

It was now Magnum's turn to be puzzled.

"Who's Llewellyn?" he demanded. "And where does he come in?"

"The man who tried to buy this land away from me at the auction sale. He wanted it for his own town house. Is it possible that
he would go so far as to try to poison myself and my family?"

"Everything's possible," returned Magnum. "But much more
likely that he wanted merely to drive you out of the house—get you
to sell it off. A very ingenious scheme."

"A very dastardly scheme, sir!" retorted Sir Julian.

"Well, that depends on the point of view. I was looking at the
scientific aspect," answered Magnum.

In his inner thoughts he was remembering that this Llewellyn
had completely mystified him—Magnum, the acknowledged head
of his profession—for six days and nights. For that he rather ad-
mired Llewellyn.

THE BOND STREET POISONING BUREAU

"It is possible to buy murder in Bond Street," said Detective-Inspector Callaghan, spacing out his words impressively.

"From whom?" asked Magnum the scientific consultant.

"'Kahmos' is what he calls himself."

"What's the difficulty in arresting him?"

Callaghan drew his chair closer.

"That's what I've come to consult you about. The man is a scoundrel of quite a remarkable kind. To begin with, he has undoubtedly the gift of mind-reading. If we've sent one, we've sent a dozen people—men and women—to sound him. He spotted every one of them for detectives."

"Were they regulars?"

"Four were regulars—the others were men and women from outside."

"Then on what grounds do you make your first statement?"

Callaghan lowered his voice, though in Magnum's private office there was no likelihood of eavesdroppers.

"At the present moment there is a lady of title in a certain private asylum in Sussex. Her history has been a very sad one. When too young to realize what it involved, she was married to a wealthy blackguard, and he made her life a hell. About a year ago she was drawn to consult Kahmos; and, in short, he advised poisoning the husband. She carried out his directions, and the remorse of it has driven her into insanity. . . . At the asylum all this has come to light. Of course, it's not legal evidence against Kahmos—it's merely

49

one of the indications we have. We've strong grounds for suspecting that he is doing to-day what Tofana, Cagliostro, and Nostra-
damus did in the past—run a society poisoning bureau. Ostensibly
he is a Bond Street crystal-gazer and clairvoyant. We could arrest
him as a fortuneteller and have him fined, but that's not worth
while. We want him on a big charge."

"You want me to devise a scientific way of getting him?"

"Yes; and if it's of any interest to you, the Commissioner asks
me to mention that there may be a knighthood as well as a heavy
consulting-fee waiting."

Magnum sniffed.

"I've no use for frills," said he.

"Very well, sir. I merely mentioned it."

"Sounds a dangerous business if you throw in that kind of in-
ducement."

"That won't deter *you*," returned Callaghan, with a shrewd
touch of flattery. "It might be dangerous if the affair were bungled,
because he'd be revengeful; but with a clean-cut job we put him
away for life."

"You want me as a battering-ram," was Magnum's dry comment.
"Not the post that a man of peace would choose."

"We want you as a scientific advisee," amended the detective.
"Frankly, this case needs something beyond the usual Yard methods. We've had his clients watched and shadowed; we've burgled
his rooms; we've arranged fake society troubles in order to trap
him. But he's damnably clever and cautious."

Magnum filled a rank-smelling, curved briar pipe with a strong
mixture of his own particular blending, lit up, and puffed in silence for some time.

"We live in a sentimental age," he remarked presently.

"Meaning that . . ."

"Meaning that in a rational age Scotland Yard would settle the
matter off-hand—take the fellow by the scruff of the neck and kick
him out of England. There's far too much flabby sentiment about
'England, the Home of Liberty.'"

"I agree," nodded Callaghan. "But Scotland Yard doesn't frame the law. We have to take it as it stands."

"Because of this flabby sentiment," continued Magnum contemptuously, "I'm to waste my brain-matter over a policeman's job."

"You'll be in good company, sir—Bertillon, Lombroso."

The scientist was human enough to be susceptible to judicious flattery.

"Very well," he conceded. "Go ahead and tell me all you know about Kahmos."

Magnum had a frank and robust scepticism of the power of "mind-reading." He did not deny its possibility—his attitude was rather that no plain, above-board, scientific proof had as yet been given to the world. He refused to believe on mere hearsay or the evidence of weak-minded, easily duped amateurs. He had once taken part in a scientific commission to investigate the question, and after six months' sifting of so-called "evidence" the result was his present attitude of mind.

Therefore he went to call on Kahmos without fear of having his inmost thoughts exposed to the psychometrist. Since it was quite likely that Kahmos would recognize such a well-known London man as the scientific consultant, Magnum attempted no disguise of name.

Kahmos occupied one of the most curious positions in London. It was a small, two-storeyed house of the Georgian period, in time-mellowed red brick, surrounded by a stone courtyard. On three sides reared up Bond Street shops and offices; at the back a very high wall fronted a quiet by-street of residential chambers. As a consequence, although the house could be overlooked, there was no possibility of anyone boring holes in party walls and overhearing, as there would have been had Kahmos occupied one of the usual flats or suites of offices. Doubtless he had chosen the position with that advantage in mind. The main ostensible entrance was in Bond Street itself, alongside a well-known picture-gallery, but there was also an inconspicuous door at the back, leading into the by-street.

Magnum was first shown into an anteroom, where a business-like young lady of foreign appearance sat at a secretarial desk with an engagement-book and telephone. The room was quietly papered with a cool green wallpaper, and furnished in rosewood. The young lady informed Magnum that Kahmos's time was so much in demand that it was necessary to make an appointment a couple of days ahead. He had expected that, and readily agreed.

Two days later he returned at the appointed hour, and was now shown into a second ante-room of a very distinctive nature. It was windowless, and hung on all sides with heavy velvet draperies of a deep blue—shot from peacock to ultramarine, according to the incidence of the light, which came from a single glow-lamp on the head of a large sphinx in pure white marble, at one end of the room. At the other end stood a brazier, from which thin fumes curled out in slow stateliness. A couch, heavily cushioned in the same deep blue, invited the visitor to rest and let his senses be seduced by the perfume from the brazier and the haunting atmosphere of mystery.

A concealed clock tolled out the hour with the deep, age-long notes of an Indian gong.

Ten minutes passed in complete silence. No sound from the outside world penetrated to that heavily curtained, windowless room. With a start, Magnum realized that his will-power was in some subtle way becoming weakened. He felt as though he would be content to lie amongst those soft cushions for ever and ever. His high-voltage energies were being tapped and drawn away.

Magnum, with his cold, scientific mind, attributed that marked lulling of the willpower to the effect of the perfume from the brazier. His keen scent had already told him that it contained some very unusual component. Reaching into his breast-pocket as though for a handkerchief—masking the significance of the movement in case he were being observed through some slit in the heavy draperies—the scientist contrived to open the top of a small vacuum flask, and take a sample of the perfumed air.

Another few moments passed without incident, while he strove to grip hold of his drugged will.

Then suddenly the velvet curtains parted at one side of the room, and revealed an open doorway into a further room hung with draperies of a brilliant flame-colour—not harsh or crude or jarring to the lulled senses, but rather uplifting, hope-inspiring, like the glory of full-flowering azaleas. It was a colour that breathed of glowing life, a colour that inspired one with confidence. At the side of the doorway stood a tall, well-built man, dressed in a plain dark European costume. He did not affect the usual crude impressiveness of flowing Oriental robes or a mask over the face, because his clients were men and women of the world, and needed a more subtle handling. He relied on the careful arrangement of colors in the two rooms, the drug from the brazier, and his own magnetic personality.

"Come in," he said gravely. "Come in, and I will tell you why you seek me."

The voice was well modulated, cultured—the voice of a man of breeding accustomed to the refinements of civilization. Magnum could well believe, according to the detective's account, that he was connected with a Spanish ducal house. There was no definitely foreign accent in his speech, but he enunciated his words with that careful spacing of one speaking an alien language.

Magnum, rising from the softnesses of the couch with a perceptible effort, obeyed, and took a seat pointed out to him at one side of a low table. On the table stood a crystal, covered by a cloth of black velvet; to one side was an electric standard lamp in burnished copper, of very graceful design. With his scientific exactness of observation, he noted that the wiring of the lamp apparently ran into the floor below—no wires trailed disharmoniously across the Persian rugs on the floor. In the background of the room was a large bureau and bookcase, also, curiously enough, fashioned of burnished copper. A few graceful ferns in copper bowls made foils to the glowing draperies on the walls.

Kahmos took a seat opposite to his client.

"Well?" asked Magnum, keeping his voice as strictly neutral and unsuggestive as possible.

"You are a scientist," answered the other, fixing his dark, heavily lashed eyes full upon him. "I should know that even if it were not given by the yellow stain of iodine on the little finger of your left hand. Science stamps itself on the aura of its earnest students with a cold whiteness. Every profession tinges the aura, but none so unmistakably as science. You have not come to me for advice or help. Your astral body does not reach out to me for aid. I see it close by your side—very cautious and reserved. You are endeavoring to sum me up. You think me a charlatan, but you are not sure. You would like to test me, for you doubt my powers, and it would afford you a certain scientific relish to prove me a charlatan. Very good; propose your own test, and if it comes within the scope of those powers which I have acquired during my long subjugation of the body and enloosenment of the soul, I will carry it out. I shall not hope to convince you entirely, because you have become engrained with the aspects of the material world. Your esoteric colour is a very hard reddish-brown, verging on mahogany."

"Clever patter," thought Magnum. Aloud he said: "I wanted your opinion on a certain scientific problem of mine."

"No!" cut in Kahmos sharply. "Do not attempt to mislead me."

"Prudent of him to keep off my own ground," thought Magnum. Aloud: "Very well; I won't press the point if it's outside your province. I've heard that you can read any sentence written on paper and sealed in an envelope. I'd like to test that, provided you leave the room while I write my sentence."

Kahmos went to the bureau and returned with pencil, paper, and envelope. These he handed to Magnum, and then withdrew.

It was the opportunity for which Magnum had been angling. Under pretence of guarding against trickery, his eyes darted about the room, seeking the point of attack for the forces of the law. Was it possible to get a man into this inmost room and concealed behind one of these draperies while Kahmos held his intimate conversations with his clients? No; out of the question. Eavesdropping via the roof? No; not practical. Then an inspiration flashed

"You are a scientist," said Kahmos, fixing his dark, heavily lashed eyes full upon him. "You have not come to me for help or advice. You are endeavouring to sum me up. You think me a charlatan, but you are not sure. You would like to test me, for you doubt my powers. Very good; propose your test."

upon the scientist. With the toe of his boot he pushed against the base of the electric standard lamp. As he expected, it remained firm—it was screwed to the floor. Excellent!

The rest of the proceedings, including the successful reading of the sentence in the sealed envelope, held no interest for him. He judged it a clever trick, but not worth puzzling one's brains over.

A fortnight later, the electric lighting in Kahmos's house suddenly went out of order. At unexpected and inconvenient moments the lights would grow dim, or become extinguished. It was highly annoying. He 'phoned up the electric lighting company and told them so.

One of Callaghan's men, placed in the office for the express purpose of hearing and answering that complaint, either by telephone or in person, declared to Kahmos that it was no fault of the company's main circuit. There were no complaints from houses adjoining his. There must be a flaw in his own house-wiring—a "short circuit" somewhere. Kahmos demanded that it be put right immediately.

Callaghan's man, in the ostensible role of an electrical engineering expert, accompanied by a genuine mechanic, proceeded to Kahmos's house with a full load of tools and electric equipment. After elaborate tests, he diagnosed the trouble as having occurred below the flooring of the inner sanctum, in the wires leading to the fixed standard lamp. It would be necessary to pull up the boarding.

Kahmos told them to do so, and as quickly as possible, so that his séances could be resumed without risk of the light going out. It was a lengthy business. When the police official and the mechanic were through, they left behind them under the floor below the table with the crystal a highly ingenious microphone, specially prepared for the purpose by Magnum. Acting as a telephone-receiver, it was connected to the ordinary electric light circuit, and could convey sounds out of the house through the minute variations it caused in the electric current.

In brief, there was now an unseen listener below Kahmos's consulting-table.

Callaghan engaged the top floor of a residential house in the by-street, and had telephone wires brought into it. While he or a subordinate sat listening to the consultations in Kahmos's sanctum, they could at the same time look down on the courtyard of his house and watch the ingoings and outgoings of clients.

Callaghan came to Magnum's office a few weeks later with the glint of battle in his eye.

"We've got the fellow!" he declared.

"In prison?"

"No, here." Callaghan opened his big fist, palm upwards, suggestively.

"Then mind he doesn't slip through your fingers," warned Magnum brusquely. He had a scientific dislike to hearing the counting of unhatched chickens.

Callaghan did not consider the warning worth attention. The affair now lay in his own province. He pursued:

"Your part of the work is through, sir, but I thought you would be interested to hear what's on foot, and, if you like, sit in the stalls to watch the last act of the drama."

"Meaning, the last act but one."

"That will be played off-stage," returned the detective, with grim allusiveness. He continued: "Two nights ago a young man who has dissipated a big fortune went to consult Kahmos for the third time. This young man has an uncle from whom he expects a heavy legacy. Needless to say, he has already mortgaged his expectations so far as anyone would lend on them. Now he wants to come into his legacy quickly. Kahmos showed him the way to do so."

"Then what are you waiting for?"

"For the last link of proof. As I told you in the first instance, we don't want a bungled job. We want a case that's solid from end to end. When that young man starts to poison off his uncle—"

"You'd wait for that?" interrupted Magnum incredulously.

"Certainly; there's no great danger. Kahmos explained to him that it has to be done very gradually, so as to give the appearance of slow illness. The first dose won't effect much. We've got a foot-man into the old man's house on watch."

"What is the poison?"

"That we don't know as yet. Kahmos gave him the stuff—we could tell from the interview as we heard over your 'phone arrange-ment—but, naturally, he didn't mention the name. When our man brings us in the coffee dregs, we'll turn them over to you to analyse."

It was not long before the latter part of the statement was ful-filled. Magnum's analysis—or, rather, the analysis as made by his right-hand laboratory man, Ivor Meredith—proved the presence of one of the higher alkaloids of the theobromine series, a drug with a depressive action on the heart. It is not an article of com-merce; it would have to be specially built up by one with an expert knowledge of organic chemistry. Magnum offered the opinion that Kahmos had not prepared it himself, but had obtained it from some confederate, possibly on the Continent.

Those details did not greatly concern Callaghan. His thoughts were now fixed on the handcuffing of the psychometrist. He looked at his watch.

"Eleven-thirty. We'll take him at lunch-time. He lunches regu-larly in a private room at the Restaurant Sevilla, not a hundred yards from his place of business. That will make a quiet job of it. I don't believe in 'sensational arrests.' 'Neat, but not gaudy,' is a professional motto of mine."

Magnum accompanied him—from other than motives of mere curiosity. He had a lurking feeling that the arrest might not be so simple and straightforward as the detective confidently expected; and if by any chance Kahmos should slip through the fingers of the law, and should know of Magnum's share in the attempt to trap him, it would create a highly uncomfortable situation for the scientist. For Kahmos was the kind of man to stick at nothing for revenge. Magnum was by no means a cowardly man, but he had a good stock of healthy, rational prudence. He wanted to make sure that the detective's staging of the penultimate act should be car-ried out to the prearranged "curtain."

At lunch-time that morning Kahmos did not take his customary meal at the Restaurant Sevilla. After a wait of nearly an hour, Callaghan 'phoned to the police observatory flat on the top floor of the residential house in the by-street. The answer came that Kahmos had not left his house, though the secretary had gone out to lunch at one o'clock, presumably to the popular café she was known to frequent.

Callaghan, after a moment's consideration, detailed one of his men to proceed there and keep watch on her, as a precautionary measure. Within ten minutes he learnt that she had not called at the café that day. A furrow deepened between the detective's eyes. He gave crisp, rapid-fire orders. The two entrances to Kahmos' house were to be quietly guarded while he himself and a trusted assistant went to make the arrest. Magnum was to proceed to the observatory flat and watch from there. A taxi was to wait in the by-street, in readiness to convey the prisoner to the police-station.

Detective-Inspector Callaghan and Sergeant Reece—the one tall, alert, briskly capable; the other a big, burly, powerfully muscled man dressed in civilian clothes, made their call at the courtyard entrance to the house of the psychometrist. The bell was answered by Kahmos' butler.

"Mr. Callaghan, is it not?" said the butler before the visitors had time to speak. "My master desired me to hand you this note."

He held out an envelope sealed with flame-colour wax—the colour which Kahmos had chosen for his inner sanctum, and had adopted as an expression of personality. Callaghan, without answering, ripped open the envelope.

> "My dear Sir," ran the message, "I much regret that an important engagement in the country prevents me from staying to receive you. I had to leave this morning. Pray excuse me. Kahmos."

This morning! Did that mockingly polite message mean that he had escaped in the guise of the girl secretary? It was quite possible.

On the other hand, it might be a "blind"—Kahmos might still be in the house, concealed in some secret biding-place.

Callaghan gripped hold of both possibilities.

"Arrest that man," said he, flashing a warrant. The sergeant carried out orders, taking his prisoner to the waiting taxi; and Callaghan went straight to the telephone on the secretarial desk, and sent instructions to headquarters to watch railway-stations and other likely resorts for Kahmos in the guise of a woman. Then he proceeded to organize a thorough search of the house.

It was a small, two-storeyed place, with cellars, but containing few rooms. They searched it with all the thoroughness and patient minuteness of Scotland Yard, tearing down draperies, tapping the walls behind for secret cupboards, pulling aside wardrobes and bureaus in order to search behind, taking up rugs and carpets for possible hiding-places under the flooring.

The search was fruitless.

"He got wind of us and escaped this morning," admitted the detective to Magnum, late that afternoon, with a curtness that rough-covered the annoyance he was feeling. "Here's the note he left for me."

Magnum examined it minutely, and then sniffed at the paper thoughtfully.

"Written in the inner rooms," he remarked. "It carries the fumes from the brazier."

"Probably got away in his woman secretary's clothes."

"And she?"

"Not in the house. Might have put on some fashionable clothes and left earlier in the morning as an ostensible client."

"Or *he* might have."

"No. He was heard over your 'phone arrangement up to twelve-thirty. The woman was reported leaving the house at one. That's how he went, d— him!"

"I'd like to examine the house myself," said Magnum.

"We've ransacked every corner."

"Still . . ."

"Then come and see for yourself."

Magnum's first action was to go to Kahmos' bedroom and turn out all his suits, sniffing at them like a hound on the scent of a quarry.

"If he changed into the girl's clothes, where is his working-suit?" asked Magnum. "It would reek with the fumes from the brazier."

Callaghan himself sniffed at the various coats and waistcoats. "Wouldn't this be the suit?"

"No—too faint," replied Magnum decisively.

"Then you think . . ."

"Find his working-suit, and I'll believe he escaped in the girl's dress. Otherwise, he's somewhere in the house."

Another long search ensued, without result. Finally, Magnum and Callaghan, the latter with a revolver ready for emergencies, proceeded to the ante-room, which was hung in blue draperies, now torn down and lying in confused heaps on the floor. The white marble sphinx stared at them with its inscrutable eyes. The brazier still sent out its fumes, more strongly than ever.

"What a reek!" exclaimed Callaghan. "It makes one dizzy. Let's get out of here!"

He moved to the door leading to the inner sanctum. It was firmly locked.

"It wasn't locked before!" exclaimed Callaghan sharply. He rushed to the door by which they had entered. That too was closed with a spring-lock.

"We're trapped!"

"He's inside the sphinx!" called Magnum with a sudden inspiration. "Quick, break it open!"

They rushed at the huge block of marble, trying to overturn it. It resisted their utmost efforts. The fumes of the brazier began to pour out more thickly than ever. Callaghan rushed desperately to the brazier in an effort to beat down the fumes. His only result was to fracture it and let the drug full out upon them.

They staggered back, coughing.

"Shoot through the lock!" cried Magnum.

The detective lurched dizzily towards the outer door, but Magnum snatched the revolver from him and fired blindly through the inner door. It might be heard by telephone.

They fell to the floor, unconscious.

Presently, from the base of the sphinx, a block of marble swung open and Kahmos appeared. He breathed through a miner's rescue-helmet connected with a small cylinder of compressed air. Quickly he stripped off the detective's clothes and changed into them. Some long-chance hope of being able to pass through the cordon in the guise of Callaghan was evidently in his mind.

But a pounding at the outer door cut short his preparations. Someone was trying to smash in the paneling. He picked up the revolver Magnum had discharged, five chambers still unused, and waited, crouching by the side of the unconscious detective.

The door burst open. The burly Reece was framed in the opening, and behind him another of the police force.

The situation stopped them on the threshold. Magnum and Callaghan lay crumpled up on the floor; Kahmos was holding the revolver against the detective's head. He could not speak because of the miner's helmet, but he quickly pointed with his left hand at the revolver, and then waved them away.

Reece understood that Callaghan was hostage.

"Get up!" called Reece, coughing at the fumes.

The helmet-eyes stared at him immovably. Set determination was in the poise of the body. If Reece moved across the threshold, Kahmos would blow out Callaghan's brains.

A terrible responsibility lay on the police-sergeant. He thought wildly for some moments.

"Give yourself up, and we'll let you out of the country," was his decision.

The open door had let in a sweep of fresh air into the drug-smothered room. Magnum, semi-unconscious, stirred to it, and his hand, reaching out, touched Kahmos' back.

Kahmos, with every nerve tensed up in this fight for freedom, judged it an attack from behind, and wheeled swiftly.

In that instant Reece saw his opportunity, and, risking his own life, rushed forward on the criminal. It was a quick, smashing struggle. A revolver-shot found Magnum's thigh, and in the next instant Reece was on the writhing Kahmos, battering at his helmet-protected face.

It was the helmet that hampered Kahmos. With eyes freed, he might have sent home the other four shots of his revolver. As it was, the twisted helmet obscured his sight. A second revolver-shot chipped marble off the head of the sphinx; he was overpowered, the weapon was captured.

In a few moments Kahmos the poison-merchant was in steel bracelets.

THE MYSTERY OF THE VANISHING GOLD

A two-horse lorry was moving sedately through the crowded traffic in Bishopsgate Street. It was a long dray, with low wooden sides, such as might be used for transporting barrels of beer. On the high front seat were a uniformed driver and his mate.

The point of interest was that the lorry contained six large ingots of dull yellow metal.

Magnum, the scientific consultant, and Ivor Meredith, his young assistant, happened to be gazing down from the upper window of a building in Bishopsgate Street—the ante-room to a client's office. "It looks like gold," remarked Meredith mildly.

"It is," returned Magnum; and with a quick mental calculation he summed up the value of the ingots. "Over two hundred thousand pounds' worth."

"I should have thought it a very dangerous way to carry gold about."

"No; the safest possible. Note those two men on either side of the road. They're Bank detectives. They watch the lorry from the docks to the Bank of England. The ingots are far too heavy for anyone to steal. There's no possibility of losing them on the way."

In a block of traffic the lorry came to a standstill for some moments. Passengers on the tops of motor-'buses looked down on the yellow ingots, open to anyone's inspection, and exchanged remarks of astonishment. Like Meredith, they did not realize that this apparently crude method of transporting gold had been decided upon by the keenest brains in the Bank of England.

65

"Suppose," mused Meredith, "that a gang of thieves had arranged to stop that lorry. They might overpower those two detectives and get them out of the way. The two men on the front seat
would know nothing of it. The thieves might—"

"Rubbish!" interrupted Magnum impatiently. "Imagine a man
staggering through Bishopsgate Street in broad daylight with a
quarter-ton ingot of gold in his arms! Might as well try to steal a
dead elephant!"

Meredith blushed and shrank into silence.

Three days later Magnum was called to the telephone in his office
at Upper Thames Street. "Yes, yes; this is Magnum. Confound that
buzzing! Exchange, d'you think I pay telephone rental in order to
listen to fantasias on the buzz-saw?"

"Sorry," murmured the exchange operator mechanically, as she
did about a hundred times a day, and replugged the connecting jack.

"That's better. Now don't cut me off ten seconds later. Give me
a chance to know who's speaking."

"Yes, the telephone service is disgraceful," said a quiet, dignified voice at the other end of the wire. "This is Sir Walter Symonds,
of the Bank of England. Will you do me the favor to come to my
office this morning for a consultation?"

"Is it urgent? I'm very busy."

"Extremely urgent, and it is a matter I cannot very well discuss
over the telephone. One never knows who may be listening."

"That's true," agreed Magnum. "Abominable service! I'll be with
you in half an hour."

Sir Walter Symonds, one of the directors of the Bank, made a
marked contrast to his visitor. The banker was quiet, leisured, and
courteously dignified under all circumstances. His white beard was
closely and neatly trimmed. Behind gold-rimmed spectacles were
mild, pleasant eyes. One could never imagine him in a hurry, whilst
Magnum suggested a continuous impatient mental bustle. The
world and its inhabitants were far too slow for Magnum.

After a few courteous commonplaces, Sir Walter entered on the
subject of the consultation.

"Three days ago, a consignment of gold from South Africa was unloaded at the East India Docks from the R.M.S. *Wicklow Castle*, and brought to the Bank by our usual method of transport, with which you are doubtless familiar."

"I saw it. Bishopsgate Street. Six ingots."

"Exactly. Now, it may seem incredible," the banker smiled quietly, as though he deprecated the sensationalism of the statement, "but on the way from the docks about twenty thousand pounds' worth of gold disappeared."

"With your detectives watching it all the way!" cried Magnum incredulously.

"Yes; and men in whom we have the utmost confidence. Six ingots left the ship, six ingots arrived at the Bank, but the difference in their weights amounted to about twenty thousand pounds sterling."

"Some mistake in weighing."

"We have, of course, cabled to Johannesburg to verify weights. They correspond to the weights registered by our men at the docks, but not to the weights given on our own scales at the bullion department."

"It seems a case for the ordinary detectives," returned Magnum without much interest.

The banker drew out a letter from a drawer in his desk.

"A very remarkable communication has reached me. The writer states that he has discovered a method for bringing about the disintegration of gold. He alleges that it is possible for him to cause an ingot of gold to vanish gradually. I should value your opinion on the possibility. I am not a scientist myself, and I do not know if one can attach any credence to his statement. Supposing the unlikely case that it were true, it would be very serious for the stability of the world's money markets, would it not?"

Magnum took up the letter and examined it intently. His interest had now been roused. It was a case within his own province.

"H'm," said the scientist non-commitently after reading it.

"What is your opinion?"

"I never deny the possibility of any new scientific discovery. The X-rays, radium, and the transmutation of elements were incredible enough when they first came to light, though they're commonplaces today."

"And your advice?"

"If it isn't true, catch him and put him in prison. If it is true, put him in a lunatic asylum."

Sir Walter laughed pleasantly.

"A drastic remedy! Though I am afraid the law is not sufficiently complaisant to allow us to carry out your suggestion."

"A man like that would be a danger to civilization."

"Exactly. The world's fabric of credit is based on the stability of gold. Therefore we, as the focus of the world's money markets, are bound to proceed cautiously. He telephoned to me yesterday, offering to sell us his secret for fifty thousand pounds. Naturally, he gives no address or clue by which we might find him. He asks for the sum to be paid in cash to a lawyer whom he will name, and the lawyer will then hand to us the document embodying the secret and the antidote. That removes the case out of the region of blackmail. We are asked to pay money for a definite legal consideration; that is to say, it would be a business transaction pure and simple. Now would you advise us, on the grounds of scientific possibility, to buy this secret for fifty thousand pounds, or any other sum?"

Magnum drew himself together from his easy, rather impersonal attitude. The case was now touching him in a very personal way. If he gave wrong advice to a director of the Bank of England, it would mean a severe blow to his reputation in the City of London.

"No scientist could express an opinion on the evidence you have given me," returned Magnum, with some asperity. "Ask him for proof."

"Twenty thousand pounds' worth of gold disappeared between the East India Docks and Threadneedle Street," reminded the banker gently.

"Does he claim to have managed that?"

"No. Naturally, he would not lay himself open to a charge of theft."

"Scarcely theft."

"Well, whatever might be the legal term for destroying the property of others."

"Ask him to destroy some of the gold in your Bank vaults."

"He said that he would telephone again to me this morning. Perhaps you might care to stay in my office for the telephone call, and speak to him yourself; that is, if you are willing to investigate this matter and give us your written opinion."

Magnum, with a very natural prudence, hedged.

"I'll talk to him and investigate further. But I shall not definitely take up the case until I see my way clearer. No fee will be due to me until I hand you a written opinion."

The banker's eyes smiled pleasantly in recognition of this cautious answer. In Magnum's place, he would have taken the same line.

Half an hour later the expected call came through. The banker, after listening for a few moments, passed the receiver to Magnum.

"I want sixty thousand pounds for my secret," said a voice, which appeared to be made deliberately husky as a matter of disguise. Otherwise it was the voice of an educated man, probably under thirty.

"You said fifty," returned Magnum.

"That was yesterday. To-day it's sixty. To-morrow the price may be seventy."

"It may not be worth seventy pence."

"Then don't buy it."

"We might be disposed to buy if we had reasonable proof."

"You've had it already."

"How?"

"I'll leave that to your recollections of the week."

"Are you prepared to destroy some of the gold in the Bank vaults?"

"Certainly not!"

"Why not?"

"Because I should have to install apparatus that would give away my secret."

"Then our gold is in no danger?"

"Except in transit," taunted the voice of the unknown. "And every week there's gold moving into or out of the Bank."

"With this warning you've kindly given us, we shall take precautions."

"Take all the precautions you could think of. Engage a squad of cavalry to protect your lorries."

"Or change the route."

"Decidedly change your route if you want to."

"Or the liners that carry the gold."

"Change the liners."

"There's something else we shall change."

"What's that?"

"That," retorted Magnum, "is our secret!"

"You'd better take my offer while the price is low," taunted the voice.

"Indicate the nature of your discovery."

"It might be a bombardment of alpha-rays from radium, suitably directed."

"Would need to be very near to the gold."

"Fishing?"

"Trying to determine what you offer us."

"You'll find that in the envelope with my lawyer."

"Who is he?"

"Before I tell you, I want to know if you are ready to pay sixty thousand in cash. Are you?"

"Will you give a week's option?"

"Certainly not!" came the decided answer. "In a week's time my secret might be worth a hundred thousand."

"Oh, go to blazes!" snapped the nettled Magnum, losing his easily lost temper.

"Right! Good-bye till Monday!"

The telephone irritations of the morning, coupled with the cocksureness of this young man, roused in Magnum an inordinate desire to fight out the mystery. Thrusting aside his previous business prudence, he told Sir Walter that he would undertake to give a definite written opinion for a fee of a thousand guineas.

"That is to say, you guarantee to give us advice which will prove sound in the outcome?" asked the banker.

"Provided I'm given a free hand in the investigation, yes!" said Magnum firmly.

His first step was to visit the gold vaults inside the citadel of the Bank of England. The head of the bullion department showed him into a steel-lined room in which ingots of gold were stored, some piled up like metal castings in a factory, others resting on low trucks Magnum unsnapped a pocket magnifying-glass and examined minutely the consignment from the *Wicklow Castle*. It was evident that the vanished gold had not been sliced or sawn away, because either of those processes would have left a type of surface easily recognizable under the magnifying-glass. On the contrary, the surface was unmistakably *corroded*—the marks of identification stamped on the ingots at Johannesburg were blurred, as with the legend on a coin which has been for a long time in circulation. He sniffed at it, but could detect no trace of corrosive acid.

As Magnum, on leaving, passed through the outer office, his eye was caught by the weighing-scale. It was a heavy machine, fashioned wholly in brass, very like the scale employed for baggage at a railway station or shipping office. Indeed, viewing the heavy weight of the gold ingots, no other type of machine could be employed.

"Correct to a quarter of an ounce," mentioned the head of the bullion department, laying an affectionate hand on his protégé.

On returning to his laboratories at Upper Thames Street, Magnum passed a generous word to young Meredith.

"You were right, and I was wrong," he said.

Meredith flushed with pleasure.

"In which matter?"

"Transporting gold through the streets of London. The Bank lost twenty thousand pounds' worth on Monday. I've undertaken to find out how." He explained briefly the conversations of the morning, and then tossed a sovereign over to the young fellow. "Make it vanish."

Magnum went sniffing round the vault in a highly impressive manner.

"In what manner?"

"That's for your ingenuity. Try the radium alpha-rays or high-power alternating currents, or anything else you can think of."

Meredith looked blank.

"I don't see how it's possible," he objected, "unless I use aqua regia."

"No; it wasn't managed with acid. I could smell the nitric in aqua regia a month old, and there was no trace of it on the ingots."

"Or mercury?"

"It would take a couple of weeks for mercury to dissolve up twenty thousand pounds' worth of gold. I want some method which will do the trick in an hour or two. Find it. Outwit that cocksure young man who wants sixty thousand for an envelope."

Meredith, roused by the spur of competition, took up the sovereign, and set to work on a campaign of scientific assault against it.

Meanwhile, Magnum entered the motor-launch moored to his backyard, and sped her at a dizzy rate down the Lower Thames to the East India Docks, restoring his equanimity by the breathless rush through the water. The *Wicklow Castle*, her white paint and trim brasswork dirtied over by the grime of the East End, was patiently enduring the process of unloading. The hawsers which held her to the quayside were rather insultingly armed with tin shields, so as to protect the wharf from any plague rats she might be carrying.

On board, the fourth officer held charge. In his oldest uniform, and collarless and smutty-faced, he made an appearance very different from the smart young dandy whose chief duty during the smooth run from Biscay to Table Bay was to provide flirtation for the pretty girls of the first saloon.

Magnum presented his credentials from Sir Walter Symonds.

"I would like to see the strong-room?" he asked.

"The detectives have done that already. You clumsy swab!" answered the fourth officer. The latter part of his remark was addressed to a stevedore.

"I want to see it also."

"The purser or his assistant has the keys, and they're both on shore leave during unloading."

"Bring them both here!" ordered Magnum, impatient of obstacles; and tapped his letter of introduction emphatically.

The fourth officer whistled up a steward in a grimy fatigue-jacket.

"Wilks, get this gentleman the moon, or anything else he asks for."

Then ensued a long period of telephoning, in order to find the purser and his assistant. It was not until nightfall that they arrived at the docks, by no means pleased at having their leave interfered with. The purser was a steady-going, middle-aged man; his subordinate, a quiet, capable-looking young fellow. No doubt they were pleasant and tactful officials during the run of the voyage, but in these circumstances politeness was hidden under a thick covering of brusqueness.

"There's nothing to show," frowned the purser, unlocking the door of the strong-room, and stepping over the two-foot-high sill. "We keep the gold here. The keys are always in my possession, or my assistant's. Nothing happened to the gold on the voyage. The weighing at the dockside proved that. Are you satisfied?"

"No!" snapped Magnum, for want of some better rejoinder. "Why do you allow the keys out of your own possession?"

"D'you accuse me?" flared the young assistant.

Magnum turned his back on him, and went sniffing round the vault in a highly impressive manner.

"Well?" demanded the purser.

"I reserve my conclusions," retorted Magnum, having formed no conclusions; and stepped out of the vault.

The purser expressed his feelings by slamming home the steel door.

Magnum sped off in the motor-launch to his home out by the Plumstead Marshes, cleaving through the light mist of the lower Thames like some phantom rider to the sea, plumed with the white foam tossed up by the razor bow. Tugs bellowed their sirens at him; ferry-boats cursed him; a police-boat sleuthing under the shadow of a deserted wharf hailed him peremptorily, then darted out in pursuit, but Magnum drove on regardless. He was intoxicated with the madness of speed, his one hobby of mental relief from the problems of his profession.

The following morning, Saturday, he was at the Bank of England, with the request that Sir Walter Symonds should have the six ingots from South Africa loaded on to a lorry, and taken down to the docks by the usual route and method.

The banker looked doubtful.

"Suppose that some more of the gold should disintegrate on the way?" he suggested.

"So much the better," returned Magnum briskly.

Sir Walter smiled at the rejoinder, and gave the required order. The six ingots were carefully weighed to a quarter of an ounce on the Bank scales, and loaded on to the lorry. The detectives accompanied on foot. Magnum followed the detectives at a discreet distance, also on foot. Nothing suspicious happened on the route.

At the docks the ingots were piled on to the official weighbridge of the Port of London Authority—a heavy, iron machine, rooted to the planking of the quayside. It was, of course, not so accurate as the scale in the Bank of England, but the weight registered corresponded closely enough. Nothing had been lost on the way.

And so back to the Bank, where a third weighing tallied with the other two.

Another morning wasted, and not a whit nearer the solution of the problem!

From Thursday to Monday morning, with only a few hours off for sleep, the patient Meredith had been continuously assaulting that golden sovereign, as well as a specimen of pure gold obtained from a jeweler, in the hope of inducing it to shrink, evaporate, or otherwise vanish. His efforts were fruitless. The gold seemed as stable as the law of gravitation.

"I'm afraid—" he suggested mildly.

Magnum tugged at his straggly, reddish beard, and furrowed his forehead with thought.

"It's not the loss of a thousand-guinea fee I object to, but being beaten by that cocksure young fellow."

Meredith said nothing. His department was the purely analytical; he left all initiative to his chief.

Magnum was in the act of setting light to a pipeful of his special evil-odored mixture, when he suddenly jumped up, and, with a curt "I'm off to the docks," bustled out of the laboratory.

The *Wicklow Castle* was now in the process of loading up for its end of week departure. Magnum paid no attention to the ship, but made straight for the official weighbridge, examining its solid impassiveness with a searching eye.

"What's below the wharf?" he asked of a Port of London harbor-master.

"The cold-storage rooms, sir," was the answer.

"Could I see over them?"

"Certainly. But I should advise you not to stay in them too long, as you would be liable to catch a chill on coming out to the open air."

He passed Magnum over to the single attendant in charge of the cold storage. Down below the wharfside Magnum was conducted to an icy rabbit-warren of passages, where frozen mutton from Australia, game, and butter were awaiting, in coverings of sacks and muslin nettings, their removal to Smithfield or Tooley Street.

"What's above here?" he asked.

"Some part of the offices or wharf—I couldn't exactly say which, sir."

"Have you a plan of the arrangement of these rooms?"

"Yes, sir; I'll fetch it."

Magnum studied the diagram intently, and made his way to one end of a passage.

"Do you happen to remember what was here last Monday morning on that top shelf?"

The attendant scratched his head to stimulate the brain inside. Magnum assisted with a half-crown.

"Sacks of game, sir," was the recollection. "They were taking them away."

"Who?"

"The firm they belonged to."

"Could you trace the firm?"

"I'll have to look up my books."

"Were you watching while the firm's men were down here?"

"No, I don't think so. I check at the outer door."

"Did you happen to notice anything peculiar about the packages they took away?"

"Now you mention it, sir, I did. One of them was so heavy that two men had to carry it. I remember saying: 'You've got a corpse there.' Of course, that was only a joke."

"What were the men like?"

"One of them was just a workman of some kind, and the other was a young fellow, a sort of manager."

"Ah! Quiet, dark, capable looking?"

"Yes, sir; that would just fit."

Magnum passed over a sovereign. "I'm going to telephone for a young man I know to come down to the docks. I'll lead him past your office, and I want you to look carefully through the window and tell me afterwards if you recognize him. Don't mention a word of this to anyone, and there may be a second sovereign for you."

Another prolonged bout with the fourth officer, Wilks the steward, and the telephone fetched the assistant purser from his home in North London, highly indignant at this further interruption to shore leave.

"What is it now?" he demanded of Magnum.

The scientist was, for this occasion only, quite apologetic.

"I'm very sorry if I'm giving you unnecessary trouble. Perhaps this fiver will compensate you?"

The young fellow waved it away. "I'm not in the habit of taking tips."

"Now tell me, the gold was weighed on a Port of London weighbridge on Monday morning?"

A careless nod.

Magnum led the way towards the machine.

"That one?"

"Probably."

The window of the cold-storage office was round the corner. Magnum led the way slowly past it.

"And they trucked the gold by this passage to the lorry?"

"Possibly. I wasn't here."

"Where were you?"

"That's not your concern. But if you want to know particularly, I was at home. I went off on leave early Monday morning."

"That's all I wanted to ask you."

When the young fellow was out of sight, Magnum returned briskly to the cold-storage attendant.

"You saw him. Was that the young man?"

"Yes, sir, it was," affirmed the attendant. "But last Monday he was wearing another suit of clothes, and a bowler hat, not a soft felt."

"You could swear it was the same man?" pursued Magnum eagerly.

"On my Bible oath, sir!"

"Then here's a fiver for you."

Sir Walter Symonds wore an air of some concern as Magnum entered his office.

"I have had another telephone message during the day," he mentioned. "We are now asked to pay a hundred thousand pounds for the secret. I have consulted with my co-directors, and we are anxious to have your opinion as early as possible."

The scientist handed over a sheet of letter paper. "Pay nothing," was its brief message, followed by Magnum's heavy-nibbed signature.

Sir Walter smiled in relief.

"And your reasons?" he asked.

"The gold did not vanish on its way from the docks to the Bank. It disappeared between Johannesburg and London—most probably on the voyage. I suspect that for a couple of weeks the strong-room of the *Wicklow Castle* was turned into a mercury bath. The vault has a high sill to the doorway, and would exactly serve that purpose. A fortnight's rocking with mercury would easily eat up twenty thousand pounds' worth of gold."

"But the weighing at the docks corresponded roughly with the Johannesburg weight!" objected Sir Walter.

"It's an *iron* weighbridge."

"I do not see the application of that point."

"In the cold-storage rooms below the wharf, one or more men manipulated a powerful electro-magnet to depress the iron scale, and so falsify the weighing. A very neat and audacious scheme. But the cleverest feature was the attempt to trail the Bank off the scent by the cock-and-bull story of a new method for disintegrating gold. That made you concentrate on the transport between the docks and Threadneedle Street. Very natural. Of course, I personally was not deceived for a moment by the story."

Magnum's recording angel may have been charitable enough to overlook this.

"I knew from the first that it was a fairy tale," pursued Magnum, "though it would not have done to let him suspect over the telephone that I saw through it."

"Who is this man?"

"The assistant purser."

"Have you had him arrested?"

"No; my duty ends with explaining to you how the scheme was planned," answered Magnum. "I have no interest in policemen's work. Frankly, I rather admire the fellow's ingenuity. If he should manage to escape arrest—well, I don't know that I should feel greatly disappointed."

THE SECRET OF THE RADIUM MAKER

Magnum returned from his laboratories to the office, holding a tiny sealed glass tube. In it were a few grains of white crystals.

"It's radium chloride right enough," he announced to his visitor.

"What is it worth?"

"The market price. About £25,000 a gramme."

"My man can produce it for £5000 a gramme."

"At that figure, I should advise buying it," returned Magnum drily. A tinge of a smile curled around his shrewd eyes, arched by bushy reddish eyebrows. As the acknowledged head of his profession of scientific consultant in London, he was entitled to his scepticism.

His visitor, Mr. J. Warren Fennimore, was a man of leisure and means. That was unmistakably conveyed by his manner and his careful dressing. The morning coat and top hat, the white slip to his vest, the immaculately-creased trousers and the gray spats exhaled the atmosphere of a club window in Piccadilly overlooking the Green Park, the *Times* and a morning glass of sherry.

Magnum, with his bushy eyebrows and straggly reddish beard, his great knobby bald head and his baggy, shapeless working clothes, made a striking contrast with him.

"You don't believe it?" asked Fennimore, stiffening.

"When I see proof, I believe."

"That brings me to my point. This fellow I've come across tells me that he has discovered an entirely new process for extracting radium from pitchblende. I don't know much about the matter, but

I understand that the high cost of radium is mostly due to the present very expensive process of extraction."

"Quite right."

"Then, on the face of it, his claim is not unreasonable?"

"It is not impossible," amended Magnum.

"If he can do what he claims, I am prepared to finance him and float a company. It would be more valuable than a gold mine."

"And you want me to examine into his process?"

"Exactly,"

Magnum, who was a shrewd business man as well as a scientist, pushed some notepaper and a pen towards his visitor. "I should want an option on ten per cent of the issued shares at half their par value, and of course my usual consulting fee in any circumstances."

"But why should I give you this option?"

"As an insurance that I would do my utmost to protect your interests," returned Magnum briskly.

"Then you suspect a fraud?"

"I've lived for twenty-five years in the City," was the dry answer.

"He seems a decent fellow. I should like to help him as well as make money myself over the discovery."

Magnum emphasized that there was pen and ink handy.

The next day, Fennimore's speckless motor drew up at Magnum's laboratories. The scientist entered the car with Ivor Meredith in his wake. This young Welsh boy was his right-hand man—a genius amongst the crucibles and beakers of the laboratory, but raw, shy and painfully self-conscious in the world of men and women. Fennimore shook hands graciously, though privately he was wondering why on earth the raw youth should be brought into the affair.

Magnum, scenting that, put Fennimore into his place. "Of course you know that Meredith is the finest analyst in England?" said he challengingly.

"Indeed!" answered Fennimore, startled and turning to view the boy once again.

Meredith colored like a ripening tomato.

"I wouldn't part with him for a fortune," snapped Magnum.

The car purred out of Upper Thames Street, snatched up pace on the Embankment with a glad relief at being away from the grime, and quickly sped them to a cottage in a back lane of Chiswick.

On their arrival followed an elaborate unbolting of the front door. The thin, meager face which showed in the doorway was framed in bandages.

"They broke in last night, Mr. Fennimore," complained the damaged inventor.

"Who?"

"I don't know who they were, because they'd got masks on, but I'm pretty certain who set them on to me—Hartley, that City man I told about my discovery before I came to you. That's who it was—Hartley!"

Hartley and Company were an important firm of manufacturing and wholesale chemists, with head offices in Moorgate Street. They practically controlled the English market for radium, buying from the producing firms and selling to scientists, doctors and hospitals, as well as to wholesale druggists.

While Fennimore plied questions about the night attack, Magnum was closely observing the inventor.

He might have been anything from thirty to thirty-five. The long, streaky, untidy hair was fading from brown to a nondescript yellowish. The carelessly-shaven face was long and thin and meager—clever but hungry might sum up the expression. The voice had a decided tinge of Cockney in it. Magnum placed him as the product of a London Polytechnic School.

In the background lurked the inventor's wife, a woman of a faded prettiness, but with decided strength of character. Evidently the two had had a hard struggle for a livelihood.

"What did these men find out?" Fennimore was asking.

"They found out what the business end of a poker feels like," replied the inventor with relish.

Fennimore proceeded to introduce: "Mr. Bertram Kimbell, Mrs. Kimbell—Mr. Magnum, the analytical consultant—Mr. Meredith, his assistant. They are going to examine into your process."

But the inventor, suspicious of all the world after recent experiences, made an distinctive movement to protect the passage leading to his workshop-laboratory.

"I *don't* think!" he retorted.

"Come, come!" protested Fennimore. "I vouch for these gentlemen. Their standing is unquestioned. Anything they may see they will regard as absolutely confidential."

"That's all very well," returned the suspicious inventor, "but if my process gets known, I'm left on the doorstep. You know I mustn't patent it. It has to be kept secret and worked secret. Then there's tons of money in it. But if everyone could go and make radium my way—!"

Mrs. Kimbell nodded agreement.

They were up against the old, old problem of the inventor and the capitalist. Who should trust the other? What kind of guarantees should be given?

"Show the gentlemen your other inventions," suggested Mrs. Kimbell, and her husband, acting promptly on her idea, produced from a bureau a sheaf of printed patent specifications which he handed to Magnum to examine.

They formed in a way a *dossier* of his life since he had left the Polytechnic. He had evidently become a professional inventor—his creations covering an astonishingly wide range of industries. The Patent Office had granted to Bertram Kimbell, Esq., B.Sc., of Laburnum Cottage, Chiswick, protection for non-refillable bottles, diabolo-spools, fire-screens, garters, safety-scaffolds, jumping-jacks, boot-fasteners, penny puzzles, non-puncturable tires, and a score of other ingenious but mostly unsalable devices.

"I see no patents on chemical processes," was Magnum's pointed comment.

"I'm a B.Sc, London," retorted Kimbell. "I did five years as works-chemist for the United Drug Company, Battersea. Ask them."

Evidently he was willing to have his whole life examined into.

The argument was interrupted by the sound of another motor drawing up before the cottage. Hartley, the radium dealer, stepped out and knocked briskly at the front door.

"Like his confounded cheek!" said Kimbell. "Shall I let him in?"

"Yes," decided Magnum.

So Hartley was brought into the parlor conference—a brisk, capable, moneyed City man, probably not overburdened with scruples. He nodded agreeably to the introductions.

"Well, gentlemen," said he, "I suppose we're all here for the same object—to decide how much money there is in Kimbell's process."

"There's a fortune in it!" stated Mrs. Kimbell defiantly.

"Possibly, madam, but none of us are going to buy a pig in a poke."

In his cool way, he seemed to identify himself with the interests of Fennimore and Magnum.

"Let's have a demonstration," he continued. "If the process is sound, we might pool capital and float a company together."

Magnum did not relish the suggestion. "Put we in the singular," he snapped.

"It's done," agreed Hartley. "Kimbell, will you give me a private demonstration?"

For once in his life the down-trodden inventor was master of the situation. Rival capitalists were contending for his favor. He swelled visibly. "How much will you pay me to show you?" he asked.

"I'll gamble a hundred pounds," said the brisk Hartley.

"Two hundred," offered Fennimore.

"Three," raised Hartley.

"Four."

"Five."

"I also offer five hundred,"—from Fennimore.

"I stand pat,"—from Hartley.

Kimbell looked at his wife, who signed to him to come and talk it over in private. They withdrew to another room.

When they returned, the inventor attempted the Napoleonic touch. "I want five thousand pounds in cash before I give up my secret," he announced, "and one thousand pounds on every gramme of radium produced by my process."

"Good-by," said the brisk Hartley, reaching for his silk hat.

"Your suggestion is ridiculous!" protested Fennimore, distinctly ruffled. "I've been trying to help you, but now you can fend for yourself!"

The capitalists left in their respective motors.

In the mysterious fashion of the press, which seems to scent out news almost as soon as the news begins to scent, Kimbell's discovery got into the daily papers. The *Daily Mirror*, for instance, took and published portraits of the inventor, the inventor's wife, the inventor's wife's cat, and the inventor's wife's cat's kitten. Another paper stated that Mr. Magnum, the well known consultant, had been investigating the process and considered it held great possibilities. All featured the point that Kimbell had demanded five thousand pounds in cash before he would disclose his secret to anyone.

Fennimore 'phoned to Magnum: "What do you advise?"

"Doing nothing!" snapped Magnum, irritated by the newspaper inaccuracies. "Sit still and let Kimbell come to you."

It was sound advice. A fortnight later, the inventor was waiting hat in hand on J. Warren Fennimore, humbled and prepared to demonstrate without any cash payment at all.

Fennimore, Magnum and Meredith repaired once again to Laburnum Cottage, Chiswick. This time, they were taken straight into the workshop-laboratory, a room with heavily-barred window and stout locks to the door. It was a hodge-podge of lathe, tools, chemical apparatus, and odds and ends of invention material.

Kimbell, after swearing them to secrecy, plunged enthusiastically into a description of his process, his wife standing by to help in the practical demonstration. He showed some pitch-blends ore; another sample ground to a flour-like state of attrition; another test-tube sample partly dissolved up according to a process he described; another test-tube containing a crystallization product; and then he came to the crux of the matter.

"That apparatus, as you'll see at once"—the inventor showed with pride a complete arrangement of specially-shaped X-ray bulbs harnessed up to a secondary electric coil—"is to ionise the radium away from the barium and other useless stuff. Everything depends on the new-shaped bulbs I've made and the composition of the kathode. But first we've got to do a special separation by osmotic pressure. Florrie, just reach me down—"

But as Mrs. Kimbell reached to a shelf above, her elbow brushed against a flask of liquid; it fell, smashing itself—exploded with a ferocious bang, and reduced the precious X-ray bulbs to scrap-glass.

The scene that followed was heartrending. While Magnum, whipping out a brown silk handkerchief, rushed to wipe away from the white-faced Mrs. Kimbell the liquid that had spurted onto her dress, the inventor broke down and wept and cursed in pitiful alternation.

"My poor fellow, don't despair!" said Fennimore, trying to console. "You'll be able to replace it. Be thankful no one was injured."

"Three months' work destroyed!" wailed Kimbell. "Just my luck!"

"I'll see that you don't lose by it," offered Fennimore generously, reaching for his pocket-book.

"No!" answered the inventor's wife, white-faced but determined. "We won't take your money for nothing. We've got our pride left, thank goodness!"

And in spite of Fennimore's protests, she proved adamant.

As the visitors left the cottage, a press photographer, waiting for them, snapped a shutter and then took off his tweed cap as a combination of asking permission and saying thank you. Magnum, by way of indicating his opinion of this cool action, thwacked a walking-stick into the vitals of the camera.

"Here, I say!" protested the indignant photographer. "What d'you mean by doing that?"

"Tells its own story," snapped Magnum, and strode straight on to the waiting motor.

In the car, Fennimore began to express regrets at the unfortunate accident. "It will mean waiting a couple of months at least, until Kimbell can make a fresh piece of apparatus. Then we must take up the matter again. You believe the fellow's genuine, don't you?"

"Quite genuine," admitted Magnum frankly.

"Not a trickster?"

"No."

"And his process?"

Magnum left the answer to Meredith, who replied diffidently that the new process for extracting radium sounded quite possible on the scientific side, but of course one had to be careful to verify all his points one by one.

"I believe in the fellow, and I shall finance him," decided Fennimore. "We mustn't let Hartley slip in ahead of us."

Magnum remained very silent during the drive.

Back in their laboratories at Upper Thames Street, Magnum flipped a sudden question at the Welsh boy; "What caused that explosion?"

"I don't know," confessed Meredith. "I was too startled to think out the matter."

"Did you smell chlorine from it?"

"No, I was thinking how lucky it was no one was injured."

"Booby! When are you going to learn to observe outside your own laboratory?"

"What does it matter what caused the explosion?" said Meredith, stung to retort.

"It may matter everything! I suspect chlorate and sulphuric acid. That's why I wiped the splashes off Mrs. Kimball's dress with my silk handkerchief instead of a duster. Take this handkerchief and analyze it."

It was not long before Meredith was able to report that his chief's guess was perfectly accurate. The explosion had been caused by the action of concentrated sulphuric acid on potassium chlorate.

"That's very significant," was Magnum's comment.

"I don't see why!" said the Welsh boy in bewilderment.

"*Intended* to explode. . . . Now listen carefully to my directions. I want Kimbell brought to me here without his wife knowing it. I want to sound him, away from his wife. You are to return to Chiswick and hang about the neighborhood of Laburnum Cottage until one or the other comes out. If he leaves first, tackle him; if she leaves first, wait until she's out of sight, then knock at the door and get Kimbell alone. Bring him straight to me."

"What reason shall I give him?"

"Say that I'll make him a direct cash offer for an option on his process. Now streak off, and don't bungle the affair."

Meredith sped away. Later in the day, he returned with the inventor in tow, distinctly pleased and proud at having carried out a diplomatic task so successfully.

Magnum put his test without waste of circumlocution. "Will you take one hundred pounds cash for a fortnight's option on your process?"

"What does the option mean?"

"That if at the end of the fortnight, I decide to buy, I pay you the five thousand pounds you ask and a royalty of one thousand pounds on every gramme of radium produced."

"Done!" answered Kimbell with unconcealed delight, and at once signed the necessary form of receipt.

"When you get home," said Magnum grimly, "tell your wife."

"Of course," returned the inventor. Then something in Magnum's look made him ask hurriedly: "Here, what's your game? Is this a trap?"

He fished the notes out of his pocket and pushed them back at Magnum. "I won't take them until I have consulted my wife!"

"I have your signed receipt for them," replied Magnum, refusing to take up the notes. "Better leave her to conduct the rest of the negotiations."

"I don't understand you, and that's flat!" shouted the angry Kimbell, and went off.

Magnum was now completely satisfied, from the inventor's demeanor, that he was no party to any trick or fraud that might center around the radium discovery.

Within an hour, Mrs. Kimbell was ringing up the scientist on the telephone. "There's some mistake about that option," said she. "Bert ought not to have taken your money."

"Exactly," returned Magnum. "But he has. And now, if you want to avoid a prosecution for criminal conspiracy, you'd better come to me here and make a clean breast of the affair."

"How dare you!"

"I do dare. Better come along and see me. It may save unpleasantness." And with that he rung off.

The Mrs. Kimbell who appeared at Magnum's office was an angrily defiant woman.

"What do you mean by threatening to prosecute for criminal conspiracy?" she demanded.

"I mean this: your husband is genuine enough, and there may possibly be something in his process. But why did you deliberately wreck his apparatus?"

"It was an accident!"

"An arranged accident!" snapped Magnum. "I know the explosion was intentional. I analyzed the handkerchief with which I wiped away the splashes on your dress. People don't keep a mixture of chlorate and strong sulphuric acid in a flask unless they intend to cause an explosion. . . . The inference is fraud. Now that I have your husband's receipt for my hundred pounds, I can prosecute him. I'll certainly do so, unless you make a clean breast of the affair."

"Here's your hundred pounds back!" She threw the notes on the desk.

"I refuse to take them."

For some moments Mrs. Kimbell stood eyeing the scientist defiantly.

"I want to know," said Magnum very slowly and deliberately, "why you planned a fraud on me—*me*, Magnum?"

"There was no fraud meant on you!"

"Ah—then you admit a fraud of some kind?"

"I never wanted to take your money, or Mr. Fennimore's either. Twice I stopped Bert from taking it."

"For some very good reason of your own. What was the reason?"

"I didn't want your money or Mr. Fennimore's at all," repeated Mrs. Kimbell obstinately.

"Then you were deliberately wasting our time—valuable time. Why?"

"Please take back the money," pleaded Mrs. Kimbell with a sudden change of front.

"Pleadings won't move me. The truth may. Try the truth. Otherwise, I shall certainly prosecute."

Her defiance had broken down before Magnum's implacable insistence. She sank into a chair.

"If I tell you the truth, will you promise not to prosecute Bert?"

"I make no promises. It depends on what you have to tell me."

"It was like this," she explained falteringly. "For years and years Bert has been inventing and inventing and scarcely making enough money to keep us from hand to mouth. You've seen all the patents he's taken out?"

"Yes, yes."

"Most of them were unsalable; and as for the others, when he did sell them, he was done out of his profits by those City men. For the last twelve months Bert has been trying to find a process for making cheap radium, and he thought he'd found it. He took it to Mr. Hartley, and Mr. Hartley told him it was no use. Bert didn't believe it; he doesn't believe it yet; he thinks he has a gold mine."

"Yes, I summed up your husband as genuine enough," admitted Magnum.

"So I thought I'd try myself to get money for us. There's not much money in making real discoveries, but I fancied I saw a way to make it out of a sham discovery. I went in private to Mr. Hartley—"

"So he's at the bottom of this affair?" interrupted Magnum.

"Yes, he arranged it all. He promised me one thousand pounds if I could make a public stir about the new process and, keep it going for two months. He told me how to approach Mr. Fennimore and the reporters, and wreck Bert's apparatus, and so on."

"The object being to juggle with the radium market?"

"Yes. People would get afraid, and sell their present stock of radium to him cheaply. In two months he could make a lot of money. . . . But I assure you on my word of honor that I didn't intend to take money, or let Bert take it, from Mr. Fennimore and yourself. You saw how I stopped him twice. That *would* have been fraud. And I assure you Bert knows nothing whatever of my arrangement with Mr. Hartley."

"I believe that," admitted Magnum. "He's not the man to be able to act a lie convincingly."

"Please don't prosecute Bert!" begged Mrs. Kimbell earnestly. "Here is your hundred pounds. If you *must* prosecute some one, take *me!*"

"Oh, run away!" answered the mollified Magnum, returning to her the inventor's signed paper. "I don't fight with women. Run away—and keep straight for the future."

THE INVISIBLE BULLET

Magnum heard the revolver-shots from the street—Sloane Street—
on one of those misty, midwinter afternoons when the sun is a mere
ball of dull-red metal passing from incandescence to sullen cold-
ness.

A single shot would be taken by any sophisticated Londoner
for a tire-burst on a motor-car; but two in rapid succession . . .!

The sound came from above, from the upper story of a tall,
pleasant-looking stone building. recently steam-cleaned, and a
trifle proud of its cleanliness compared with untubbed neighbours.
The ground floor housed Madame Pauline, "Modes," evidenced in
three Paris hats backed by a curtain of écru lace which screened
the rest of the establishment from the public view. There were never
more than three hats in the show-window, thus conveying the necessary suggestion of exclusiveness to the moneyed shoppers of
Sloane Street. A few choice flowers out of season, in costly Japa-
nese vases, emphasized the point.

On the first floor, as Magnum looked upwards, was the sober
announcement in plain block lettering of 'Arkwright Nugent, Solicitors and Commissioners for Oaths'; above that, in larger and
more fanciful lettering, 'Nurse Palmer, Massage and Electric
Baths'; and on the top story, 'Gymnastic and Fencing Academy,
Sergeant McIntosh', swung outwards on a hanging sign.

Magnum, grasping a stout umbrella, darted for the open stair-
way at the side of Madame Pauline's entrance. He moved quickly
but not recklessly, with an ear alive to the possible hasty descent

93

of a murderer with four shots still in his revolver. In that case the scientist would have stood aside and contented himself with registering the appearance of the criminal. He had no intention of foolhardy bravery.

On the first floor, at a quarter-opened doorway, a flabby little solicitor's clerk peered out. "What's-the-matter-is-anyone-shot-who-is-it?" he asked all in one quavering breath.

Magnum, without wasting time in answering, pushed upwards. The second-floor landing was empty, and the door of Nurse Palmer's establishment closed. On the third floor, a woman's scream rang out—in high-pitched hysteria rather than in sheer terror. The scientist quickly threw open the door, to find himself in a gymnasium, a broad open room, high and arched by an ample skylight, through which the misted sun sent a pinkish glow like a stage dawn. Two slight young girls in fencing masks, short skirts and leather jackets were endeavoring to carry to a couch a middle-aged woman in hysterical convulsions.

"Are you a doctor? In there," called one of the girls, pointing to the farther end of the gymnasium, curtained off by hanging cretonne in cheerful blue and white, reaching two-thirds of the way up to the arched roof.

No," answered Magnum, releasing his umbrella and snatching up a bar-bell. He hastened to the curtain, and with a belligerent grip on his weapon, pulled it aside.

Lying on the bare wooden floor of a second gymnasium—or, rather, the continuation of the same room—was an elderly man, stout, pasty-faced, bald, in white flannels with a gaudy scarf girt about his waist. A spreading pool of blood around him, and on his white flannel shirt, told the story. Bending over him, trying to staunch the blood with a towel, was Sergeant McIntosh, also in gymnastic flannels.

"It's impossible! It's just impossible!" rasped the Sergeant, middle-aged, greying, stiff in attitude from long military training, even in this moment of tragedy.

"Have you shot him?"

"*I*, man?" His amazement cut out any further questioning along the line of Magnum's first thought.

"Who?" demanded Magnum.

"I don't know."

"Which way did he escape? It wasn't by the staircase."

"Which way? I ask you that myself!" cried the agonized Sergeant.

From beyond the blue and white of the cretonne curtain, so incongruously cheerful, came the sound of one of the girls demanding a telephone number. Evidently she was calling up a doctor.

"It'll just ruin me!" cried the Sergeant.

"He's dead?"

"Stone dead, and never a word!"

Magnum, with his bar-bell, peered cautiously round an open door leading off from the side of the gymnasium, the only door in sight. It led into a small dressing-room with a shower-bath. Quite empty. The window at the end of the room was shut and the catch locked in. Nevertheless, Magnum opened it and looked round for a possible method of escape for the criminal. The wall went down sheer three stories to a back-yard. There were no fire-escapes, no staples in the wall up or down or sideways, no convenient water-pipes.

The Sergeant had followed. "I tell you, man, the room was empty! And the window shut! And there's no way of getting down from the window!"

"Or up to the roof?"

"I was here within three seconds of hearing the shots. I was just beyond the curtain with the young ladies when I heard them. I ran in at once."

"With a weapon?"

"No—as I was."

Magnum made an unspoken compliment to the Sergeant's courage. He strode back to the gymnasium and pointed up questioningly to the roof with its half-open skylight.

"I tell you, man, I was up yon rope to the skylight in a brace of jiffs. There was no one on the roof. Go up yourself and look. Oh, but it's just impossible!"

Magnum threw off his coat and swarmed up the pendent gymnasium rope till he had reached the skylight. He established a foothold and looked out over the roof, heavily grimed with London soot, able to carry traces which no criminal could efface. It seemed impossible that the shots could have been fired by a man crouching near the skylight. Indeed, when the doctor appeared, that point was corroborated in a startling manner.

"He was shot at point-blank," said the doctor. "Look at the scorching on his shirt."

Two shots from behind, through the lungs, had killed the man. One of them had passed clean through the body.

"It might possibly have been suicide," suggested the doctor doubtfully.

But no weapon had been found.

The police speedily appeared. There was a babel of cross-examination, through which the agonized Sergeant repeated at intervals: "It'll just ruin me!"

Out of the welter of questions and answers the facts of the tragedy came into bold silhouette. Sergeant McIntosh had been engaged in instructing the Hon. Sybil and Winifred Lennox in the art of the foils. The secretary, she of the hysteria, was in her front office. Beyond the cretonne curtain, Mr. Barclay Walsh, the dead man, had been going through a course of dumb-bell exercises alone. Then the two shots, the Sergeant rushing in to the rescue, and the astounding mystery of the gymnasium empty save for Walsh lying gasping on the floor, and the empty dressing-room.

A gruff police inspector made a notebook sketch of the floor arrangement, "A" representing the position in which the dead man was found, and "B" where the fencing-lesson was proceeding.

There was naturally a search into every nook and cranny of the suite of rooms. A hiding mouse could not have remained undiscovered.

"Must have escaped by that open back window," muttered the gruff inspector.

"I tell you, man, the window was shut when I ran in!" protested the Sergeant. "To avoid draughts. Shut, and the catch locked."

The inspector looked open disbelief.

"Why should I lie to you?"

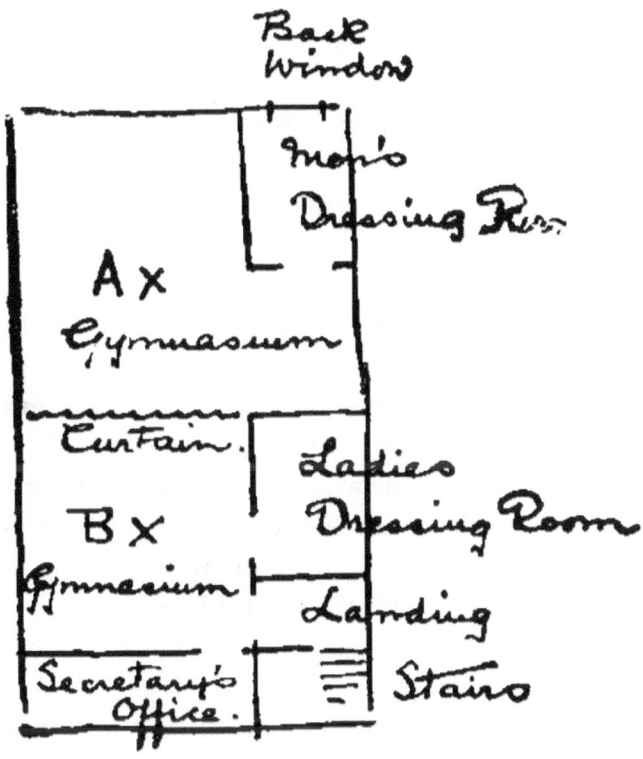

"My-duty-to-warn-you-that-anything-you-say-may-be-used-in-evidence-against-you," rattled off the officer in three words.

"I've nothing to hide!"

The inspector shut up his notebook with a professional snap. "Pretty evident how the fellow got away. Ran into the dressing-room and hid behind the door. You came in; then left the room to climb up the rope. While you were doing that, out he goes by the window. Easily fooled *you*."

The Sergeant's stiff shoulders bowed sadly. The tragedy on his premises might ruin his academy and sweep away the savings of a lifetime. On top of that, he was suspected of complicity—or at the best, of crass foolishness—in letting the criminal escape.

Magnum, remembering the Sergeant's courage, felt a sudden wave of sympathy for him. Therefore he interposed, remarking authoritatively: "The window was shut and locked."

"Who are you, sir?" demanded the inspector.

Magnum passed over his card.

"Doesn't tell me anything," said the officer curtly.

"Drafted in lately from Devonshire?" inquired Magnum, stung in his very human vanity.

"My-duty-to-warn-you that-anything-you-say may-be-used-in-evidence-against-you."

"Very good. Make a note of that question of mine. Hand my card to the Commissioner, and ask him for some elementary information about me. Now listen to me, inspector, or whatever you are. When I entered that dressing-room, less than a minute after the shots were fired"—Magnum strode to the room and finished his sentence at the window—"the window was shut and the catch locked in. I had to press back the catch in order to open it and look out."

"Then the fellow must have shut the window from the outside and pushed home the catch with a knife-blade."

"Will—you stand out on the window-sill and demonstrate how it was done?" asked Magnum:

The tension of the tragedy was broken by a light laugh from the doctor. "Better have a mattress in the backyard," he suggested.

The inspector scowled on Magnum. "If the fellow didn't escape this way, then tell me how he *did* escape!"

For once Magnum had no ready reply to make. The only reasonable solution of the mystery had been choked off by his evidence. Where could the criminal have hidden in a few seconds, and how could he have escaped except by the window, the skylight, or the curtain leading to the first half of the gymnasium? In the latter room were the two Misses Lennox and the secretary—how could he have passed them unobserved?

Grudgingly, Magnum suggested the rope leading up to the skylight. The sun had now disappeared sullenly in a bank of grey, half cloud, half mist. The electric lights were switched on, and the inspector clambered up the rope to examine the roof.

But he could find no trace there of an escaping man.

"You can both come with me to the station," he told the Sergeant and Magnum curtly; and gave orders that a policeman should remain to keep guard over the gymnasium, leaving everything precisely in the position in which it was found.

The dead man had, of course, been removed; round where he had fallen, the crimson pool had blackened into a dark, ugly clot, gleaming dully under the electric lights.

Magnum and the Sergeant were speedily released from the police-station, the former after a telephone message to the Commissioner of Police, the latter on Magnum's bail. But the scientist was not one to lie down tamely under such an insult.

"You can write out an apology or a resignation," he snapped at the inspector.

"Only did my duty," was the sullen answer.

"Your duty," retorted Magnum, who rather liked lecturing, "was to remain on the spot until you discovered how the crime was committed and how the criminal escaped."

"If you can prove to me how he escaped," flared back the inspector, "except by the back window, I'll write you an apology *and* a resignation."

Magnum, having no tenable theory whatever, ignored this challenge. But it remained in his thoughts, thrusting itself disturbingly between his ordinary professional work and himself. The murder, as Sergeant McIntosh had phrased it, seemed "impossible." A man shot at point-blank in a well-lighted gymnasium, and the criminal to escape within a few seconds without leaving the remotest clue!

There was no doubt of the essential correctness of part of the Sergeant's story. Aside from the evidence of his secretary, there were the two Misses Lennox, whose word was indisputable. They testified that the Sergeant, on hearing the shots, had rushed at once through the curtain, unarmed.

But they had not followed him. For what happened beyond the curtain the police had only the word of the Sergeant and Magnum, who arrived a minute or so later. The police theory was either suicide and the concealment of the weapon by Sergeant McIntosh, or complicity in the criminal's escape. After the inquest the case began to look very black against the unfortunate gymnastic master.

He was re-arrested and charged with being "an accessory after the fact."

Magnum, who prided himself on his judgment of men, was completely satisfied of the Sergeant's innocence. And, pitying him, the scientist found himself irresistibly drawn towards the unravelment of the mystery. It was bad business to do this, a sheer waste of professional time, but, for once, Magnum laid aside his usual attitude of profitable money-making.

"This thing worries me," he told young Meredith, his chief assistant, hunching his bushy, reddish eyebrows. "I can't get it out of my thoughts. I must put Stacey on to defend the man."

A note from the Sergeant thanked him gratefully for the offer of legal help. Magnum then rang up the offices of East, East and Stacey, solicitors.

"Is that Stacey? . . . Magnum speaking. I want you to defend Sergeant McIntosh—the Barclay Walsh case. . . . Don't run away with the idea that there's big money in it for you. I'm paying costs, and if you pile up a stiff bill. . . . I'm asking it as a personal favor. A return for that help I gave you in the Jonasson case. . . . You're a sportsman! Thanks. Now get busy."

A few days later, young Stacey, brisk and trim, came to Magnum's laboratories with a not very hopeful report.

"We'll do our best for the Sergeant," said Stacey, "and he's got a clean record in his favor, *but* . . . it's devilish awkward to find a plausible defence. I'm beginning to think there's something in the police theory."

"You reckon that he let the criminal escape?"

"He might have thought it would hush up a scandal. Foolish, but natural."

"I don't believe it!"

"It doesn't depend on what you believe, but what the jury believe."

"It depends on what *you make* the jury believe," retorted Magnum. "Or your counsel, which comes to the same thing."

"Of course, we throw the onus of proof on to the other side. The case will rest on circumstantial evidence. But you can't get away from the fact that the criminal escaped *somehow*. Suicide is out of the question. Walsh had no reason for suicide. He was a prosperous business man, a sleeping partner, with not a financial worry in the world. He was doing exercises in the gymnasium to reduce his figure. There was no hidden disease—the p.m. proved that. He must have been shot by someone with a grievance against him."

"By the way, have they found the second bullet, the one that passed clean through the body?"

"No. Every inch of the gymnasium was searched, but it hasn't been found. Curious point."

"Another mystery!" growled the irritated Magnum. "This case annoys me. I hate mysteries which won't clear up. I'll have to search for that bullet myself."

But professional matters of urgency prevented him for a full week. He was called up to Scotland, and returned to London barely in time to give his evidence on the opening day of the trial.

The following morning, accompanied by Meredith—whose sight, trained by the exacting standards of the laboratory, was abundantly keen—Magnum went to search the now deserted gymnasium. A permit from the police allowed them in. They attacked their task with mathematical precision, dividing the wall-area of the room into sections, and examining one section at a time. After that, they went over the furniture and the gymnastic apparatus with similar care. But the missing bullet remained invisible. It had vanished as mysteriously as the criminal had vanished.

"Damnation!!" concluded Magnum.

"Two unknowns in an equation. The one might be a function of the other," suggested Meredith mildly.

"We'll go down to the yard and have a look at the back window."

"Will that help?"

"Probably not. But I want to satisfy myself as to whether the fellow could have escaped that way."

By permission of Madame Pauline they passed through the millinery establishment on the ground-floor out to the yard—a small, grimy enclosure used for dustbins and the storing of shop rubbish. Magnum gazed up to the window three stories above, furrowing his forehead in an effort to visualize the escaping criminal.

"I don't see it," he concluded growlingly. "A cat could hardly have escaped from that window. Let's go."

As they moved away, Meredith suddenly exclaimed: "Why, here it is!"

"What?"

"The bullet."

Meredith had picked it up at his feet. He passed it to his chief, who examined the object as though it had been a diamond of the first water. Undoubtedly it was a twin to the bullet which had been extracted from the body of Mr. Barclay Walsh, imbedded in the spinal column. How came it to be lying in that yard?

"Could someone have thrown it out of the window?" suggested the young fellow.

"Even a policeman wouldn't be so idiotic as to throw away evidence of this importance," mused Magnum.

"Would the criminal have dropped it, do you think?"

Magnum ignored this suggestion.

"Or the Sergeant?"

"What earthly reason could he have for doing so?"

"Then how—"

A mighty slap on the shoulder from Magnum sent Meredith reeling. "Whatever is the matter?" he inquired patiently while rubbing the affected part.

"Upstairs again to the gymnasium!" cried Magnum, now as eager as a ferret.

"Why?"

"To get the trajectory of the bullet. I believe you're right in what you said—two unknowns in an equation, and the one dependent on the other!"

The art of the advertisement lies largely in making the public believe that the advertiser has goods or natural gifts far beyond the ordinary ruck. Magnum was fully alive to this truism. Even lawyers and barristers, hedged in by professional etiquette, are not above utilizing the chances of life in a dramatic form which will arrest public attention, and procure for themselves an advertisement to which their professional censors can raise no objection.

Accordingly, Stacey and his counsel held the winning card in hiding until the Crown prosecutor had exhausted every effort towards the piling up of argument against the unfortunate Sergeant, and the case seemed at its blackest. Counsel's speeches had been made on both sides; there remained only the summing-up by the judge and the consideration of their verdict by the jury before Sergeant McIntosh would be convicted of being an accessory after the fact, an accomplice in the criminal's escape.

Just as the judge, clearing his throat and turning sideways towards the jury, was about to deliver his summary of the case, counsel for the defence jumped up after a whispered consultation with Stacey.

"I ask your ludship's permission to recall Mr. Magnum for further evidence!" he interposed hurriedly.

"Very unusual," frowned his lordship.

"Most important evidence has just come to our knowledge."

The judge looked inquiringly at the Crown prosecutor, and the latter, following the traditions of British justice, answered: "I raise no objection. Of course, your lordship will permit me to cross-examine."

"Then proceed to call your witness."

"Mr. Magnum," called counsel for the defence; and the scientist, by no means displeased at having the searchlight of publicity focused upon himself, mounted briskly to the witness-box and took the oath, ignoring the unsanitary custom of kissing the Book, and, instead, swearing with uplifted hand in Scotch fashion.

"You are Mr. Magnum, the scientific consultant, of Upper Thames Street, E.C.?" rattled off the barrister.

A nod.

"You were recently endeavoring to find the missing bullet, the one which passed through the body of the deceased?"

"Yes."

"You failed to discover it in the gymnasium?"

A nod.

"You then proceeded to the yard at the back of the accused's premises, and found it there?"

"I did."

"Is this the bullet in question?" Holding it up.

"It is."

"You believe it to be the second bullet fired by the murderer?"

"Undoubtedly."

The object was handed round by an usher for the inspection of the Crown prosecutor, the judge, and the jury.

"Why," inquired the judge, "did you look for it in such an unlikely situation as the yard?"

"Because it was bound to be somewhere. Bullets don't vanish into thin air. Having exhausted the likely places, I continued a systematic search into the unlikely. That is merely a commonplace of the scientific method." Magnum looked as though the innermost secrets of nature were an open book to him.

"Confirmatory evidence will be given by Mr. Ivor Meredith, the witness' assistant," mentioned counsel, and then proceeded: "Have you any theory as to how the bullet came to be lying in the backyard?"

"Dropped there."

"In what manner?"

"After passing through the body of the deceased, it left the gymnasium by the open skylight, and fell to earth in the yard."

"How came it to travel upwards through the skylight?"

"Obviously it was fired from *underneath* the deceased."

"By someone in the gymnasium?"

"The criminal was not in the gymnasium."

A buzz of excited whisperings broke out amongst the spectators. "Silence!" ordered an usher.

"Explain to the court how the tragedy, in your opinion, took place."

"It is not a matter of opinion," corrected Magnum. "It is a question of fact. Mr. Walsh was engaged in carrying out a course of health exercises. One of the exercises set for him was to lie on the floor, face upwards, and raise himself repeatedly into a sitting posture. He was doing so at the moment when the two shots were fired at him, *through the floor*."

"That would leave shot marks in the flooring," interposed the judge.

"No," returned Magnum. "To be exact, the shots were fired through a knot-hole in the wooden flooring. The criminal reached it through the ceiling of the room below. She was never in the gymnasium at the time of the murder. That is how she escaped detection."

"But this knot-hole you speak of—" objected the judge.

"Obviously the knot was replaced in position after the firing. An elementary precaution on her part. It was kept in position by a bradawl. I know that because I sawed through a portion of the planking and took it up."

"My lord, I assured you I was innocent!" burst from the Sergeant.

"Please be silent," rebuked the judge, and proceeded to consult a plan of the building. "I see that the floor below is occupied by a Nurse Palmer, Massage and Electric Baths."

"At this very moment," interposed counsel for the defence, "the police are taking possession of her rooms. We have discovered that the name 'Palmer' is an alias; that her profession was not precisely that of 'nurse'; and that her past relations with the dead man give an ample motive for the revenge she took on him."

The judge nodded comprehension, but added: "There must be no further statement made about this Nurse Palmer in court. The present case deals solely with the innocence or guilt of the prisoner in the dock."

"Now, Mr. Magnum." continued counsel, "let us have further details of your discovery."

The details were merely an elaboration of the central fact. Meredith's timid evidence was hardly necessary. The Crown prosecutor wasted little time in cross-examination, and half-an-hour later, Sergeant McIntosh left the court in triumphant acquittal.

He grasped Magnum's hand in overflowing gratitude.

"You are marvelous, sir!" he exclaimed.

"Merely an application of the scientific method," said Magnum in an off-hand manner. He had no intention of letting the world know that his discovery was the result of an outrageous fluke. "Now you'd better transfer your academy to some other building, and I expect you'll work up a fine business again. Good luck to you! You understand that I pay the legal costs?"

"That's most generous of you, sir."

But the advertisement for Magnum was fully worth the monetary loss.

THE ROUGH FIST OF REASON

At the phrase "spirit photographs," Magnum interrupted his client brusquely. "Spirit photographs!" he repeated. "My dear young lady, I can get them made for you seven and six pence a dozen, cabinet size, platinotype, finished off with an art mount. It's a mere question of faking the plates—taking a double exposure. Any raw amateur could turn the trick. When I was on the Occult Investigation Committee, a couple of years back, we had hundreds of such photographs submitted to us. Sent, mark you, in perfect good faith. The people who had them believed them to be indisputable evidence of spirit visitations. Utter rubbish! Trickery, and transparent trickery at that! Why, the so-called spirit-faces were demonstrably taken from existing pictures or photographs. The same pose of head, the same turn of expression."

It was an unusually long speech for Magnum to make. With his quick impatience, his habit of condensing a quart of thought into a thimbleful of crystalized concentrate, he would customarily have answered an inquiry of obvious foolishness with an emphatic "*Rubbish!*" and allowed his tone of voice to drive home the reason behind the summary. But in this instance he felt very strongly and lengthily on the matter. He was an inveterate opponent of superstition or nebulous fancy presented to the world in the garments of science, and, wherever possible, liked to smash a fist into it.

His client, a Miss Cicely Cotterell, was a modern young woman, one of those bright-hard college girls who are not abashed by any authoritativeness on the part of man. She answered quietly: "I knew you had been on the Occult Investigation Committee, and that is why I came to consult you. You would be able to see at once through any of the customary trickery—anything that had been done beforehand by spirit mediums. But before I explain further, tell me this: do you believe in the possibility of supernatural happenings?"

"There is no supernatural," retorted Magnum, a little discomposed by this quiet self-assurance. "Anything that happens is *ipso facto* natural. There is the supernormal—something outside the range of ordinary experience."

"We mean the same thing," said Miss Cotterell, "though your wording is more accurate."

"Go on."

"Do you believe that the soul can leave the body and travel through space?"

"Beliefs are outside my province. Science deals with facts—verifiable, repeatable facts. I'd have no quarrel with all that theosophical, astral farrago if they'd put it forward as theory instead of assertion. Now my time's valuable, so come down to your particular case."

He glanced up at a large, bold-faced clock which was a conspicuous feature among his plain, workmanlike office appointments.

"My aunt, Miss Dallas, has been dabbling with theosophy and spiritualism for a year past. Up to now we have regarded it as a harmless hobby—"

"We?" interrupted Magnum.

"I am representing her family."

"And heirs?" asked Magnum pointedly. He had no liking for the modern young woman in general, and in regard to Miss Cotterell in particular, he wished to see her decently subdued.

"I want you to understand clearly that any interest in the matter is not mercenary. I'm very fond of my aunt. I want her to live as long as she can naturally live, happily and peacefully. I don't care if she never leaves me a penny. I have my profession—I'm independent."

"School?"

"Inspector of factories. However, that's beside the point. I was saying that my interest in the matter was not mercenary. I hate to see her fooled or tricked, that's all."

"And you want me to expose the trickery?"

"Yes, if it *is* trickery." Miss Cotterell added a barbed point: "And if you are able to see through it."

That found Magnum in a tender spot. He had been about to refuse the request, but this doubt of his abilities spurred him to action. "Get down to the facts," he snapped.

Miss Cotterell produced from her purse-bag a rough-trimmed silver-print and handed it over to the consultant. It represented an impression of a woman's form in a seated position—showing as through the vague outlines of the clothing—and to one side and above it, another form apparently issuing from the first, smaller and less definite in outline, like a cloud of vapor. The rest of the photograph was plain darkness.

"My aunt," she explained. "What is your opinion of the photograph?"

"There are many ways of faking a print," answered Magnum cautiously.

"I took it myself," was the quiet reply. "I exposed the film myself, and developed and printed it myself. I bought all supplies without his knowledge of where they came from."

"His. The medium's?"

"Mr. Slivinski is not exactly a medium."

"Sounds a tricky name."

"He's rather a famous man in the occult world, and leads a psychic society in London. He *may* be genuine—frankly, I don't know. But if this photograph of mine is the result of some trickery I want it explained and my aunt taken away from his influence, before she becomes obsessed by it."

"Can I see the room where this photograph of yours was taken?"

"It was at Slivinski's own house."

"That's awkward. If I went there he would be sure to recognize me." Magnum was under the impression all London would know him by sight.

"I don't think so. You might take an assumed name and pass off as an earnest inquirer. He holds weekly meetings for his circle. The next gathering is to-morrow night, at nine o'clock."

Magnum hunched his bushy eyebrows at the strange photograph she had passed to him, so suggestive of an "astral body" leaving the material body of Miss Dallas. In view of the girl's explanation of having exposed and developed and printed it herself, it was something quite beyond his previous experiences in the chicanery of spirit mediums. It was no faked film, no faked print. The "cloud of vapor" might conceivably be accounted for by the painting of the background with concentrated sulphate of quinine, which, invisible itself to the human eye, would yet affect a photographic plate. But no such theory would account for the unearthly manner in which the body of Miss Dallas gleamed through the vague outlines of her clothing. It was ridiculous to suppose that she would have painted herself from head to foot with sulphate of quinine; even granting such a supposition, the drug could not send its ultraviolet rays through the layers of a lady's clothing. The mystery of it piqued Magnum. Was it possible that this was an instance of the "supernormal" which he was ready to admit? Or was it merely some up-to-date development of the spiritualist's armory of illusion? If so, he felt keenly roused to expose the fraud and deal another fist-blow in the face of superstition.

"I'll come," decided Magnum.

"It would be best first to call at my aunt's house," suggested Miss Cotterell. "She dines at seven. After dinner we can drive together to Slivinski's."

He nodded assent, and announced his fee for the investigation.

At seven prompt, Magnum's taxi was at the door of the quiet residence on the height of Campden Hill occupied by Miss Dallas. Outside and inside it suggested leisured dignity of age and amply sufficing means. Miss Dallas herself, a woman of sixty, silver-haired, delicately framed, almost childlike in her simplicity of thought—in a word, Victorian—made a striking contrast to her self-reliant young niece. Miss Dallas belonged essentially to the class of the "leaners," those who must have some stronger will to obey and rely on. Her confidential maid, her niece and no doubt this fellow Slivinski were at present the dominants in her life. One could imagine that if her supports were suddenly removed, she would fall to the ground.

This, however, was not Magnum's thought. He was concentrating on the one problem of that strange "astral" photograph. He decided without hesitation that if some fraud had been perpetrated, there had been no connivance on the part of Miss Dallas or the confidential maid, an elderly woman devoted to her interests. It was equally evident that Miss Cotterell was sincerely attached to the aunt, and in her bright-hard, modern way, anxious to make her happy.

The dinner was somewhat of a trial to Magnum, whose gastronomic tastes ran to large porterhouse steaks or hearty beefsteak pies, solid substantial puddings and strong cheeses. At Miss Dallas' table no meat was served, or any heavy dish, and only for Magnum's benefit was wine introduced. She herself drank a bottled table-water imported from the Caucasus and supposed to have very special medicinal qualities, in the manner of all high-priced table-waters.

"My health has improved so wonderfully since I came to know Mr. Slivinski," she informed Magnum. "I am so glad you are coming with us to see him. You will like him, I am sure. His teachings are so restful and so beautifully expressed. I always feel that merely to listen to his voice is to be carried to a higher plane."

"I'm interested in that photograph taken by your niece," responded Magnum, feeling a trifle uncomfortable under his assumed name of the evening, and wishing to make his status clear. "I'm frankly a skeptic."

"Yes the photograph—isn't it wonderful? I had always felt the truth of Mr. Slivinski's teachings about the astral plane, and now that I have the evidence of it in my own person—now that I have seen my own astral body emerging from the shell of the material body—I am comforted beyond measure."

"I suppose Mr. Slivinski will be building a temple to house the society," suggested Magnum, groping for the mercenary interest he imputed to the spiritualist. "Something large and costly."

"No, I don't think so," returned Miss Dallas. "Our modest little circle contents us all."

Disbelief was in Miss Cotterell's features. She also, worldly-wise looked for the mercenary motives behind the astral teachings.

After dinner, Miss Dallas' pair-horse carriage came to the door—the modern motor jarred against her tastes—and they drove across London to Slivinski's flat in Hampstead. This was furnished simply and tastefully, nor was there any open evidence of the paraphernalia of the medium. Magnum expected to see the familiar black cabinet with black velvet curtains from which the "spirits" usually emerge under cover of a kindly darkness, or the trick pictures on the wall. They were conspicuously absent from the drawing-room into which the visitors were shown. About a dozen others of the circle were already present, nearly all women, and this number presently filled out to twenty-five or thirty.

"Where did you take the photograph?" whispered Magnum to Miss Cotterell.

"Over there," she answered, pointing to a side wall papered in a sober, self-colored grayish-green.

"Any curtain or screen behind your aunt's chair?"

"Nothing—only the bare wall."

"Lights down, of course?"

"Not entirely. I could see quite plainly."

"Was Slivinski in the room?"

"Yes—over by the fireplace."

"All the time you were exposing the film?"

"Yes."

"A time exposure?"

"He told me to allow five minutes."

Anton Slivinski entered to take his seat at an open reading-desk raised on a platform and flanked by a pair of palms. He had the face of an ascetic and dreamy, far-away eyes. He made his way silently to the desk and sat there in dreamy immobility while a lady at the grand piano played a nocturne of Chopin. Then, without formal preface, he began to read from a translated work of Indian mysticism. His voice—as Miss Dallas had indicated—was musical and finely modulated.

At the conclusion of the reading there was another pianoforte selection, and that was followed by an address from Slivinski. His subject was "The Cosmic Consciousness," and his thoughts on it were mystical in the extreme, vaguely nebulous like a misted scene from a far-away realm of fancy. To the practical Magnum it was a core of nothing wrapped round and round by swathings of beautiful, meaningless words, but the audience seemed to find in it some comfort he was totally unable to appreciate. They applauded at the finish in a manner of subdued heartiness, as though they wished to express their thanks but considered it indecorous to do so loudly.

The gathering broke up into knots, and coffee was handed round. Magnum edged away to the side wall against which the photograph of Miss Dallas had been taken, and scrutinized it for some evidence of trick paneling. He could find nothing to bolster up his suspicions.

Presently he was introduced to Slivinski. To Magnum's mingled relief and disappointment, the mystic did not penetrate his alias, but welcomed him as an earnest inquirer, with courteous words and offers to elucidate any point in the lecture which might have caused difficulty or doubt.

Magnum had nothing to ask about the address, which was far too involved and nebulous to offer opportunity for attack, but he went directly at the subject of the mysterious photograph.

"Do not let us lay too much stress on that," replied Slivinski gently.

"Why not? It seems to me highly important. As a skeptic, I welcome any form of material proof."

"Ah, you are a materialist, and so you value the unessential. I would like you to develop the thought that the true essential is the existence of an astral body which those of us who have purified the inner vision can see as plainly as you perceive the material body. The photograph tells me nothing new. I have long since arrived at the purification of the inner vision. My life-work is to train others to the same end. Such a photograph is merely a proof to those who half-believe, and in itself it has no true value."

He was winding words around Magnum. The scientist cut into the web with the rejoinder: "Could such a photograph be repeated? Could I, for instance, obtain that effect with a camera?"

"Undoubtedly you could, under the right conditions. Miss Dallas had very carefully prepared herself with fasting and with prayer, and when I perceived that her aura was in the condition of being able to impress itself on a photographic emulsion—which is only rarely in the case of an initiate—I asked her niece, who like yourself is a materialistic skeptic, to expose a film and so register the condition in a visible form."

"Could I obtain that effect with Miss Dallas?"

"I must repeat, sir, that the necessary conditions are but rarely obtainable, and since the test was only made to satisfy Miss Dallas, I cannot see any valid reason for repeating it. It would merely distress her, and it could prove no more than has already been proved."

"Could I obtain that effect in your own person?" persisted Magnum.

"With myself, yes, almost at any time, for I have long passed the stage of the initiate."

"Then will you allow me to do so?"

"To what end?"

"To convince myself."

"You sincerely wish to be convinced?"

"I am always open to conviction."

"I must repeat, sir: do you sincerely wish to be convinced?"

For all this gentleness of speech and courtesy of manner, Magnum realized that the mystic was a man of strong will and determined purpose. He was forced to answer, "Yes."

"And receiving the proof you desire, will you be prepared to withdraw your doubting, freely and without reservation?"

Magnum was little used to being cross-examined in that fashion. In his ordinary professional work, it was he who did the probing; but in this instance, hiding identity under an alias, he was at a disadvantage. "Yes, yes!" he answered impatiently, and after further parleying, an arrangement was made to carry out the test on an evening of the same week, at Slivinski's flat.

Magnum neglected no possible precaution that occurred to him. He armed himself with a stereoscopic camera instead of a single-lens instrument; he bought his supplies with extreme circumspection and tested them minutely; he took with him to the flat a screen to place behind Slivinski, backed with a coating of metallic lead; and he had young Meredith, his laboratory man, to accompany him and watch for any discoverable trickery. He had Slivinski stand for the photograph in a part of the room chosen by himself and not satisfied with one exposure, he took three separate photographs with different exposure-times.

Late that night, Magnum and Meredith were eagerly developing the plates and printing them bromide paper. In silence they surveyed the result through a stereoscopic projector; it showed the figure of Slivinski in full solidity gleaming through the vague outlines of his clothing in the same fashion as Miss Dallas, but more strongly defined—a weirdly impressive effect. The only important difference was that "no cloud of vapor" showed to one side.

"Damnation!" was Magnum's very unscientific comment.

"I have never heard of such an effect before," said Meredith mildly. "Do you think it possible that this is really the aura of the man?"

Magnum began to pace the laboratory, puffing furiously at his curved briar pipe; and he went on and on with this pacing until the patient Meredith fell asleep at the bench. The scientist awakened him without ceremony. "I'll take photographs of ourselves under the same conditions of lighting," he announced, and proceeded to do so. The result was entirely negative—a mere vague outline of clothing and head.

"You'd better go to sleep on the couch," offered Magnum with belated humanity. "I'll wrestle this out myself."

The wash-leather dawn of misty London, peering in timidly through the grimed skylight of the laboratory and shading his eyes against the glare of the electrics, found Magnum sleepless, tousled, reeking of rank tobacco, with smarting tongue and eyelids and harsh skin, perplexed, baffled—but not beaten.

"There *must* be some simple explanation!" he kept repeating to himself. "Both of them giving the same effect, the old lady and Slivinski. . . . Same effect, same cause."

The dawn, gathering courage, was now staring unwinkingly at the unwashed, disreputable figure of Magnum. St. Paul's boomed out the hour of six and a host of City churches hastened to confirm the news. Magnum suddenly realized that another working day had begun. Switching out the lights in the laboratory, he went to the office, found Meredith heavily asleep, silently replaced a fallen rug over him, and pinned a notice to the outside of the door to state that the young fellow must not be disturbed. Magnum's motor-launch was locked in a little water-kennel at the back of the laboratories. Magnum unmoored her and sped up the river to Westminster, whence he repaired to a Turkish bath near Victoria Street.

An hour later, he was lying on a couch in the cooling-off room, combining that process with breakfast and a chat with the masseur.

"You're looking off-color, sir," mentioned the bath attendant, who knew him well. "You ought to try a half-bottle of Koslof Liman water."

"What's that?"

"One of our regular clients, a Russian gentleman from the Embassy, told me about it, and since then I've recommended it to a lot of other gentlemen, and they all find it does them good after—" he was about to say "a night out," but discreetly changed it to "—when they're off-color."

"Let me see it," said Magnum idly. "All these waters are wonder-workers, every single one of them, if you believe the advertisements."

The attendant brought a small bottle in characteristic dark-blue glass, decorated with a label in Russian characters and poured out a tumblerful.

"I've seen that stuff before," exclaimed Magnum. "Quite recently. . . . It was at—"

"The Embassy gentleman says it's full of radium, sir."

"How many bottles have you got here?" asked Magnum sharply.

"Nearly two dozen, I think."

"I'll take them all."

"Very good, sir," said the pleased attendant. This was a per-quisite of his own. "Shall I forward them to your house?"

"No, I'll carry them with me."

On the evening of the next day, Magnum was again, by appoint-ment, at Slivinski's flat.

"These are the prints of the photos I took of yourself," said Magnum.

The mystic glanced at them without interest. "They tell me nothing new," he answered, "though doubtless they would seem wonderful to you. I trust you are now satisfied."

Magnum produced another print. "And this is one taken of myself in my laboratory. As you will see, I also seem to have a strongly-developed aura."

Slivinski's brow contracted slightly as he looked at the bromide print of Magnum. "You are a man of intense personality," he re-plied, "and by training you would pass quickly through the stage of the initiate to the state of the adept."

"And here," pursued Magnum, "is one of my office cat, wrapped in an old coat. She also seems to have a strongly developed aura."

The mystic remained silent.

"And finally," clinched the triumphant Magnum, "here is a photograph of a bottle of table-water wrapped in brown paper. Its aura is more powerful than yours or mine or the cat's. . . . Koslof Liman water, the same as you recommended to Miss Dallas."

Slivinski remained stock-still for many moments, his dreamy eyes fixed on some far-away vision.

"Well?" asked Magnum sharply, "What have you to say for your-self? All these photographs correspond to the one taken of Miss Dallas, with the exception of the 'cloud of vapor' effect, and no doubt you got that by smearing some of the water on the wall to the side of her chair. That water contains something new to me.

It's not radium emanation alone. When I've time to spare I shall investigate it further, and then write about the matter to the *Times*, *Nature* and the *J. C. S.*, mentioning how it's used for 'astral' effects."

"What I have taught is the truth," said the mystic with slow, religious intonation in his voice. "An eternal, imperishable truth—but not provable to the materialistic skeptic. In order to help one of weak faith, I arranged to show the invisible in visible form. I told you on our first acquaintance that I laid no stress on the photograph. You have discovered the method, but you have not disproved the essential verity of my teachings. Let me beg you to let the matter rest."

"Most decidedly not!"

"Faith has wings of gossamer—do not crush them with your rough fist of reason."

"These photographs of mine will be placed before Miss Dallas, and she will draw her own conclusions."

"You fool!" flung out Slivinski with sudden white-hot passion. "You blind fool!"

That was not the type of wording to influence Magnum. He replaced his bromide prints in his pocket, left the flat, sent the results of the investigation to Miss Cotterell, and turned to his ordinary professional work.

It was a week later when Miss Cotterell came to see him at the Upper Thames Street office. She was dressed all in black, and her features were drawn with pain.

"I wish I'd never shown you that photograph or asked you to investigate," she told him with a break in her voice.

"You don't mean that . . . ?"

"Yes. You and I—between us we have killed my aunt, and I shall never forgive myself."

"Good God!" exclaimed the horrified Magnum. "I didn't dream she—"

"When I told her, it brought on a heart attack, and she never recovered from it."

"It seems incredible that a mere revelation of trickery should produce such a result!"

"There was more behind than I knew of," she continued with bitter self-reproach. "An early love affair . . . something she had always cherished . . . and Slivinski told her that when she came to the stage of the adept she would be able to soar into space and meet *him* again on the astral plane. That was how his teachings gave her such comfort. . . . And I shattered her hope. She had nothing more to live for. . . Oh, why, why did I ever presume to interfere!"

"The gossamer wings of faith," murmured Magnum.

THE THREE ENDS OF THE THREAD

Magnum had had no training in art, and his crude lines of drawing never joined properly; nevertheless, his sketches commanded a higher price per square inch than a masterpiece by Velasquez or Rembrandt.

His client, an ordnance manufacturer, watched with absorbed attention while Magnum sketched out in pencil what looked like the section of a honeycomb, showing three cells; peppered it with NH_2's, OH's and N-N's; and scribbled underneath it a name like a coupled-up freight train, composed mostly of *amido's*, *hydroxy's* and *diazo's*, with an emphatic underlined *iso* about six inches from the beginning and four and a half inches from the end, The manufacturer seemed to appreciate these crypticisms, and departed with the precious sketch, for which he had paid a hundred guineas, fully satisfied.

That same afternoon, Magnum was slamming down the slats of his roll-top desk preparatory to leaving for the day, when a telephone bell shrilled imperiously for his attention. He took up the receiver and answered in his save-time manner, "Magnum speaking."

"You're a chemist, aren't you?" asked the voice with a perceptible twang in it.

"If you mean a chemist's shop—no. If you mean an analyst—yes," snapped Magnum.

"If chemist's shop means drug store—not wanted, if analyst means chemist—you *are* wanted."

"When I need to learn the American language," retorted Magnum, "I'll hire a professor."

This case seemed to be no exception, for the voice through the wire took on an apologetic tone. "I want to consult you, and if you can find the end of my skein of thread, I'll pay well."

"My fees come in advance," mentioned the consultant. "If I should happen to fail on an analysis—highly unlikely—I should return you your money for the sake of my reputation."

"That's agreeable to me. Can you come to my hotel, the Savoy?"

"To-night?"

"Yes—the matter's urgent."

"I'll be with you after dinner."

"Dine with me."

"Very well, but don't expect me in evening dress. What name?"

"William H. Cleveland."

Half an hour later, Magnum's taxi drew up inside the courtyard of the Savoy Hotel.

A page-boy, curling his snub nose at the scientists' tweed suit, led him to a seat in the lounge where Mr. Cleveland was sipping at a Manhattan.

"Very pleased to make your acquaintance," said Mr. Cleveland, who looked twenty years of hard-hit business experience. "Join me in a cocktail?"

"Thanks—I never need appetizers."

The American produced a check, filled in except for the amount, and a fountain-pen. "What's your evening worth to you?" he asked.

Magnum's fees were elastic, being reckoned at what he judged "the traffic would bear." He replied: "Call it a hundred."

"Pounds."

"No—guineas."

Cleveland laughed lightly as he filled in the sum. "You Britishers are very smart with that guinea device. You use a coin that doesn't exist in order to tack an extra five per cent on to your prices. . . . I take it that you'll return my check if you don't solve my problem?"

"Decidedly."

"Then let's trickle along to the dining-room and discuss the affair over dinner."

A quiet table in a far corner had been reserved for them—indeed, the head waiter preferred to pack these tweed-suit people as far as possible out of the sight of his well-dressed diners, and if he could have done so without offense, would have enforested them with palms.

Cleveland's story was a peculiar one. After asking for and obtaining a promise that Magnum would regard the matter as absolutely confidential, the American proceeded to explain that he was a negotiator representing a syndicate of fellow-countrymen interested in the leather industry. A new method of tanning leather had been invented in England, and he had crossed the Atlantic to buy the secret of it. After delicate and lengthy negotiations, he had managed to come to terms.

"With the head of the firm?" interjected Magnum, who had little faith in human nature.

Cleveland's hard-bit features tightened. "If I had bought this information from an employee of the firm," he asked, "would you prefer to return me my check and let it go at that?"

"I'm not a court of morals," rejoined Magnum.

"Well, in this case you've no need to be. My dealings were with the head of the firm, and if it were necessary, I'd give you his name." Looking Magnum straight in the eye, he paused to allow a request for the name.

But the consultant was not greatly interested in the private business ethics of William H. Cleveland, except in so far as they affected himself. He made a gesture expressive of curiosity satisfied, and the American proceeded:

"This man brought me the details of the process in a recipe occupying both sides of a sheet of the firm's letter-heading, too complicated to carry in one's head. I locked it away in the safe in my bedroom, and paid him the sum agreed upon in the form of a draft on London. That was last night. This morning, when I opened the safe, the recipe had disappeared. My first impression was that

I must have been mistaken as to locking it in the safe, and I can assure you that I made a search through my effects which would have brought to light a missing cent. My next thought was that the safe must have been burgled during the night, though this seemed mighty unlikely. It stands in my bedroom and has a combination lock. However, I took a train to the country town where the firm have their tannery, and asked the man for a duplicate of the recipe. He refused to give it—declared that I was trying to trick him in some way."

"Under the circumstances, a not unreasonable attitude."

"I returned to London and tried to stop the draft. But it had already been cleared through the bank. That, combined with his refusal to give me a duplicate, roused my suspicions. Up to then I had taken him for an honest—"

"What's the point of all this?" asked Magnum brusquely. "Do you want me to reproduce the recipe? If so, that's out of all practical question. I'm an analyst and not a clairvoyant."

Cleveland laughed pleasantly. "It does sound as though I needed a clairvoyant."

"Or a Scotland Yard man."

"Yes, it listens that way, but as a matter of cold fact I need *you*."

"How?"

"We'll come to my room after this dinner's through. and I'll show you."

The bedroom lead out of a private sitting-room. Both were very ordinary hotel rooms, having no more individuality than any other resting-plate for thousands of transients. The only unusual object was the small steel safe.

"Your own?" asked Magnum, pointing to it.

"No—I borrowed it from the hotel people."

Magnum examined the combination lock. "It would take an expert to pick this," he remarked presently.

"To my mind it would take a miracle-worker to do it. I'm a light sleeper, and any unusual noise would waken me at once. I'm positive no man entered my bedroom last night; and the more I think it over, the more I'm positive that I locked the paper inside the safe last night. Now I wonder if you're reaching out for the same conclusion as I've come to? Personally, I don't know if it's possible, because I'm a plain business man and not a scientific expert." He paused suggestively.

Magnum began to get irritated at these circumlocutory methods of a "plain business man," and he snapped out: "It would save a couple of hours if you came to the point now."

"The point is right here: I believe that the fellow must have dipped the recipe in some chemical which would eat it up silently into vapor during the night. And what I want from you is this: is it possible, and how?"

If Magnum had not been an excellent businessman as well as a scientific expert, he would have laughed aloud. By a most extraordinary coincidence, the compound he had just been analyzing for the ordnance manufacturer had precisely this property. Never was a hundred-guinea fee more easily earned. He had only to say "yes" and reel off that railroad train name which began with *tripyridyl-amido-hydroxy-diazo-etc.*, *etc.*, and ended eventually with *-glycerate*. But since he was a shrewd businessman, Magnum decided instanter to give nothing away until he had cleared Cleveland's check.

So he knotted his brow, proceeded to stuff a pipe, and pretended to delve into a mental encyclopaedia of chemical knowledge.

"Let me examine the inside of the safe," he suggested presently.

"Sure!" and the American unlocked the combination.

Magnum sniffed inside. "I don't get any smell," he remarked.

"Perhaps that's because I left the safe-door open for a spell while I hunted through my grips—the fumes may have escaped."

"H'm," said the scientist noncommittally.

"Is the thing possible?"

"H'm—yes."

"Then how was it done? Could you bring me a sheet of letter-heading written over in ink on both sides, lock it up in the safe, and make it disappear during the night?"

"It will need considerable preparation on my part," replied Magnum importantly. "In two days' time—"

"I'd like to be certain of this as soon as possible."

"I must have a clear two days," declared Magnum firmly, his inner eye fixed on the clearing of his check.

"Very well. You'll be here the evening after next and demonstrate?"

The scientist nodded assent.

The hundred-guinea check having been satisfactorily turned into cash, Magnum arrived as promised with a sheet of his professional letter-heading caked in the railway-train compound, dried, and written over with ink. This was placed in the safe and locked up. The next morning they met again; the safe was opened and the paper had completely disappeared, leaving no trace but a faint odor of oxides of nitrogen.

"You're a marvel!" declared the delighted American. "Now I can pinch that fellow for sure. Thought he'd get my money for nothing, did he? I'm going to make him feel mighty sorry for himself! . . . What's the nature of this stuff of yours?"

"It's a new compound belonging to a client of mine, and I don't sell client's secrets. However, I could give you an impressionist sketch of its composition, because that would be harmless without a knowledge of the precise method of synthesis."

"Well?"

"It's a derivative of *tripyridyl-amido-hydroxy-diazo—*" began Magnum, and continued with gusto for some moments until he arrived at the caboose of "*-glycerate.*"

"Gosh!" exclaimed the American. "That's a Marathon runner! . . . Who's the trainer, if you can tell me without breaking professional etiquette? You see, if this fellow of mine bought the stuff from your client, I'd have the proof all bound up and indexed."

Magnum took on a very professional air. "I can't give you his name without his permission."

"Of course. But you might ask him."

"I'll ask him if he wants to see you. If he doesn't, the matter must end there."

"Thanks—that's all I need. Tell him I might want to do business."

Magnum carried out his promise—put the two men into touch with one another, and promptly dismissed the matter from his thoughts.

In New York, a few weeks later, there happened an incident which has a direct bearing on this story, though Magnum only came to know of it at the very tail of the case. To preserve the sequence of events it is inserted here.

At eleven o'clock on a Saturday morning, a young man with the air of a clerk pushed a wad of yellow-backs through the cashier's wicket of the Manhattan Trust Company, and demanded a draft on London for eight thousand pounds.

"You're too late for the mail," mentioned the cashier. "The *Olympic* sails at eleven o'clock. Our advice note to the London bank won't go until next week."

"That's annoying. However, let's have the draft."

The cashier scrutinized the wad of bills, and then made out the draft in duplicate, the one copy being overprinted with the word *Original* and the other copy overprinted with the word *Duplicate*. It is the business custom to send the one and keep back the other, in case of a possible loss by shipwreck. Either is cashable, and is reckoned by a London bank, on the receipt of the advice note, as good as gold.

The young man left the draft, hastened to Battery Point, stepped on board a fast motor-boat awaiting him, caught up with the *Olympic*, and posted a letter on board.

That ended his work.

A week later, Magnum happened to be in telephone conversation with his client the ordnance manufacturer.

"Done anything further with the *tripyridyl* compound?" asked the consultant.

"I've made it the starting-point for a whole set of new compounds, and I believe I shall get out something great from it presently. If you want a good investment, buy up a few shares in my company."

"Thanks for the tip," answered Magnum. "By the way, did you do any business with that William H. Cleveland?"

"No. I gave him a little of the stuff for testing, but I've heard nothing further from him."

"I'll see my broker this morning about your shares," said Magnum, and prudently went to make inquiries.

He was kept waiting in the broker's ante-room for a full half-hour, and when he was finally ushered into the private office, he did not hesitate to express his opinion of this treatment.

"You needn't pretend to me that you're occupied with affairs of state," snapped Magnum, "even if you do strew your office with papers." He waved his hand satirically at the litter.

"Sorry," answered the worried-looking broker, "but as a matter of fact I've been searching all over the place for a missing paper."

"Poor system of filing!"

"Nothing to do with filing."

"What then?"

"I thought I locked it up last night."

"What?"

"A draft."

"Well, if I were in your place I shouldn't let a client know that I was so abominably careless. If you can't manage your own money, how can you expect them to believe that you can manage theirs?" chaffed Magnum.

The broker did not take kindly to this pleasantry. "The money's safe enough," he retorted. "The draft was an Original. I've just 'phoned to my client, and he's cabling for the duplicate to be sent over. Get it next week."

"Suppose the original had been stolen. If it's endorsed, it's cashable."

"We brokers are not so innocent as you imagine. I 'phoned up the bank at once, gave them full particulars, and told them to hold anyone who might attempt to cash it. But as a matter of fact they haven't yet received the advice note from New York. Get it next mail, I suppose."

"Then why the worry?"

"Well, the draft was for a large amount—eighty thousand pounds—and I was positive I placed it in the safe last night."

"Why didn't you take it to the bank?"

"After closing hours. My client came in with it at six o'clock, and paid it over in exchange for a batch of Rio Tinto bonds. Most extraordinary where it could have got to. I could swear on oath I placed it in the safe last night." He pointed to a substantial-looking steel receptacle in a corner of the room.

A chord of memory quivered in Magnum's mind. "Can I see inside the safe?" he asked.

"Certainly." The broker unlocked it and threw open the heavy steel door.

Magnum sniffed inside.

"If you care to pay me a hundred guineas, I'll tell you where that draft is," he remarked,

The broker looked at him suspiciously and then went to re-examine the inside of the safe.

"And for a further hundred guineas," pursued Magnum, "I'll tell you the profession of your client."

"Are you a *Sherlock Holmes*, or did you happen to overhear me telephoning to him?"

"No, until a moment ago I had no idea who your client was."

A stockbroker is usually ready to take a sporting wager on any subject on earth. "Make them both bets, and I'll take you on," he challenged.

"Done!" chuckled Magnum "First, your client is engaged in the tanning business. The tannery is in a country town not very far from London."

"Wrong!"

"But—"

"You lose. My client has no tannery in this country. He's an American, and his name is William H. Cleveland."

"Cleveland!" A great light broke upon Magnum, and for a few moments his wrath overpowered him. He had been fooled as neatly

as any man had ever been fooled. The story of the leather tannery
secret was the merest device to get Magnum to give up, unsus-
pectingly, a piece of very valuable scientific knowledge. No paper
had disappeared inside Cleveland's safe. He only wanted to know
if the thing were possible; and if so, how. And he had used this
knowledge to make a draft for eighty thousand pounds disappear
into thin air, after he had acquired in exchange for it securities
cashable in any of a dozen European bourses. Magnum's racing
mind saw that draft as a forgery. "Eighty thousand" pounds might
have left New York as "eight thousand." Until the advice note
reached the London bank next week, no one would suspect a "raising" of the draft. All trace of it had disappeared into vapor. And
meanwhile, with a week's grace, he had eighty thousand pounds'
worth of sound Rio Tinto bonds to turn into cash.

"Well?" queried the broker. "You lose one bet, don't you? Now
where's the draft?"

Magnum slammed home the door of the safe and caught at his
arm. "I'll tell you that in the taxi as we go along. Quick—hurry!"

"Where to?"

"Scotland Yard first, and then to the Savoy. We've got to catch
Cleveland before he gets off to the Continent with those Rio Tintos."

"But—"

"Don't argue—hurry! Thought he could fool me—*me*, Magnum!
The colossal impertinence of the fellow!"

THE EMPTY FLASK

The complex of glass flasks and glass tubes and india-rubber jointings on the laboratory bench ended in a pinhole opening from which a tiny blue flame jetted with an upward curl.

While Magnum watched, Ivor Meredith, his assistant, placed against the flame the cold white porcelain of a crucible-cover. The porcelain slowly darkened to a circle of a glistening gray-black. It was not the velvety, lusterless black of soot. Technically, that stain on the virgin porcelain was known as an "arsenic mirror," and it proved conclusively that the human remains they were analyzing held arsenical poisoning.

The boy Meredith shivered slightly. His sensitive mind leaped from that glistening stain to its inevitable corollary—the noose of the law around the neck of a fellow-being.

But with Magnum, blunted in fiber by his twenty-five years of consultant practice and many criminal cases in which his scientific help had been sought, the train of thought suggested was very different.

"Another of those arsenic bunglers," he remarked with seeming callousness. "Will people never learn that arsenic is the easiest poison in the world to trace? Sheep! The same old method ever since the days of the Early Egyptians. No credit for us in that kind of high-school analysis!"

And since the remainder of the testing was purely a matter of routine, calling for no special exercise of wits, Magnum left for the

office to change his disreputable laboratory coat and to motor-boat
to his home out by the Plumstead Marshes.

In the office, an imperious call of the telephone bell interrupted
him in shirtsleeves. He took up the receiver with a curt, "Magnum
speaking. Who's that?" As he listened, his rugged features lighted
up with the zeal of the investigator. "Sounds as if it were a case
worth my time," he answered crisply. "Yes, come straight here and
bring the whole facts with you."

Some fifteen minutes later, Detective-Inspector Callaghan was
laying before the scientist one of the strangest cases that had ever
baffled Scotland Yard and the medical experts retained in its
service.

"The valet found him in the morning, stone-dead. The electric
light was burning. Apparently the Baron had switched it on in the
middle of the night in order to take his usual drink from the vacuum
flask on a table by the bedside."

"Where's the flask?"

"Here." Callaghan produced it from its careful wrappings—an
ordinary leather-covered vacuum flask. "The valet's story is that
he found it lying on the bedroom carpet, as if the Baron had let it
fall to the floor. And the flask was *empty*."

"Why emphasize the 'empty?'"

"That's the astonishing feature of the case. The valet had filled
it as usual with iced *tisane*—a kind of Continental orange-flower
water. Not a single drop remained."

"The Baron had drunk it off."

"Apparently not."

"How do you know he didn't?" challenged Magnum.

"Because we've already had the contents of the stomach and
renal organs analyzed."

"By whom?" demanded the scientist with marked asperity.

Into Callaghan's professional voice of authority crept an
apologetic note: "Dr. Alfred Cresswell. As you know, sir, we usually
take analyses to him."

Magnum retorted frowningly: "The interesting ones. Leaving
to me the kind of schoolboy analysis for arsenic I've been carrying

out in there this afternoon." He jerked his hand toward the laboratory. "Or else I'm expected to clean up after Dr. Alfred Cresswell has muddied a case."

The detective owned a sufficiency of tact. He answered soothingly: "It's because Dr. Cresswell has failed that we come to a higher authority. He can find no trace whatever of poison. Probably his range of knowledge is more limited than your own."

"Well, return to this empty flask. The liquid would have spilt on the floor or carpet when the Baron dropped the flask."

"I have the floor-rug outside in my taxi. There was not a spot of liquid found on it. Nor was there a single drop left in the flask."

Magnum unscrewed the stopper and sniffed thoughtfully.

"Well, sir?" queried the detective.

"A stone-cold scent by now," replied Magnum, speaking metaphorically. Then he shot a darting glance at Callaghan from under his bristling penthouse eyebrows. "What makes you believe that Baron von Neuhausen was poisoned? He might have died of fright or shock, natural heart disease or—"

"Heart disease was the first conclusion of the doctor they called to the hotel bedroom. Certainly the man had a weak heart—one could tell that from the general flabbiness of the body and the heavy-pouched eyes. But"—the detective paused impressively—"the doctor had the sense to listen to the valet's story and examine further. He found the tongue puffed and distended and the palate blistered. You'll see that for yourself. The medical experts can make nothing of it."

"What was this story of the valet's?"

"It turns around a Viennese cabaret singer. She's now starring at the Palace Vaudeville Theatre. Mitzi Sorel is the name—no doubt you have seen it."

"I'm not interested in music-hall doings."

"Well, for those who like the snaky, white-devil style of Continental beauty, the woman is fascinating. The Baron undoubtedly followed her to London—on the chase. Then Mitzi's husband came over and told him to clear out. The Baron persisted in staying. And now he is dead. That's the framework of the valet's accusation."

"Have you arrested the husband?"

"Not yet. We can lay hands on him at any moment. First we want our evidence. We want to know what caused the Baron's death. Name the poison, and the tracing of the rest will be easy. The more unusual the poison, the simpler to find out where it was bought and by whom."

"Bring in the rug," said Magnum. "I'll turn it over to Meredith for analysis, and then you can drive me to the P.-M. room and the hotel, and show me the scene at first-hand."

After the grisly detail of the post-mortem room, they proceeded to the Hotel Monopole—one of the great caravansaries that string from Charing Cross, making first claim on the custom of travelers from the Continent. Though Callaghan was received with deference by the *maître d'hôtel*, it was easy to read that the hotel people were bitterly annoyed by the occurrence of the death under their roof, causing scandal and loss of trade.

Callaghan philosophized: "These big hotels might have been planned for crime. The one aim of the management is to *hush up*. They would have made that doctor called in give a certificate of death by natural heart failure if the valet hadn't raised such a loud protest. Lord knows how many people die mysteriously or disappear mysteriously at the big hotels of the big capitals like London and Paris."

They proceeded to the locked suite of apartments which had been in the occupation of the Austrian nobleman. Under the orders of Scotland Yard, the rooms had been left exactly in their condition of the morning when the Baron von Neuhausen had been found lying dead in the big double bed of inlaid rosewood. Pillows, bed-coverings, toilet accessories, trunks—all these were left in place, and across a chair had been laid the delicate lavender silk night-attire taken from the corpse.

Magnum, with his abnormally developed sense of smell, went nosing about the room like a hound on the trail.

"Phew! He used perfumes," remarked the scientist with an air of disgust. He pursued aloud: "The liquid from the flask might have fallen onto the pajama jacket or onto the sheets. We'll analyze these as well."

"I'll have them taken to your laboratories at once," answered the detective, turning to the telephone.

"And Cresswell's material."

"Certainly."

"What have you done with the valet?"

"He's in custody, as a matter of routine, but you may take it from me that the man is quite innocent."

"I'd like to question him for myself," returned Magnum, who did not believe in taking second-hand opinions from anyone.

The room itself, an ordinary hotel bedroom furnished with conventional luxury, offered no suggestion toward elucidating the mystery of the crime beyond the fact that one door opened into the sitting-room and another door direct into the corridor.

"A poisoner might have entered that way, easily," said Callaghan.

"Then the Baron kept his doors unlocked?"

"The valet says that he rarely troubled to lock them. Few people realize the dangers of these great hotels."

While Meredith, with his infinity of patience worked on the analysis of the materials given to him, Magnum, went to cross-question the valet. The scientist had never had an aptitude for foreign languages and had never forced himself to learn them. A police-court interpreter acted as intermediary.

The valet proved to be an oldish, shrunken little fellow, crumpled up with the blow of his master's death and the ignominy of his own arrest, yet when roused to speech, garrulous, expostulative, vehement in gesture, repetitious, irrelevant. It required far more than the scant patience of Magnum to deal with him, and very little was gained from the interview. According to custom, the man had prepared his master's *tisane*, and left it by the bedside and gone to his own rest. The Baron had returned home late, without awakening his servant. The rest was vehement theory.

"A fool, but loyal," was Magnum's mental summary.

He left, and acting on a sudden impulse, made for the Palace Theatre to witness the performance of the Viennese *diseuse*. He was just in time for Mitzi Sorel's "ten o'clock turn." The curtain rose to a stage hooped with hangings of a brilliant petunia; very quietly the hangings parted and there glided before the audience a slim figure gowned in dead black of panne velvet, unrelieved. The face had the ivory-white pallor of a magnolia; the hands were thin almost to the point of translucency; the eyes, deep-lashed, were cast downward. A strange exotic flower was this Viennese singer. Before she was half through her first song—or rather, recital of a Heine poem translated into English and set to music—Magnum knew that he was in the presence of a stage genius. This woman could *create*. The grim tragedy of the poem pictured itself on the stage as vividly as if reality were being lived through. Every movement of her head and hands stood for atmosphere.

"A woman who would attract many lovers," he meditated. "The wrong kind and the right kind—both. One could understand her driving a lover to suicide or crime."

He began to speculate on what sort of man the husband might be. Callaghan had mentioned him, but had given no description. It struck Magnum, that if the husband were still in London, he would be seeing his wife home at the end of the performance. If one waited outside the stage door—

Magnum left the auditorium and made for the quiet side-street onto which the stage door of the theatre opened. He found he was not the only one to wait for the appearance of the performers. Loungers were gathered there—some out-of-elbows; some in evening dress and opera hat, with the conventional Inverness thrown over the arm on this warm night of June; some neither gutter-cats nor *jeunesse dorée*, but apparently average citizens of sober purpose.

Presently the two halves of the stage door swung outward, and the *diseuse* and her husband moved quickly through the waiting crowd to their electric brougham drawn up by the pavement. A thick-set, heavily bearded man was this husband, unprepossessing, carrying himself with a somewhat exaggerated air of protective-ness, and at the same time of defiance, as though he dared anyone to address his wife. Magnum, usually a quick reader of character, hesitated to draw conclusions.

The husband was holding open the door of the brougham when suddenly Mitzi Sorel, glancing casually in Magnum's direction, gave an involuntary gasp and swayed as though about to faint. It was momentary only—the next instant she had regained control of herself, and with tightened lips stepped through the door into the dark interior of the brougham. The husband followed, and with the silent, cat-like movement of an electric-driven vehicle, the brougham slid away to the yellow glare of Cambridge Circus.

Magnum, most unusually, felt nonplused. He had never before met the *diseuse*, and even his strong tinge of human vanity could not make him believe that she recognized him by reputation.

Could it have been some one behind his shoulder who had caused that most unmistakable start of fear? Magnum wheeled round, to find the crowd of loungers mostly dispersing. A young fellow in a gray lounge-suit and straw hat remained still, gazing intently after the receding brougham.

"An extraordinary woman," remarked Magnum casually.

The young man seemed to start out of a reverie. "Extraordinary? Yes, of course," he answered, and without further word moved off.

"Another moth!" thought Magnum. And then as a venture he followed, keeping a discreet distance.

The young fellow turned northward up Shaftesbury Avenue and on toward the gloomy region of Gower Street, where the lodgings of London University students cluster. He fitted his latchkey into a quiet house of trim respectability and let himself in.

For the greater part of that night and the whole of the two following days, Magnum and his protégé worked at the analysis of the material supplied to them by Scotland Yard.

The results were unsatisfactory in the extreme. Where Dr. Cresswell had found nothing toxic, Magnum found nothing. The solution made from the washings of the bedroom rug and sheets also yielded nothing of interest.

Magnum, puffing furiously at his rank briar pipe, plodded up and down the laboratory, while the patient Meredith, sitting on a bench-stool, waited for the conclusions of the master-mind. His task was to carry out with a perfection of technique the analyses entrusted to him; deductions he left to Magnum.

Presently the consultant stopped short in his pacing and thundered out: "I believe there *was* no liquid in the flask—not a drop of it!"

"But the blistering of the dead man's mouth—" objected Meredith.

"Some poisonous gas in the bottle."

"What gas would that be?" (They used the word in its scientific meaning of any substance in a condition of vapor.)

The question seemed unanswerable. No odorless gas that Magnum knew of could produce such a result, and corrosives like hydrofluoric acid or acetyl chloride would have left unmistakable traces in the flask besides their characteristic odors. A lengthy search through works of reference brought no clue to light. Never-theless, they exhausted the flask and analyzed the air withdrawn. It proved to be ordinary, commonplace air. Apparently their investigations had come to the end of a *cul-de-sac*. A blank wall faced them.

"And yet I believe Callaghan is right," mused Magnum. "That empty flask is the key to the mystery. Find out what was inside it, and the rest would be easy."

"Suppose we were to cut it open," suggested Meredith.

Magnum smiled grimly. "Try, if you like."

Meredith worked with chisel and hammer until he had cut a jagged split through the stout leather cover and the double layer of aluminum of the vacuum flask. But only bland and odorless emptiness was there to mock them for their trouble.

"Go off to bed and leave me to puzzle this out," said Magnum with a sudden kindliness. "You're looking fagged to death."

"To bed? But it's only six o'clock and daylight!"

"Is it?" The scientist had completely forgotten whether it were night or day. "Well, put your watch on six hours and make believe it's midnight."

When young Meredith had left, Magnum drew some scribbling-paper toward him and began to diagram the possible ways of solving the mystery. His mind worked most easily in the medium of diagrams and, formulæ. In ordinary language, the case resolved itself finally to this: find the poison or find the poisoner. Either would lead to the other. Since he had not found the poison and loathed to let Scotland Yard know that he was beaten, Magnum began to concentrate his thoughts on Mitzi Sorel and her husband.

They seemed very close to the crime. What was the exact connection? A husband's revenge from jealousy; a passionate woman's fit of hatred; a frail woman's fear of revelations?

Yet this fact pressed itself to the foreground: the crime had been carried out by a method so novel, so far removed from the ordinary, that it had completely baffled Magnum. Could such a method be devised by a music-hall artiste or her stocky, unimaginative husband? Their procedure would surely be the usual arsenic, vitriol, strychnine or prussic acid, all easily recognizable in the post-mortem testing—unless some one with special scientific knowledge had devised for husband or for wife a method of poisoning unknown to toxicologists.

Magnum's thoughts switched to the young fellow in the gray tweed suit he had spoken to outside the stage door of the Palace. Did this man know anything relevant? Gower Street and the University of London held a suggestiveness of scientific knowledge. Magnum resolved to pay a call at the Gower Street lodging, of which he had noted the number, and went forthwith to do so. The first difficulty was that he neither knew the man's name, nor had any valid excuse for introducing himself into the house. However, Magnum was not to be stopped by trifles of that kind. When the door was opened to him by a maidservant, he ordered authoritatively:

"Take my card to your lodger."

"Which one, sir?"

"The clean-shaven young man who wears a gray suit."

"Would you mean Mr. Heath?"

"Yes. And tell him my call is important."

"He's out, sir. He always has his dinner out."

"Then I'll wait in his room until he returns."

The girl, London-trained, looked at Magnum suspiciously. "We couldn't allow that, sir," she returned. "But if you'd like to call again at about nine o'clock—"

"Are you sure he is not at the University?" demanded Magnum.

"Quite sure, sir. Mr. Heath only gives his evening lectures Tuesdays and Fridays."

"Must be a demonstrator or assistant lecturer," was the easy mental deduction. Aloud: "Leave my card in his room and tell him I'll call later."

Thence he proceeded to the University Buildings higher up on Gower Street, where he asked to see the University calendar and a syllabus of the term's lectures. From these the status of Ralph Heath was quickly found: a demonstrator in the department of physical chemistry. Magnum glanced casually over the printed summary of the lectures he had to deliver during the term—an advanced course covering a number of lines of modern research.

Suddenly Magnum crunched the syllabus in his hand with brusque vehemence. "Good heavens, what a fool not to have thought of that before! The empty flask—of course it was found empty! Three days searching for something extraordinary in the poison line, and all the time it was the most ordinary substance in the world. No smell, no stain, or corrosion, no trace of liquid left—what else could it be?"

He made at once to a public telephone, and after some delay got a connection through to Callaghan.

"The mystery is solved," he told the detective authoritatively. "You can go straight ahead and arrest Mitzi Sorel and her husband."

"Both of them?"

"I can't be sure for an hour or so which of the two is the guilty party. Be on the safe side and have them both arrested."

"What was the poison used?"

Magnum had a keen sense of dramatic value in the presentation of his results. "There are tons of the substance all over London," he answered cryptically. "You can tell Dr. Cresswell he has plenty of it in his own laboratory."

"Then it will be difficult to prove when and where they obtained it?"

"Not at all. Leave that to me. I'm now going to call on the man who supplied it in its concentrated form to either Mitzi Sorel or her husband."

And before the detective could press further questions, Magnum rang off and walked briskly to the house where Ralph Heath had his apartments. The maidservant, answering the bell, gave the reply that Mr. Heath had returned from his dinner, had taken up Magnum's card, had made no comment on it, and had gone out without leaving any message behind.

This was unexpected and annoying. There seemed nothing to be done but wait about the neighborhood until the young demonstrator should return home. Residential Gower Street is not a convenient neighborhood for loitering in, but Magnum solved that point by hiring a taxi and sitting in it.

By midnight Heath had not put in an appearance, and reluctantly Magnum gave up this policeman's work of watching and went to a hotel for the night. In the morning he called early at the apartment-house, only to be met with the reply, obviously genuine, that the young man had not returned home since nine o'clock on the evening before.

Then it was that a glimpse of the inner story came to Magnum, and he made haste to Scotland Yard to have the authorities scatter broadcast a description of the missing man.

It was not from Ralph Heath that the hidden motive of that strange crime came to light. Without doubt he had linked up Magnum's call at his house with the arrest the same evening of the two Viennese, and fearing that his secret had been discovered, he fled to the Continent by the midnight boat-train. Hunted by the police of France as well as England, he finally threw himself into the swift-flowing Rhone at Lyons.

Mitzi Sorel, on her arrest, had persistently refused to answer any question relative to the young demonstrator, but when the news of Heath's suicide came, her control broke down into passionate self-reproaches:

"That dear boy, how he love me! Never can I forgive myself! Never! He love me, you understand, for the good motive. But the Baron"—her eyes blazed out into hatred—"that was different. There was a moment when I thought I loved the Baron, and . . . one is foolish sometimes. My husband suspect, and he follow me to London. The Baron will not go away. I implore him to go away, but he refuse. He smile at me—so." With a rapid play of feature and shoulders, the actress had brought before her listeners the scene in vivid life. "What to do? It is my husband that I truly love. I want to keep him for always. He begin to accuse me. . . . And that poor boy who is dead knew of my trouble. I say to him, cannot you make the Baron go away from London? He answer that for me he would do anything. I give him a kiss—the kiss of a sister, you understand—and he goes to see the Baron. But never, never did I dream that the poor boy would do that violence! I swear to you that I would not send him did I even for one moment suspect!" Her passionate sobbing carried away her words like chips on the stream of a mountain torrent.

Callaghan supplied more of the story, pieced together from his investigations. "Heath had a fruitless interview with the Baron. Then, the following evening, he returned, entered the Baron's bedroom at the Monopole, and substituted for the flask of iced *tisane* a similar vacuum flask of his own. There are thousands of them in use, and one would look much the same as another. With the lax system of observation at those big hotels, it was a simple matter for him to slip in without arousing suspicion."

Magnum completed the tale: "You can inform Dr. Alfred Cresswell that the poison he totally failed to discover was *air*. Liquid air. One gulp of that stuff would kill any man not of an iron constitution. Heath got it from the University laboratories, where they specialize in low-temperature research work."

"But why was there not a drop of it left when the flask was found on the bedroom floor?" Callaghan had asked.

The scientist, contemptuous of this layman's ignorance, answered brusquely: "Evaporated! The stuff would keep liquid in a closed vacuum flask; but if spilt, or if the stopper were not screwed home, liquid air would simply become air. It wouldn't leave a trace behind. The empty flask—it never contained anything but air."

And he added loftily: "Only a medical dunderhead could have missed such an obvious solution!"

He said nothing of his own three days of fruitless testing.

THE SECRET ANALYSIS

One foggy afternoon in November, Magnum carried to the Admiralty a written report of a highly confidential and vitally important nature relative to a certain new torpedo charge explosive. Being a man of prudence, Magnum also carried with him a loaded revolver. He did not expect to have to protect his person and his precious charge in law-abiding London, yet carrying a revolver was a cheap and practical form of insurance.

He left Meredith at the Upper Thames Street laboratories.

The young Welshman was an analyst of genius, but he was no man of affairs. In the rough, tough world outside the sheltered laboratories, he might easily have been outwitted by a schoolboy. Probably that was shrewdly reckoned upon by the unknown who called up Meredith on the telephone and announced, with a note of authority overlaying the guttural of the voice, that he was the secretary to the First Sea Lord.

"Mr. Magnum is here with his report on the torpedo matter," said the unknown.

"Yes," answered Meredith.

"The duplicate of the report is wanted."

"It's locked away in the safe, I think, and I haven't the key."

"Mr. Magnum is under the impression that he left it in his desk."

"I'll see. Hold the line, please."

Presently: "No, it's not there."

The unknown clicked his annoyance. "I must get the key from Mr. Magnum and come down to your office myself. . . . But perhaps it would be safer if you drove to the Admiralty and took me back with you."

"Certainly," answered the young fellow. "I'll come at once."

He hurried on his overcoat and tucked his white silk muffler around his neck, then went out into Upper Thames Street. It is a gloomy, grimy lane in the cheeriest circumstances of weather, lined with warehouses of ancient pattern and choked with heavy, rumbling lorries; under the blanket of a sullen November fog, it seemed a region of subterranean cellars. Meredith made in the direction of Blackfriars Station. There he would be certain to find a taxi; Upper Thames Street is no region for cabs. But, most unusually, a taxi happened to be prowling in the lane. Meredith, much pleased with his good luck, hailed the chauffeur, gave the Admiralty address, and stepped inside without the slightest suspicion that the cab might be there for the express purpose of conveying him.

It should have been a straight-line drive past Blackfriars Station and along the Embankment to Whitehall. The chauffeur turned, however, over Blackfriars Bridge to the south of the Thames, driving recklessly through the choking fog. Meredith called through the speaking-tube: "The shortest way is along the Embankment."

"Embankment is 'up,' sir. Just as quick by Stamford Street."

Stamford Street was once reckoned as one of the most unsavory neighborhoods in London. At the time of this episode, its vice-rotted houses—blank and tenantless, with broken windows showing glimpses of rooms where the drab paper had blistered away from the walls, and spiders competed undisturbed for their harvest of insect-life—were being pulled down to make way for Government buildings. The engine of the taxi suddenly rasped and spluttered angrily; the chauffeur pulled up short.

"What's the matter?" asked Meredith through the speaking-tube.

At that moment the near-side door of the taxi opened and a thick-set, heavy-jawed man jumped in.

The struggle was very brief. Meredith, with his slight frame and weak muscles, stood no chance. He was quickly stunned and carried into one of a row of empty, three-storied houses.

That portion of the scheme had worked with the smoothness of oiled machinery. But on a further point the unknown had miscalculated. He had judged that Meredith would be in Magnum's full confidence over the matter of the torpedo explosive. As it happened, Magnum had carried out the investigation entirely by himself, not caring to let his protégé run risks. It had been a case of *noblesse oblige*—Magnum had stationed himself on the danger line.

What young Meredith knew of this highly important and confidential analysis was therefore the most general impression.

They tried to force a betrayal out of him; he had nothing to betray.

Magnum returned from the Admiralty pleased with himself. He had been able to give a flat contradiction to a staff expert and to back up his words with undeniable scientific proof. That satisfied the belligerent side of his temperament. Further, it was his first Admiralty case. It formed a most useful business connection. He now proposed to take Meredith with him to celebrate the evening with an old English dinner at the "Cheshire Cheese"—turtle soup, beefsteak pudding, pancakes and toasted cheese—and seats at the latest successful farce. Magnum's taste in gastronomy and in drama was unsubtle. A champagne supper would conclude the night.

At the laboratories, they told him that the young fellow had been called away by a telephone message. Probably some client, thought Magnum, and sat down to wait. Afternoon shaded imperceptibly into night, and no word came from Meredith. The scientist had perforce to make his celebration alone, and he did not enjoy it. The boy was like a son to him.

On the following day Meredith was still missing, and the housekeeper at his rooms knew nothing of his whereabouts. Magnum became seriously alarmed. He went to Scotland Yard and enlisted the help of his friend Detective-Inspector Callaghan.

Callaghan affected cheeriness. "Probably a case of temporary loss of memory, sir. It's not an unusual thing. Let me have Mr. Meredith's photograph, and I'll find him for you within twenty-four hours."

Three days went by fruitlessly, while Callaghan circulated descriptions of the young fellow, and fine-combed the known resorts of criminals for some possible clue. Magnum became frantically anxious. The one soft spot in that hard, rough-edged temperament was affection for his protégé. He kept the telephone wire to Scotland Yard sizzling with repeated inquiries and suggestions at all hours of the day and night. He made in person the round of every warehouse in Upper Thames Street, asking if no one had seen Meredith leave on the afternoon of the fog. One lorry-driver mentioned a prowling taxi, and on that slender clue Magnum ordered Callaghan the herculean task of questioning every one of the ten thousand taxi chauffeurs in London.

On the fourth day, a call of the telephone bell sent Magnum hurrying to the instrument. A heavy voice, the voice of one who spoke English with a smear of guttural, spoke over the wire:

"Is that Mr. Magnum?"

"Yes, yes!"

"You want to know where your young friend is?"

"I'm offering a public reward for information."

"He is staying with me."

Magnum's eagerness checked abruptly. An intuition of what was to come bade him guard his words. He answered coldly: "Speak out what you want."

"Your reward of five hundred pounds is not sufficient."

Magnum swiftly reached over for the dictaphone on his desk, placed the second receiver of the telephone against the mouthpiece of the recording instrument, and switched on the electric purr of the driving mechanism that revolved the wax cylinder.

"Speak up, please! I can scarcely hear you."

The voice of the unknown repeated louder: "The reward you offer is not sufficient."

"You'll have to share it with others," bluffed Magnum brusquely. "Your taxi was noted in Upper Thames Street by three separate people."

An incredulous laugh was the answer. Then silence.

The scientist was driven to ask: "Well, say out what you want to say."

"Your young friend will be given back to you in exchange for a complete copy of the report you made to the Admiralty on the torpedo matter. Otherwise, not."

"A threat?"

"I do not threaten. I act. From this hour your Mr. Meredith will have no food or drink until the report is in my hands. Good-by till to-morrow!"

Magnum hastened with the dictaphone record to find Callaghan and ask him if he could recognize the voice from amongst his memory of blackmailers. Callaghan listened to the record and shook his head; he called in all his detective force at various times during the day to try it with them.

No one at Scotland Yard could place the voice.

"This is foreign secret service work," was the obvious conclusion of the detective. He added reassuringly to Magnum: "But don't worry—we'll get him for certain within the next few days."

"How?"

"Your wire is from Bank Exchange. We'll give instructions to the order-line operators at Bank to trace back the issuing-point of all calls to you to-morrow."

"They won't carry that out," rasped Magnum, remembering a previous experience with the telephone authorities.

"This order will go from the Commissioner's office," replied the detective firmly.

"Even then, the man will probably 'phone from a public call-box. Tracing back the number will tell us nothing."

"It will give us the neighborhood."

"He could cross London to 'phone, if he wanted to."

"I don't think he would go to that extra trouble," said Callaghan, and with forced optimism in his voice began to tell of previous cases where blackmailers had been outwitted by the detective force.

The scientist, usually so utterly self-reliant, strong and masterful, broke down under the strain of his anxiety into bitter railing at the helplessness of the situation. "This cursed telephone system! It might have been invented for the very purpose of blackmailing! And while we're pottering about and wasting time, they'll be starving the poor boy! Heaven knows what they've done to him already!"

"When the man 'phones to-morrow, try to arrange a meeting with him," suggested the detective.

"If I get face to face with him—" said Magnum, and completed his thought by drawing his loaded revolver out of his pocket. "He won't find any squeamish scruples in me."

The expected call did not come through until the following afternoon.

"Good-day," said the voice of the unknown. "Have you thought over my offer of yesterday?"

"My report to the Admiralty was confidential," replied Magnum warily.

"Naturally."

"I ought not to divulge its contents to anyone."

The voice on the wire became brisk. "If you do so, no one at the Admiralty need ever know. You can say that your young friend was held to ransom, and that you paid one thousand pounds to get him back. That is a story they will believe."

"It's a possibility," assented Magnum with careful hesitancy. "You would have to give me your written promise that—"

"I give nothing in writing. It must be a gentleman's agreement."

"Where would you want me to send a copy of this report?"

"To an address in Cologne."

Magnum clenched his free hand in silent rage. It would be out of practical question to get foreign police to trap the negotiator. In Cologne, he or his intermediary would be safe.

"Well?" queried the voice sharply.

"I must think out my position. If we could meet somewhere and—"

"Decidedly not! Good-by till tomorrow!"

Magnum rang up the supervisor at Bank, and presently learnt that the call had come from a Mayfair number, a public call-box at the Dover Street tube station. It was just as he had expected. And though he hurried at once to the point, there was no clue to be obtained. The call-box was situated in an exit open to the street, with only a bookstall boy within range of sight. The boy had taken no notice of the many casual users of the call-box. Dover Street, in the midst of the fashionable club district, suggested nothing as to the locality where Meredith might be hidden.

Though Magnum waited wearily in his office all the following day, no telephone message came from the unknown. But in the evening, as he was giving up hope and preparing to leave, a letter was delivered by the postman, with the envelope in Meredith's thin, boyish writing. That point was certain, but this difference stood out sharply to Magnum's eyes: it seemed the writing of a man on a sick-bed. Eagerly he slit open the envelope. The only message, on a half-sheet of very ordinary note paper, was a brief sentence:

Wednesday

I am being at starved to death

Ivor Meredith

No address on the sheet; the postmark on the envelope the G. P. O.; very evident that Meredith had been allowed to write it under surveillance, and it had then been taken from him and posted.

Magnum, strong and full-blooded as he was, could not repress a shiver as he looked on the message. The weakness of the writing told its own story.

He took it at once to Callaghan with the faint hope that the detective might find in the paper or envelope some clue which he himself failed to see. But though Callaghan examined and re-examined a score of times, he could gain no hint of service to them. Note-paper such as that might have been bought at any one of a thousand stationer's shops. The fact that the envelope had been posted at the General Post Office, a couple of miles distant from Dover Street, crumpled up any theory of locality. Nor did an investigation under the microscope reveal finger-marks.

"There's only one possible course left to you, sir," summed up Callaghan. "That is to fake a report which will pass muster, and send it to the Cologne address as they direct."

No man can say of what baseness of action he is incapable under the stress of violent circumstance. History teems with pregnant examples. Magnum felt that he could not trust himself, if the worst came to the worst, to keep back the secret information in the report—information of national value—and let Meredith be slowly killed. He foresaw a point where his own iron resolution to keep faith with the Admiralty might melt in the fire of compulsion.

He therefore took the matter to the First Sea Lord—careless of the damage to his reputation which might ensue—and asked that the latter should draft out a faked report to be sent to the black-mailer.

The old sailor, grizzled and stern, looked keenly at Magnum for some moments.

"This matter is extremely serious for us," he said. "Your man may not believe what you send him."

"That's why I'm here."

"I understand. And believe me, I sympathize deeply. But,"—his voice vibrated with feeling—"no private interest can be allowed to stand before the national interest. I had an only son in the Navy. He asked me to let him volunteer for submarine duty in the very early days of the craft. I allowed it. He perished in the first submarine disaster. I did not grudge him to my country."

He held out a hand to Magnum, and the scientist took it in silence.

On the same day, another telephone message from the unknown came through to Magnum.

"Did you get the letter from your young friend?"

"Yes."

"Have you any proposal to make?"

"I agree to yours."

"Good! But play me no trick. Your Mr. Meredith will remain here with me until I know from Cologne that the report you send is quite satisfactory. Do not hope to deceive us with false information."

"I will send the report. What address?"

"Marktgasse, 18 III."

"And the name?"

"No name."

"I agree to send it at once."

"I am glad you are reasonable. Meanwhile, I will give your young friend a drink of milk. He is so very hungry and thirsty."

"Will you tell him what I am doing?"

"Perhaps I may. Good-by!"

By the same night train which carried the document Cologne-wards, Magnum also traveled. A letter of introduction to the British Consul was with him—and his revolver. He had no definite plan of action yet in mind; he must build on his interview with the Consul.

A gale from the east, ice-edged, flailed upon the Admiralty pier at Dover. Even the optimistic stewards could not offer their usual forecast of a fair passage to Ostend. Outside, in the neck of the Channel, legions of angry waves lashed against the bows of the mail-packet; and though Magnum was a natural-born "good sailor," he succumbed like every other traveler on board.

Towards the end of the four-hour passage, exhausted by the seasickness but feeling quieter, Magnum took out from his pocket-book that pathetic message from Meredith, to read it for the fiftieth time. It may have been that the strain of the sickness had altered his focus of vision; whatever the explanation, a detail in the writing gripped at his attention for the first time. In the word *starved*, the *s*, *t* and *d* were formed in a different manner to those letters in the rest of the sentence. And that *st* over which the pen had spluttered! It was a message within a message. Something Street. St—d Street. Stafford Street, perhaps, if there were a thoroughfare of such name ... or ... yes, it might be Stamford Street!

Immediately he hurried upstairs to the Marconi operator and sent off a wireless message to Scotland Yard:

> Am returning by next boat. Have found a clue. Investigate at once any street beginning with *S T* and ending in *D*. Strongly suspect Stamford Street.
>
> Magnum.

It was eleven o'clock in the morning before he was back in London and in Callaghan's office, and a subordinate at once gave him good news: "Yes, sir, we believe you're right. Mr. Callaghan has been combing the neighborhood of Stamford Street, and he's heard of lights being seen in a row of empty houses there. If you care to wait here, sir, there may be fresh news coming in at any moment."

Magnum took a blank check from his pocket and filled it in for five hundred pounds. "If Meredith is found there," he said, "you can turn this over to the Police Orphanage Fund."

An hour later, the expected message from Callaghan came in over the telephone.

"I've got word of a man with a slight foreign accent, guttural, buying milk at a dairy near Stamford Street. I'm certain it's our man."

"Thank God!" exclaimed Magnum fervently.

"Probably he's got Mr. Meredith in one of those empty houses. It's an ideal place for concealing him. No neighbors, no chance callers. But we'll have to proceed very cautiously, because I size up the man as dangerous."

"I'm not afraid of risks. I'll search the houses myself."

"There's the young fellow to consider. He's being held as hostage, remember. He would be the one in danger."

Magnum considered rapidly for a few moments. "Do you think there is more than one of these blackmailers in the house?"

"I've only heard of a single foreigner hereabouts."

"In that case, Meredith would be alone if the man went out. I'll return to my own office to wait for a possible telephone call. When that comes, I'll 'phone at once to you or an assistant of yours waiting near Stamford Street."

"Yes, at the Waterloo Hospital for Children. That's quite close."

"And while you're searching the houses, I'll try to keep the man busy in another direction."

"Excellent!"

"You'll string a cordon round that district?"

"Rely on me for that."

Magnum returned to his laboratory at Upper Thames Street in a fever of impatience, though he realized the necessity for the caution emphasized by Callaghan. There was nothing to be done but to wait for a message from the unknown. Meanwhile, he set to work to devise a possible plan for keeping the man away from Stamford Street while the detectives were at their search.

A plan of convenient simplicity suggested itself. When the unknown 'phoned to Magnum's office, a laboratory assistant would answer the call and state that the consultant had just gone out, but was expected back any moment. This would probably have the effect of keeping the man hanging around telephone call-boxes for a half-hour at least, and a clear space of time would be obtained which should prove sufficient for the police purposes.

Towards seven o'clock in the evening, the 'phone bell in Magnum's office rang for attention. Starting out of a half-doze, he beckoned to the laboratory boy to answer it as arranged. But events had taken an unforeseen turn. The assistant sent a troubled look over to the scientist, and with a request to "hold the line," came to whisper rapidly:

"This is somebody else on the wire, sir, not the man whose voice you got on the dictaphone. He says I'm to tell you they don't accept the report, and unless you send a genuine copy by tonight's post, there will be trouble. What shall I answer him, sir?"

"That you're sent to find Mr. Magnum at dinner, and he will be back within ten minutes. Say, 'phone again presently. Then keep him on the wire as long as possible."

Magnum jammed on his hat, hurried into a cab he had kept
ready waiting for him, and sped to the Waterloo Hospital. To his
relief, Callaghan himself was there, faithful to the post of responsibility. They conferred rapidly over the unexpected turn in the
situation. There were now two men to deal with, and in all prob-
ability one of them was remaining to guard Meredith.

"I'll take the house where the lights were seen," said Magnum,
"and enter it myself from the front. At the same time get your men
on the roof of the row of houses and enter by that way. It's dark,
and the gale will drown noises."

"It would be safer to wait for midnight," answered Callaghan
with the cautiousness of long experience. "We might catch them
asleep. Remember the Sidney Street affair—three men with auto-
matics, and it needed a whole company of military as well as the
police force to handle them."

But Magnum, torn with anxiety and forebodings over the fate
of his young protégé, would not hear of delay.

"There's only one man now in the house to deal with," he
rasped. "Good heavens, we *must* be incapables if we can't surprise
him back or front!"

To Meredith, lying in an attic chained up hand and foot to heavy
staples in the floor, and gagged securely against any possibility of
crying out, came the sound of breaking glass from down below.
Worn by that interminable week of ill-treatment and starvation,
tears of relief came to his eyes. At last they had come to rescue
him!

The thick-set, heavy-jawed man with him in the room started
up and grasped his automatic, then with infinite caution passed
out and descended the stairs.

An eternity of silence ensued. Meredith could do nothing. His
position had always been helpless beyond any possibility of escape.

Presently a face, grotesquely upside down, appeared at the
grimy window. It was Callaghan, being lowered from the roof by
men holding his heels. Meredith clamped his chains to indicate

that he was alone in the attic. Callaghan understood. A minute later, he was prizing up the window and effecting an entrance.

Meredith was safe.

But down below in that silent, lightless house, a tense drama was working to its conclusion. Magnum had deliberately smashed the glass of a front ground-floor window, and had stumbled heavily against a door leading from the hallway, in order to call attention to his presence and draw the unknown away from Meredith. That done, he drew behind a fragment of frowsy curtain in the hall and waited for footsteps.

The blackness of night was in this lightless house; the tearing of the gale outside surfed over all lesser noises.

Yet the creak of a strained board on the stairs above cut shrilly to Magnum's ear, and made him draw closer within the shelter of the curtain and hold his breath. The man above was very cautiously descending.

Magnum wondered with a curious, numb impersonality if he would be alive ten minutes later.

But while he listened, there came another sound, as of some one ascending from the underground region of the kitchen. What did this mean? Had Callaghan's assistants forced an entrance into the basement? Or was one of them the man descending from above? Magnum began to reproach himself that he had arranged no signal with the detectives by which they might recognize one another during a possible encounter inside the blackness of the house. A mistake in identity might be disastrous. He decided to be very wary before his finger pressed home the trigger of the revolver.

A slapping noise came from the head of the kitchen stairs, as of a man who expected one step more and found it non-existent.

Instantly from above, on the first-floor, a shattering roar like a mine explosion—an automatic in action. And then the blaze back from the automatic of the man below, a yell of pain, and a headlong flight down the kitchen stairs. The man above leapt down in a pursuit of vicious ferocity. Magnum caught a flying glimpse of a thick frame and heavy jaw; with unused revolver in hand, he warily followed.

But his weapon never came to trigger-point.

Leading from the kitchen-cellar to a Thames-side wharf (he afterwards found) was an underground passage, a relic of Stamford Street's history of crime, through which the blackmailers had been able to make their entrances and exits to the deserted house without the knowledge of neighbors or police. At the door of this passage, the final scene of the duel between the two men came to an ending of death.

They were the two partners. The one, returning from his telephone message to Magnum, had heard the smashing of glass and the stumbling, and had come upstairs from the kitchen fully prepared to find a detective in the house. The other, creeping down from above, had the same thought in mind. Their mistake was mutual.

It probably saved Magnum.

THE MYSTERY OF BOX 218

The system at the Holborn Safe Deposit is extremely simple and is (or was) reckoned perfect. For a couple of guineas a year you rent a strong box in the vault, in itself surrounded by such foundations of steel and concrete as would make dynamite feel dubious. The single entrance to the vault is via a steel grille, the openings of the lattice-work allowing a clear view of the whole interior. The key to this grille is in the possession of a uniformed commissionaire, who watches while you transfer valuables to or from your strong-box. And access to the commissionaire is via another locked gate, of which the key is held by the secretary of the company, on duty during business hours. In order to reach the vault, every caller has therefore to pass the secretary, the locked gate, the commissionaire, and the locked grille. During the night a watchman keeps guard.

Up to the day when the managing director of the company called on Magnum, the system of the Safe Deposit had worked with oil-smooth perfection. There had been no "incidents," no complaints, no suggestion of unreliability. The reputation of the Safe Deposit stood as high, in its respective line, as the Bank of England's.

Pleydell, the managing director, had little to do but sign checks for the salaries of the staff of three and himself. His real activities lay with bank directorates. He was a man of solidity—both financial and physical—and his name was usually prominent on the lists of Mansion House Funds and other national charities.

"I with to state," he began, "that the matter I have to place before you is extremely confidential." There was a quintessence of board-room manner about Pleydell.

Magnum nodded brusquely. "I'm a safe-deposit for clients' secrets," he answered.

"That is not a very happy analogy, Mr. Magnum. I am very much afraid there is some loophole in our system. Yesterday, it seemed impossible; but to-day, after all the evidence I've heard—I want you to realize that the reputation of a safe deposit company has to be beyond suspicion—like Caesar's wife, beyond suspicion."

"If my memory of Roman history is correct," put in Magnum, "that analogy is also somewhat unhappy."

Pleydell did not approve of jesting inside business hours. "Be that as it may," he answered stiffly, "I am extremely anxious to avoid publicity. If a breath of scandal affecting us should reach the newspapers, it would be a very serious matter. That is why I am not at present calling in the services of the police. They are too much in touch with the reporters. No doubt some of them receive a monetary reward for passing on items of information."

"Is this a scientific problem—something inside my province? I'm not an ordinary criminal-chaser."

"Your reputation, Mr. Magnum, is thoroughly well known to me. That is why I am here confiding in you. Whether the matter has a scientific bearing or no, I cannot at present say. It is extremely mysterious. I suspect some new scientific discovery criminally applied. The modern criminal goes to science for his weapons."

"The crux of the matter?" demanded Magnum abruptly.

"I must first explain the system under which we work," replied Pleydell, who was accustomed to having people listen to him with deference; and he proceeded to expound in great detail. Eventually he came to the point:

"Box No. 218, on the third row of the right-hand side, is rented by a Mr. Michaelis, dealer in precious stones. He has used it for many years. On Wednesday of last week, he entered the vault with a client of his, a Paris dealer, and deposited a valuable pearl necklace. The operation was seen by our commissionaire, Collinson, in whom I have hitherto placed great confidence. On Tuesday of this week, Mr. Michaelis and his client again repair to the vault to take away the necklace, and find—or allege that they find—it missing. Between those dates, neither of the dealers has entered the vault, according to the evidence of both the commissionaire and the secretary. I cannot suppose that both of our staff would lie over such a matter. They have comfortable positions, and I can see no reason why they should jeopardize their livelihood."

"Michaelis has the only key to 218?"

"Decidedly."

"A criminal might have got an impression of that key, made a duplicate, rented a box near to 218, and opened 218 as if it were his own."

"Collinson watches every access to the strong-boxes. That is in the routine of his duties."

"Routine is always liable to suffer from temporary aberration of mind."

"But each box is prominently marked in white with its number, and Collinson accompanies every caller inside the vault and stands near to him while he opens a box. My life-long experience has given me, I venture to think, more than a little knowledge of human nature, and I do not believe that Collinson would let himself be tricked in such an obvious manner."

Magnum sniffed, He took no secondhand opinions from anyone. "Science exhausts the obvious before it proceeds to the abnormal," he remarked sententiously.

"Further," clinched Pleydell, "no box near to 218 has been newly rented within the past four months."

"What is your liability towards a renter?" asked the scientist abruptly.

"There is no definite liability on the part of the company. But what I fear is that Mr. Michaelis will make a public notification of his loss, and this would very seriously affect the reputation of the Safe Deposit. Confidence in us would be shattered."

"Naturally. And meanwhile you're trying to keep him from shouting. Has he asked you to make good the loss of the necklace?"

"Not precisely, as yet, but I can foresee such a claim on his part."

"Pay up, or public scandal. And you want me to devise an explanation for Caesar's wife?" Magnum was not greatly interested in the case, which seemed on the face of it an ordinary criminal matter, and he did not care whether Pleydell took offence at his words or not.

But this offhandedness had the effect of increasing the director's eagerness to have Magnum solve the mystery. "I want the truth," he replied, "and with your acumen and specialized knowledge, I believe you can give it me. I myself have exhausted all the ordinary explanations."

"Including chicanery on the part of this jewel merchant?"

"I make no allegation," answered Pleydell with characteristic caution, "yet I have thought over that possibility very seriously. I cannot see how fraud—if fraud there were—has been carried through."

Unlike the usual scientist, Magnum was an excellent man of business. "Well," he responded brusquely, "I see nothing in this case, so far, but ordinary police work. I'd better warn you that means a heavier fee than usual."

"I fail to follow you."

"If you asked Sargent to paint you an advertisement for bottled stout, you couldn't expect to get it for less than a double fee, could you?"

The remainder of the interview was barter.

Magnum's first procedure was to call at the Holborn Safe Deposit in the character of a would-be renter of a strong-box, in order to observe the normal sequence of events. He found that they corresponded exactly to the abundant details given by the managing director. He then revealed himself abruptly as the investigator, producing a signed authorization.

Collinson, the commissionaire, a conspicuously honest-looking old soldier with a row of service medals across his left breast, went pale at Magnum's words.

"This affair will ruin us, sir," he muttered. "I shall never get another job if I'm discharged from here."

"Not if you tell me frankly all you know and get the mystery straightened," returned Magnum with a sudden kindliness.

"I told everything to Mr. Pleydell, sir—every single thing I know! I haven't an idea how a robbery could possibly have happened." He hesitated for a moment. "And I don't believe it did happen."

"Ah! They pocketed the necklace and then claimed it wasn't in the safe?"

"That's it, sir. That foreign gentleman from Paris."

"Or Michaelis."

"Well. I wouldn't exactly say that. I've known him coming here for years, and he always seemed to me straightforward."

"Bring the secretary here," ordered Magnum.

The commissionaire hesitated again. "I mustn't leave you in the vault alone," he answered.

"Quite right! Then I'll wait in the passage outside the grille."

Presently Collinson was back with the message that the secretary must not leave his office.

Magnum made no demur to this obedience to rules. He went himself to the secretary's slip of an office abutting on the entrance, and began a cross-examination of that formal and tepid official, a young-oldish man of such a colorless and hairless facial aspect that he suggested a recent visit to a bleaching-tub.

In guarded terms, the secretary voiced the same theory as Collinson. He was suspicious of jewel-merchants in general. Many of them were a—er—shady lot, especially men like Mr. Michaelis, who had no office of their own and did business in restaurants and on the curbstone. Magnum heard him through without comment, though he knew that this curious method of transacting business was quite usual both in London and in Paris, and that there were office-less jewel merchants of excellent reputation. In fact, a man who exercises his calling in the public view has necessarily to keep a rein on himself.

"Show me your night arrangements and Sunday arrangements," Magnum then asked.

The bleached secretary routed himself to a pale semblance of enthusiasm, and demonstrated the treble lockings at night-time, the word-combination and time locks, the burglar alarms, and the everything-proof doors. He considered the night-watchman's post a pure formality. Magnum delved minutely into this aspect of the system: examined locks with a powerful magnifying-glass; sniffed around like a hound in a covert; sprang surprise questions on the secretary, in whose capabilities he felt no confidence; and in general raked the system of the Safe Deposit with a volley of mental analysis.

But he could find nothing on which to grip his teeth.

"Where can I see Michaelis?" he finally asked.

The secretary suggested his inquiring at the Café Leduc, near Hatton Garden. That undistinguished-looking street, the focus of London's trade in precious stones, probably houses more diverse nationalities than any other thoroughfare of similar length. The Café Leduc, thoroughly Continental in aspect, is filled at all hours of the day with inordinately shrewd-looking men who sit at small three-legged tables sipping strong black coffee, gulping lager, stirring syrupy drinks, casually unrolling wash-leather bands containing jewels of the value of thousands of pounds, and conversing in guarded whispers in half a dozen languages. Magnum made his way to the bar-counter and inquired for his man. The answer was that if he would sit down and wait, Mr. Michaelis would be sure to turn up eventually.

Magnum decided to wait, though waiting was not a specialty of his temperament, and the super-shrewd, cosmopolitan atmosphere of this jewel exchange rasped against his tastes. Several men approached his table at various times and inquired ingratiatingly if he were "in the market" for diamonds or emeralds or sapphires. Magnum froze them.

Two hours of the afternoon went by fruitlessly, and with overflowing irritation he was about to pay his score and leave, when the head waiter brought up to the table a well-built man of thirty odd, with a neat, dark, close-trimmed mustache, a healthy color, a brisk, direct glance, and a decidedly pleasant smile. Magnum, expecting to meet a crook whom his instincts would at once detect, felt taken aback.

"What can I do for *you*, sir?" greeted the jewel merchant in the customary formula of business.

Magnum, forgetting his irritation in his surprise, passed across politely enough his letter of authorization from the managing director of the Safe Deposit.

Michaelis, looking him over with a frankness which carried no offence, remarked: "I should not have taken you for a detective."

"I'm not. I'm a consulting chemist."

"Good! What can I tell you?"

"Your side of the case."

The jewel merchant lowered his voice to the customary whisper of the Café Leduc, but his words were frank and open. He gave his narrative crisply and clearly. Monsieur Antoine, his Paris client, was a jewel dealer of reputation, and however the robbery had been carried out, it could be taken for granted that the Frenchman had no complicity in it.

"What's the value of the necklace?"

"Fifteen thousand, roughly."

"And if you don't get it back?"

A shadow passed over the features of the jewel merchant, leaving them gray and cold like a dead fire. "In that case," he answered, "I should have to begin all over again. I should have lost ten years of my life. And there's a girl I'm engaged to—"

Down below the hard outer shell of the consultant was a core of human feelings. These words vibrated within him.

"Pearls are not like cut stones," he remarked sympathetically. "They can't he disguised by further cutting. If yours are offered for sale in London or Paris, they would be recognized."

"Probably shipped out to India or the Far East," returned the jewel merchant with bitterness.

"What's your theory of the disappearance?"

"To my mind, there's only one possible explanation."

"And that is—"

"The secretary at the Safe Deposit."

"Your reasons?"

"Four pounds a week, or thereabouts, and no prospects. Too much of a temptation to be in charge of all those valuables."

"And Collinson?"

"He always looks to me the essence of honesty. I don't accuse him. But that secretary fellow—" He pursed up his lips suggestively.

Magnum felt as though he were swimming in a sea shrouded by mist, with no indication as to the direction where land lay. His investigation had so far given him no tangible clue whatever. These mutual suspicions were the merest theories. He was outside his own special province. If there were only some scientific fact at which he could grasp and use for a hand-hold!

His eye caught the glint of a steel chain leading into the jewel merchant's right-hand trouser-pocket. "Is that where you keep your keys?" He pointed.

"Yes. Where else should I keep them?" Michaelis fished out the chain and showed that it was securely fastened at one end. At the other end was a ring with three keys, one obviously a latchkey, the other a bureau key, the third a Yale lock key.

"For box. 218?" inquired Magnum, pointing again.

"Yes."

"Let me see them."

He unsnapped his pocket magnifying-glass and examined all three minutely.

"Looking for wax marks?" suggested Michaelis. "I had thought of that myself. But there's nothing to be seen."

Magnum's face suddenly lighted up with the zeal of the investigator. "Wrap these keys carefully in tissue-paper," he ordered, "and come to my laboratory."

"What do you propose to do with them?"

"Nickel-plate them."

"I don't see the object—"

But Magnum was already picking up his hat and thrusting a coin towards the waiter.

In a small glass tank was a colorless solution of nickel sulphate. Electric wires led at one end to a rod of pure nickel pendant in the solution, and at the other end to hooks from which the three keys hung. For over an hour a very tiny current of electricity had been ferrying ions of metal from the anode of nickel to the cathode formed by the keys.

Magnum now removed them carefully, dried them in a gas oven, and showed them one by one to Michaelis. "These two," he demonstrated, "show the polish of nickel-plating all round, but the Yale key, you note, is plated on one side only."

"What does that convey?"

"It means that one side of it has been pressed against wax, which has left an invisible film on the metal. But that minute film has been sufficient to resist the electric current."

"There might have been grease in my pocket."

"Then all three keys would have been affected. No," deduced Magnum triumphantly, "there's been a wax impression taken of your Yale key."

"But who . . . ? That secretary fellow?"

"You sit about in cafés with your keys in your trouser-pocket," rasped Magnum. "What could be simpler for a trained pickpocket than to pull them out gently, take a wax impression, and replace them? One man holds you in conversation while the other does the trick."

Michaelis became very thoughtful. He was evidently searching his memory for an occasion when this would have been possible.

"Frankly," added Magnum, "I wouldn't trust myself with valuables inside the Café Leduc."

"We always have to run risks in the jewel trade," answered Michaelis. "We get calloused . . . Wait while I think."

But eventually he gave up the task of searching his recollections. "One meets and talks with so many men. It's hopeless to work the case from that end."

"Then we must put your recollections alongside of Collinson's," said Magnum sanguinely. "If he has recently shown someone into the vault who corresponds with someone you've talked business to recently, we're hot on the scent."

They drove forthwith to the Holborn Safe Deposit, but found it closed for the day. The night-watchman explained that Collinson and the secretary had just left. Yes, he knew the commissionaire's address. It was 16, Ethelberta Road, Fulham. Magnum and the jewel-merchant re-entered their taxi and drove to a row of two-storied brick houses in the "respectable poverty" area of Fulham. The cab had evidently outpaced Collinson's bus or train, for the landlady who opened the door informed them that he had not yet returned from his work.

"Is his wife in?"

"No, sir, 'e's a widower. I couldn't let you wait in 'is room, but if you like to sit in my parlor—" She opened, with pride, the door of her state room, reserved for the local curate and other distinguished visitors. Then, with the morbid curiosity of the lower classes, always ready to put the worst interpretation on any event, she inquired sidlingly: 'I 'ope 'e's not been doing anything wrong, 'as 'e?"

"Nothing!" said Magnum firmly.

She looked a trifle disappointed. "'E's always been so regular in 'is 'abits, but last Thursday when 'e went out for the night and didn't return till Saturday afternoon, I kept wondering-like what 'ad 'appened to 'im."

"Did you ask him?"

"Oh no, sir! I knows 'ow to keep myself to myself."

"You say he has always been very regular in his habits. Rent punctual?"

"Yes, sir."

"Drink?"

"'Course 'e goes to the White 'Art of a night like any other man, but I can't say as I've ever seen 'im the worse for drink."

"Women?"

"Oh no, sir! I wouldn't allow such a thing in my 'ouse!"

A heavy step in the passage outside indicated the return of Collinson. The landlady went out to inform him of the visitors. He seemed surprised to see Magnum and Michaelis, but invited them politely to come upstairs to his room—a bed-sitting-room plainly furnished, but kept with scrupulous neatness and decorated with his trophies of former service in India, regimental portraits, Afghan weapons, and trifles of native workmanship.

Magnum had already whispered to the jewel merchant to keep silent and allow him to conduct all the questioning. He began: "I want to compare your recollections of recent callers at the Safe Deposit with men whom Mr. Michaelis has done business with lately."

"Yes, sir, with pleasure."

"First, you were on duty every day last week and this week?"

"Yes, sir."

"Quite sure."

"I've never missed a day for the past two years—not a single day."

"If you were ill, who would replace you?"

"Mr. Pleydell would be told, and he would send one of his bank messengers to take my place."

Magnum turned to the jewel merchant. "Now give close descriptions of every man or woman you can remember meeting during the three weeks before the necklace was discovered to be missing."

It was a lengthy and tedious task. Collinson was evidently concentrating his mind intently, but he could match no recollection against that of Michaelis. Then they tried the reverse way round, the commissionaire endeavoring to describe the callers at the Safe Deposit, and Michaelis listening. Nothing tangible resulted.

Magnum had meanwhile been observing them both, on the keen watch for some clue. He was forced to the conclusion that they were both honest men, and both of them eager to have the mystery cleared up. Any lingering suspicion of the *bona fides* of Michaelis vanished, while Collinson's truthfulness seemed transparent.

Yet the landlady's words reverberated in Magnum's sub-consciousness. He asked abruptly. "You stayed out one night last week, didn't you?"

The answer came without hesitation: "Yes, sir, at my brother's house."

"And went to work from there, returning home Saturday afternoon?"

"That's quite right. He lives over in Camden Town, so it was quicker to go straight to work from there."

"But you don't go about of an evening in your uniform?"

"No, sir, I took it with me in a bag. I went to stay the night because he was ill and asked me to come."

The ring of sincerity was in every word uttered by the commissionaire. It was impossible to doubt that he was speaking the truth. Magnum had been elated over his discovery in connection with the Yale key, but now disappointment settled upon him. He sighed and rose to leave.

Collinson accompanied them downstairs to the front door of the house. "Is there nothing more I can tell you, sir?" he asked earnestly. "It means a great deal to me to have this matter cleared up."

"You might give me your brother's address."

Collinson took out an old envelope and penciled the address on the back.

It was a silent drive townwards in the taxi. Magnum made no comment on the evening's disappointment, and the jewel merchant was too tactful to force unwanted questions. But nearing the Strand he ventured to ask: "What's to be the next move? Would anything be gained by calling on Collinson's brother?"

Magnum, for want of a reply, took out the envelope to scan the address written on it, holding the paper close to his eyes in the dim light

Suddenly a faint tinge of some unusual odor tanged his extraordinarily keen sense of smell. He sniffed at the envelope—sniffed again hard, rolled, as it were, that infinitesimal fragment of odor on the sensitive membranes of his nostrils, furrowed his forehead in thought . . . then ordered the chauffeur to drive to Woodford Square, Camden Town.

"What have you discovered?" asked Michaelis eagerly.

But the scientist was so absorbed in his new-born theory of the mystery that the question passed over him totally unheard.

The district of Camden Town is compounded mostly of the sordid and the sinister. Woodford Square proved to be an oasis in the desert, a group of terraced houses of a substantial stuccoed mid-Victorian aspect, occupied by teachers of music, cheap dentistry exponents, dressmakers, and other home businesses.

Magnum left the taxi at one end of the square, ordered it to wait for him, and walked with Michaelis to No. 23. He gave a postman's *rat-tat* with the knocker, knowing that this would always bring some one speedily in answer. The door was opened by a young woman—pretty, but sharp-featured and with an indefinable aspect of the *déclassée.* "What do you want?" she asked suspiciously.

"Mr. Collinson," answered Magnum.

"There's no Mr. Collinson living here."

"This is No. 23, isn't it?"

"Yes."

"Do you know anyone of that name living in the square?"

"No." She held the door as though to close it on them.

"I must have made a mistake," said Magnum. "Sorry to have troubled you."

"Queer!" commented the jewel merchant as they returned towards the waiting taxi.

Magnum answered briskly: "I want you to drive to Fulham and bring Collinson back with you. Meanwhile I'll stay round here and wait. Don't question him on the way—leave that to me."

"Right! I'll hurry."

It was over an hour before Michaelis returned with the commissionaire. Obeying orders, he had entered into no conversation beyond generalities.

Magnum at once took up the questioning: "Your brother lives at No. 23, doesn't he?"

"Yes, sir; but what do you want me here for?"

"To give exact answers to my questions!" snapped Magnum. "Is he a man of about your own age and rather like you in appearance?"

"When we were younger we used to be taken for one another, but now time has changed us a good deal."

"There's a young woman, rather pretty, living at No. 23. Who is she—your brother's daughter, or wife, or what?"

Collinson hesitated before answering— "Not exactly his wife."

"Now about yourself: You came to 23 to stay the night on Thursday evening last?"

"On Friday evening, sir."

"Thursday, your landlady mentioned."

"That's a mistake of hers. I came on Friday, stayed the night because my brother was ill and wanted me near him, went to work on Saturday morning, came back to here after work, found him very much better, and then back to my own room at Fulham."

"Were you feeling in good health on the Saturday?"

"Not very good, somehow, sir. I had a disturbed night, and felt a bit muzzy."

"'Do you ever take chloral for sleeplessness?"

"Never!" returned Collinson with genuine surprise at the question. "Why should I? I sleep sound enough."

"You're positive about Friday and not Thursday?"

"Of course I am! I've told you several times that I only went to my brother's for a single night."

"And one last question," pursued Magnum, looking at him searchingly. "What does your brother do for a living?"

"You'd better ask him yourself," retorted Collinson resentfully.

"That's all I want from you," Magnum passed over a sovereign. "This is to pay your fare back to Fulham and recompense you for the trouble I've put you to."

The commissionaire hesitated, but decided to take the coin.

"Well?" queried Michaelis eagerly when they were alone,

"The method of the robbery is perfectly clear now," said Magnum with his air of being superior to any mystery on earth or in heaven.

"I don't see it."

"While you were fetching Collinson, I waited about the Square. I saw the brother entering 23. There's a striking resemblance between the two."

"Well?"

"That's the man who stole your necklace," returned Magnum with dramatic abruptness.

"But how on earth—"

"They drugged Collinson with chloral. Kept him unconscious at 23 during the whole of the Friday. He's honestly under the impression that he was there for one night only; but he was actually there for two nights and a day."

Michaelis had now caught on to the line of deduction. He joined in: "And on the Friday this brother dressed himself in Collinson's uniform—"

Magnum, who preferred to make all deductions himself, took possession of the uncoiling of the chain of events: "And went in his place to the Safe Deposit. Walked in calmly at the opening hour in Collinson's uniform. That bleached secretary is a dull fool, and he wouldn't have noticed the difference. Brainless routine deadens a man's perceptions. . . . Once in the commissionaire's place, the rest was perfectly simple for the brother. He had merely to unlock your strong-box at some quiet hour of the day, and pocket your necklace."

"But how would he get the duplicate of my key?"

"Probably he was not the one who took the wax impression, I suspect an organized gang of them—a man with brains to plan, a man with hands to get the key, and a man with a lucky resemblance to get inside the vault. Given a passable disguise, the rest was child's play."

"Of course! But you're a marvel to have unraveled it so quickly!" exclaimed Michaelis gratefully. "Now to get the police on to them."

"First to Pleydell," amended Magnum. "My commission is from him. He's naturally anxious to avoid publicity, and I must leave to him any further steps."

"My necklace may be at Number 23 at this very moment!"

"It may. Wherever it is, we'll get it back sure enough. Don't worry any further. If you'll take my advice, you'll go straight to the young lady you're engaged to and—"

But Michaelis needed no prompting on that aspect of the case.

THE MESSAGE OF THE TIDE

The Thames tide, yellow-brownish in its capacity of universal col-
lector and carrier, rippled briskly up-river against a westerly summer breeze, exchanging coolness and warmth, salt and sooty
smoke, a faint tinge of marsh odor against a lingering reminiscence
of meadow.

A squat-shaped bottle came bobbing along with the brisk tide.
There is a peculiar appeal in a corked bottle floating on water. It
touches the core of human curiosity. What does it carry? Merely
emptiness, or liquor, or perchance some message from a ship-
wrecked vessel? A temperance league once organized a campaign
of propaganda by means of corked bottles containing its special
tract. So far as getting the appeal read, the scheme was an admi-
rable one; though it is to be feared that the conversion effect was
minutely small.

Many people saw the bottle that was carried on this up-river
tide: mid-day loungers on the Embankment, taking their lunch
interval in the open air; saunterers along the bridges, looking down
at whatever of novelty the river-traffic might present for their special entertainment; men on barges taking economical advantage
of the tide to dispense with tug-power; the voyagers on an occasional river-steamer, which for London has an exotic and out-of-
place appearance; and the river-police slowly chugging in a motor-
launch on their routine beats.

The bottle, by perversity, avoided all who might be near enough
to water-level to capture it, until it came with a swirling rush under

Westminster Bridge. To one side was the stately fretted pile of the Houses of Parliament; to the other side, in front of the arch-episcopal Lambeth Palace, was a small area of shingly beach from which slum urchins bathed nudely in the July sunshine. They sighted the bottle with glee. One of them swam boldly out to capture it.

Triumphant, he brought it to shore and opened it. What he found inside sent him to hurried dressing and a march on Lambeth police station. The bobbies ought to give him a few coppers for this!

From the police station the bottle and its message went to Scotland Yard, and in the course of time to Magnum, scientific consultant.

"I'll tell you what we've done already," said Callaghan, inspector in the detective force. "First we had to make sure that the message was not a hoax. That kind of thing has been done before, in order to get a rise out of us. Well, it appears that there does exist a Mr. Lester Oakeshott of Vancouver. He banks with the Union Bank of Canada. He made a fortune out there in Vancouver over land—'real estate,' as they call it—and he came to Europe to have a good time with his money. That was three years ago. Since then they have been regularly cashing checks for him, sent from all parts of Europe, up to his fixed limit of three thousand dollars a month. But they haven't heard from him, except by these checks; and relatives have been sending inquiries from Vancouver about him, which of course the bank couldn't answer."

Magnum inserted a comment: "The bank would know to whom the checks were paid."

"For the last eighteen months the checks have been drawn to 'Self or bearer,' and cashed by bearer," replied Callaghan, and continued with his narrative: "You must understand, sir, that Mr. Oakeshott was a gentleman of rather overbearing manners and temper—the kind of man who means to have his own way, and won't take advice. Men who make fortunes quickly often get that way."

The scientist nodded assent.

"That's what we found from the bank and from Cook's, who supplied him with a courier for the first year of his travels about Europe. Then he quarreled with the courier and went about by himself in dubious company. He would not be the first man to fall into the hands of a gang of international crooks. Judging from the message in the bottle, that is what happened to him. They have held him in confinement and forced him to go on signing checks every month. It seems to me a perfectly likely story. I don't see it as a hoax message."

Magnum held the scrap of paper—a label from a liquor bottle—up to the light, and read again the prickings which formed the piteous cry for rescue.

"Yes," he agreed. "And what next?"

"We have to find out where he is now. The bottle might have been thrown overboard from a boat in the Thames—a private yacht, say—or it's just possible that Mr. Oakeshott might be held up in some underground vault in the docks district. As you probably know, there's miles and miles of those vaults. We don't want to waste energies combing the whole of the river and the riverside. I thought you might be able to give us a line of approach—something about the bottle or the paper we might have missed."

A call of the 'phone turned Magnum to the desk instrument. He listened, and then said: "Hold the line a moment . . . For you, Callaghan."

The detective took up the receiver, and presently repeated the message aloud: "The relatives in Vancouver have cabled us an offer of fifty thousand dollars reward for Mr. Oakeshott produced alive. The money would come out of his property. Of course, sir, the Commissioner would see that you had your proper share."

Magnum never affected to despise the monetary end of his profession, and he usually assessed his services at a substantial figure. "You can count on me," he answered. "Leave the bottle and the message, and I'll put my energies into the affair."

It is commonly supposed that Scotland Yard is an autocratic and self-sufficient body of men. This is not true of recent years. The

authorities pursue a broad-minded policy of calling on specialized
help whenever it seems likely that outside brains will supplement
the knowledge and intelligence of the force. Magnum had been able
to help them from the scientific angle on many occasions, and his
connection with the Yard was close and cordial. What they needed
now was some short cut in the troubled problem of search for the
missing man. A bottle floating at the caprice of the tide—whence
had it come? Magnum might be able to deduce.

After Callaghan's departure, the scientist proceeded to examine the data in his own thorough and minute fashion. The bottle
was of the squat, monastically corpulent shape and the dark green
glass associated with bénédictine liqueur. The labels had become
ungummed and licked away by the tongues of the tide, but the
molded glass name remained, whilst inside there was quite definitely the sweetly-pungent odors of bénédictine. They—the captors—had evidently allowed this luxury to the man they held in
captivity. They would treat him reasonably because every month
he represented to them an income of some six hundred pounds.

One identification mark suggested itself as missing to
Magnum's keen memory—the red wax seal affixed to the shoulders of the bottle. It had been completely chipped off. One could
deduce that the bottle had made a long journey, rubbing shoulders against river-craft or bridge-piers. A seal would not be loos-
ened by water as a label would be.

The discolored cork held a salty odor. Magnum proceeded to
cut the cork in two, and from the upper half, which would have
projected from the bottle and be washed by the water, to make a
solution. This he handed to young Meredith, his chief assistant,
for detailed analysis, and turned his own attention to the paper
which carried the cry for help.

It was a printed label, round in shape, ungummed from the
bottle itself. The captive had pricked it with dots to form the letters of his message, had enclosed it in the bottle, and had either
thrown it into the water or, more likely, trusted to its being thrown
away as rubbish by those who cleared his meals. "They have kept
me here over a year," he wrote. "I have lost count of dates. By the

warmth it must be June or July. I do not know where I am. They threaten to kill me if I do not sign checks."

Scarcely a message that a clever business man who had a small fortune for himself should write. He ought to have given such particulars of his place of captivity as would help the police to narrow down the search. But it must be taken into account, Magnum reflected, that a year's close captivity under the menace of constant threats might have worked on his nerves to make him a mental wreck. Further, there was little space on the label for a long description. The remainder of the message was a plan for instant rescue. It ended off with the name of Lester H. Oakeshott and the Vancouver address on the very edge of the label.

Magnum puffed heavily at a curved briar pipe, rank with strong tobacco and long usage, as he pondered over the wording. If the man had been on a yacht, the inevitable motion of the vessel would have told him of that fact, and he would surely have mentioned it. One must deduce that he was on shore. A vault in the docks district, Callaghan had suggested. That was quite possible: but the sentence "By the warmth it must be June or July," threw doubt on the suggestion. Magnum knew the storage vaults of the docks. Interned in one of them, a man would not know whether it were midwinter or midsummer.

If the captive had given a definite and recent date, one might deduce from tidal statistics the maximum distance the bottle could have traveled. "June or July," was altogether too vague to serve any practical deduction. The bottle might have been days or weeks on its journey. From the chipping off of the red wax seal and the moldy appearance of the cork, a considerable and adventurous travel seemed probable.

Up river or down? The analysis of the solution made from the cork should help to settle that point.

Working intently, Meredith had completed by late that night the detailed chemical analysis of the solution made from the cork. Magnum studied the symbols and figures with a concentration of his bristling reddish eyebrows.

"We must take samples," he mused, "from here to the mouth of the Thames. To compare with these figures. . . . Get the launch ready with petrol for fifty miles."

Meredith, wearied by his long and patient work of analysis, tried to suppress a yawn of sheer exhaustion.

Magnum caught the action with the tail of his eye, and he abruptly amended his order: "No, get straight off to bed. I'll see to this myself."

The motor-launch was Magnum's hobby—and a means of transit to and from his home. He was accustomed to racing it at a dizzy pace through the crowded traffic of the lower Thames and out to the freedom of the broad estuary. He knew the many reaches well, and the small shipping and yachting harbors on each side and the islands and marshlands of Essex and Kent.

The night was one of full moon, with a clear, unruffled sky. Navigation was simple. He had opportunity to concentrate on the problem of the case as he speeded down river, stopping every few miles to bottle a sample of the water, becoming more and more salty as it approached the sea.

Out of his meditations came a plan. He drafted out an advertisement to be inserted in the "agony column" of every London newspaper. It was an announcement of an exceedingly legal-dry character: "*In re* the Estate of Charles Harding Oakeshott, deceased, of Victoria, British Columbia. The Executors of the Estate request information of the present address of Lester Harding Oakeshott, chief legatee. Communications should be addressed to the Union Bank of Canada, Threadneedle Street, E. C."

It was possible that the captors, scenting fresh booty from the announcements, might guardedly get into touch with the bank. But reliance must not be placed on this alone. A third avenue of approach to the problem must be devised.

And during that night of glorious speeding down and up the Thames, it came upon Magnum with the flush of an inspiration.

A week later, Magnum and Callaghan were installed at Sheerness, the dockyard town on the Isle of Sheppey, at the mouth of the Thames, as their base of strategical operation. Comparisons of water analyses had proved that the bottle with its contained message had been thrown into the water within the region where river meets sea. That narrowed down the problem of search. It was unnecessary to undertake the tremendous task of combing the riverside of London itself. On the other hand, the advertisement in the newspapers had brought no reply.

The third plan of attack was now in operation. That was, in brief, to "beat the coverts" and scare out the game. All the local papers of North Kent and South Essex had been supplied from Scotland Yard with a highly-colored story of a spy-hunt. Two mysterious men, believed to be foreigners, so the story ran, had been seen loitering around the fortifications of the Thames mouth. The local police were hot after them. The provincial officers were requested to assist. Any suspicious circumstance was at once to be reported to local authorities.

Magnum shrewdly reckoned that this man-hunt must be read or heard of by the captors of the unfortunate Oakeshott, and that they would be scared into moving their captive to a safe region. It was unlikely that they would make away with him, because so long as he could sign checks, cashable all over Great Britain and the Continent, he represented to them a very comfortable income. They would be more likely to preserve him at all hazards.

The detective and the scientist sat as it were in the center of a web of telegraph and telephone wires, weighing the merits of the reports sent in to them from the region of riverside and marshland roundabout, and despatching police by motor-cycle and motor-launch to investigate.

They had been there three days when Callaghan came at midnight into Magnum's bedroom and brusquely wakened him from sleep.

"We've got the right report in now!" declared the detective triumphantly. "The bridge-keeper at the crossing over the Swale stopped a closed motor-car containing two men and what seemed to him a third man rolled up in blankets and lying asleep inside. He began to ask questions, and they tried to drive on over the bridge in the direction of the mainland. He closed the gate against them, and they seemed to get frightened, backed off, and drove on to the island again."

The Swale is a tidal stream separating the Isle of Sheppey from the mainland of Kent.

"And that's the only bridge," continued the detective rapidly. "We've got them! I've sent out scouts to guard the roads to Queenboro' and Sheerness, and to scour the rest of the Isle."

Magnum, now awake and immensely alert, interjected: "They'll try to get off by boat: Send a launch round the seaward of the Isle, and we'll take the Swale ourselves." He hurried on clothes with remarkable vigor, and within ten minutes the two were in Magnum's motor-boat, speeding off through a miscellany of small craft, nodding drowsily to the gentle heave of the harbor waters, and the gray hulls of warships, which by a trick of elfin moonlight seemed of cardboard thinness.

Soon they were threading the channel of the Swale. To each side slept a stretch of lush mainland—a "salting" in the local vernacular—with now and again the dark, irregular shape of a farm-house nursing its brood of outbuildings. A sheep-dog, vigilant even in slumber, awoke as the *putt-putt* of the motor-boat came unfamiliarly to its ears, and barked a challenge.

It was lonely, eerie country. Magnum realized how fittingly it would be adapted to the holding of a prisoner. In one of those four farmhouses, separated from neighbors by miles of marsh-meadows intersected with creeks and sluggish streams, any crime might be committed with perfect security.

The barking of the sheep-dog suggested that the sound of the motor-launch must be carrying far through the still night. Magnum shut down power, and let the boat glide on in comparative silence.

Over the levels of salt-marsh a yellow star of light bobbed like a bottle on a brisk tide. Some one was tracing a path across the treacherous network of creeks, making for the western end of the Isle, where by day an ancient and weatherbeaten hulk ferries infrequent travelers across the Swale.

The two men exchanged glances, without need for an open expression of thought. It was well within the probabilities that Oakeshott's captors would abandon their motor-car, easily traceable in the narrow confines of the island, and strike out across the marshland for the ferry-boat, lying deserted and ready for their purpose. Magnum ran his launch to the ferry, a mere suggestion of a pier to either side of the muddy banks of the Swale. The heavy ferry-boat slept hoggishly on the mainland shore. Magnum untethered it and towed it across to the island side, thus building a golden bridge for their game. He then glided the motor-launch into the shelter of a neighboring creek. Both men sat still and listened intently.

A half-hour passed before the *squelch* of footsteps, dulled by distance, told them of an approach across the marsh-meadows. Presently the sounds changed to a firm and crisp note. Men were now on the paved road that led down to the ferry. There was no need to risk premature discovery by climbing the bank of the creek and observing by eye. Ears told them that the footsteps were those of three men. The bridge-keeper had mentioned only two, and one lying asleep or unconscious—presumably Oakeshott. Was the latter now conscious again and walking with his captors? That would greatly simplify the work of arrest.

The detective's trained ears told him more than reached Magnum.

"Two men in exact step, carrying a burden between them, and a third man walking in advance," he whispered.

"The bridge-keeper might have forgotten to mention the chauffeur," suggested Magnum in his knowledge of the fallibility of human evidence.

"Yes," agreed Callaghan. "And we must assume they carry revolvers. Now I don't suppose, sir, that you want to run unnecessary risks?"

"I don't," admitted Magnum frankly.

"Then we must wait until they are in mid-stream, working at the oars. If you will crouch down in the boat and see to the levers,

I'll tell you when to rush them." He took out his own service revolver and handled it fondly. "Leave any shooting work to me."

The scientist obeyed. It was not in his province to run the risks that fall within the normal duty of a detective. He had his own revolver loosed, but he lay crouched in the launch and awaited orders.

They heard the party of men tread into the ferry-boat, take up the heavy oars, pull out across the Swale.

"Now!" ordered Callaghan. "Straight across their stern."

As a surprise maneuver it was perfect. The startled game dropped their oars in utter confusion as Callaghan, standing up with revolver plainly in view, shouted at them: "In the name of the King!" He had them completely at a disadvantage. In another few moments they must surrender to *force majeure.*

And then the unexpected happened. A rope trailing meaninglessly under the water from the moldy pier fouled the propeller of the launch. It pulled up with a jerk that threw Callaghan off his feet and sideways into the muddy waters. The captors of Oakeshott shouted wildly to one another at the mishap.

Magnum was torn between two duties: to rescue Callaghan and to effect the arrest. He had to decide without the delay of precious moments. Intuition told him that the detective should be able to look after himself. It was close to shore. Callaghan must be left to swim or grope through the mud for it.

The scientist fired his revolver haphazard, by way of warning rather than attempting any aim; and with a vigor that did every credit to a sedentary man of forty-five, he leaped from the launch onto the ferry-boat.

It was a maneuver unexpected and menacing. For a second time the captors of Oakeshott were taken by surprise.

"Hands up!" growled Magnum in his bassest voice, like a grizzly in fury at trespass, and flourished his revolver with terrorizing ruthlessness.

Three pair of hands went hastily skywards. The figure in the bottom of the boat, sack-high, did not stir.

Magnum waited to hear sounds behind him. There came a splashing and a gurgling and then a most welcome swearing of a man angry but safe. Callaghan was clambering aboard the launch.

"Splendid, sir!" he called out when he realized the new situation. "Keep them like that till I get to you!"

The rest lay in the routine of the detective service.

Oakeshott had been heavily drugged in order to keep him quiet during the removal to safer quarters. When he recovered consciousness, he explained matters with the stammering incoherence of a man whose nerves had been shattered by long-drawn terror and despair.

It was as Magnum had shrewdly deduced. He had been confined in the loft of a lonely farmhouse on the Sheppey salting, given the food and drink he asked for, but kept rigorously in captivity. The entrapment in the first place had been made at Nice. An invitation to a gay little yacht-party from some casual acquaintance of the Riviera—how harmless it had seemed to the self-confident, self-sufficient man from Vancouver! Others besides Oakeshott had gone to destruction by the same path.

Oakeshott, in charge of a capable nurse-attendant, was shipped back to his home-town in Canada. In heartfelt gratitude for the rescue, he doubled the reward offered by his relatives.

And Magnum came to believe that he had by himself effected the rescue, the arrest, and the delivery to justice of the three men who had terrorized Oakeshott. Callaghan's share in the work receded into the dim background.

It was a very human illusion.

THE SECRET OF THE TOWER HOUSE

In every great port of the world there now and again comes into the papers an obscure paragraph telling of some seaman from an Eastern trading ship being taken to the hospital with symptoms resembling those of plague. The sensation-hardened newspaper reader skims over it lightly. It does not affect himself. The case is reported (say) from the East End of London, which is a continent removed from the comfortable West End or the trim suburb where the reader lives. Unless the event arises where a whole county is set to the task of rat-exterminating, the menace of Oriental plague does not impinge on his imagination. He promptly forgets that obscure paragraph.

But there are men—public officers of health and consulting analysts—to whom the menace looms large. They stamp on that sporadic outbreak with all the resources of medical and sanitary science. But for their ceaseless vigilance, a whole city, a whole nation might be decimated.

It was in the spring of a year when a King of England was to be crowned with all the pomp of complex traditional rites. The occasion would "make" the London season. Visitors from all over the world were already pouring in by thousands. At the very least computation, ten million dollars in extra trade would gladden the hearts of London hotel-keepers, landlords and retail merchants. Pray Heaven that there would be no royal mourning or national calamity to ruin the season! At Lloyds', a stream of business was being done in insurances against such an eventuality. For a premium of ten guineas per cent, the underwriters of the great insurance exchange were comforting a nervous London. They reckon it at the moment nine to one against any untoward event. A rumor of royal illness might send that rate leaping to twenty or thirty per cent. The "rate at Lloyds'" was the barometer of the London season.

Magnum, opening his daily paper one morning in early May, noted that the glass was "set fair" at ten guineas per cent. It did not affect him personally in a business direction, since his work was independent of season, but he was lightly pleased that things looked like going smoothly for anxious London.

An underwriter at Lloyds' who occasionally employed his services rang him up on the 'phone. "Everything sound with London's health?" was the inquiry. "No suspicious disease-cases brought to you?"

"Nothing; and if there were, I'm not sure that I should tell you," replied Magnum brusquely.

"I'm not asking for professional secrets."

"Sounds very like it."

"Sorry!"

"Good-by."

Magnum had found by experience that his particular brand of brusqueness did not lose him clients.

Later that same morning, the telephone bell called Magnum again to his office.

"Is that Mr. Magnum, the analyst?" asked a stranger's voice.

"It is."

"Your name has been mentioned to me. A very mysterious case of poisoning has happened in my house. Could you come at once to investigate?"

"I'm very busy."

"I'm very anxious."

"I could perhaps put off my present work, but my fee would be heavy," answered Magnum the business man.

"Please come. The address is The Tower House, Wensleydale Gardens, W. My name is Anstruther."

May was all opalescent sunshine and joyously twittering sparrows as Magnum drove westwards through the pleasure heart of
London. The main streets were already being palisaded with the
wooden stands which were to accommodate the sightseers at the
Royal procession in June. Even the churches were seizing the fore-
lock of the occasion and hiding themselves behind escalades of
wooden seats prominently advertised as "From One Guinea Upwards." The building trades, also seizing the occasion, were con-
templating a strike, and union buttons were blatant on the coats
of carpenters and scaffold workers.

The taxi wormed through the feverish traffic of the West End,
and with a sigh of relief entered the clearer stretches of the
Kensington district. Wensleydale Gardens proved to be a quiet bye-
street of houses of a mid-Victorian pattern, solid, substantial, built
for large families and the leisured life. The term "Gardens" was
somewhat of a landlord's flight of fancy, for the only greenery to
be seen was a tiny triangle of railed-in grass and trees at the end
of the street, flanking the first house. It was a public domain in
that it was not attached to the house, but it was too small to be of
service even for nursemaids and children, and in any case there
was no entrance gate. The domain seemed to be purposeless—perhaps a relic of some ancient public right in a district which was
once a village outside London.

The house it flanked was The Tower House, evidently so called
from an astronomical dome built by a former owner. Magnum
noted that the residence was newly painted and decorated and win-
dow-boxed and tussore-silk-curtained from top to bottom, and
mentally raised the fee he was to ask to a comfortable figure. His
charges were elastic, based on "what the traffic would bear."

As the door opened to his ring, a sound of the yelping of terriers
penetrated through the house to the hall. The parlor-maid ushered him into Mr. Anstruther's study, quite newly-furnished and
redolent of new paint.

Mr. Anstruther entered, a man of fifty with a curiously soft and
gentle air and manner. His hair and beard, graying, suggested in

their cut something of the artist, but a precision in the room contradicted that. His eyes were mild, and he wore bifocal spectacles. Magnum found it difficult to place him, but in the course of conversation enlightenment speedily came.

"I have just returned to the Old Country after thirty years in Australia," explained Mr. Anstruther. "My eldest daughter is with me, and my wife and the rest of my family are expected next week."

"Government civil servant, retired," thought Magnum.

"I have taken the house to settle down in."

"And marry off his daughters," deduced Magnum.

"I have also brought with me my Aberdeen terriers—my hobby, I should explain. I had entered them for the Dog Show, and was hopeful of carrying off some first prizes, for they are splendid animals, though I say it myself. But now—" His mouth contracted with pain.

"Poisoned?"

"Two of them are dead. The veterinary surgeon I called in seems to be uncertain over the cause of death, but I myself suspect that they have been deliberately poisoned."

"By whom?"

"How can I say? I may have jealous rivals without knowing it. My dogs are such splendid animals—"

"You want an analysis made?" interrupted Magnum.

"That is why I have called on your services."

"The dogs were quarantined before landing, of course?"

"Yes, for two months. During that period my daughter and myself were searching for a suitable London residence and having it decorated and furnished. Being Coronation year, London houses are scarce, and I consider myself very fortunate in being able to secure this one at a reasonable rental without difficulty."

"You're only just in?" said Magnum, sniffing at the odor of the new paint.

"Only ten days in the house."

"Let me see the bodies of the animals."

"Jock, who died five days ago, is already buried; but Scottie died only yesterday, and his body is down below in the cellars."

Mr. Anstruther leading, they made their way to the mid-Victorian basement of the house, a region of kitchen, scullery and underground cellars. In what had evidently been intended by a former owner for a wine-cellar, the body of the unfortunate animal was laid out on a wooden shelf, decently covered over by a holland cloth.

Magnum, with prudence, lifted off the cloth by means of a fragment of wood, and sniffed closely at the dead body, distended and forbidding. He gazed at it long and thoughtfully.

"Do you recognize the signs of poison?" questioned Mr. Anstruther.

Magnum did not answer. He was not accustomed to committing himself before he had definite evidence. He turned over the body of the dog with his fragment of wood, and withdrawing, studied it from a distance. Finally he replied: "I must make a detailed laboratory examination. But first I want to question your vet."

"Certainly. He lives quite near."

They went together to a neighboring mews in process of conversion—sign of the times—to a motor garage. At one end, the sign of "Animal Hospital" swung out prominently. Mr. Henry Gedge, veterinary surgeon, proved to be a knowing little horsey man, full of talk and anxious to command the situation by reason of technical knowledge. Magnum quickly subdued him with a few searching questions tinged with sarcasm. Mr. Henry Gedge's theories crumpled up. He was forced to an admission that in all his practice he had never had a case of animal death with symptoms similar to those of Jock and Scottie. He had made a post-mortem of Jock and it had given him no definite information.

"Where were the remains buried?" asked Magnum.

"In the Dogs' Cemetery, Kensington Gardens," was the reply.

On the way back to The Tower House, Magnum looked unusually grave. As they entered the house, he said abruptly: "Can you move out today?"

"Move out!" exclaimed Mr. Anstruther in surprise and, for a man of mildness, some indignation.

"Decidedly. Yourself, your daughter and your household. The dogs must be sent away to,"—he considered rapidly—"to Canvey Island, at the mouth of the Thames."

"But we have invited guests for dinner to-night!"

"There is the telephone," replied Magnum pointedly.

"You think that there is some grave disease in the house?"

"I make no definite statement at present."

"The whole house has been cleansed and redecorated from cellar to attic!"

"It's open to you to refuse my advice," said Magnum curtly.

"I must consult my daughter. It is extremely inconvenient to move at such short notice." He was much upset at the development of affairs.

"While you're doing so, I'll make use of your telephone."

Magnum carefully closed the study door, and calling up Meredith, his chief assistant, at the Upper Thames Street laboratories, ordered him to collect and to bring to The Tower House a quantity of bacteriological apparatus and special reagents.

"It sounds like plague," commented young Meredith over the 'phone.

"S'sh!" whispered Magnum imperatively. "Don't breathe that word!"

That evening, in an empty house, the consultant undertook his examination of the dead Scottie. He himself had been inoculated against plague a couple of years back, and Meredith also, but he preferred that his young protégé should run no risks. It is well known that the disease is not communicated by direct handling, but through the agency of the rat-flea; in the course of a laboratory examination there is always the danger of an infected fleabite.

By midnight he knew that his diagnosis was accurate. This was a case of Oriental plague, not in its most virulent form, but highly dangerous and a startling menace to London. If Magnum had been unscrupulous, he could have used his knowledge to "play the market" at Lloyds', and reaped a fortune in a few days. However, the thought was never allowed to penetrate "beyond the threshold" of consciousness. His position of consulting analyst involved moral obligations. As far as it rested with himself, the knowledge should be kept rigorously from the general public. His duty now was to trace the source of infection, communicate with the officers of health, and have the outbreak isolated and buried under an avalanche of germicides.

Where could plague have come from? The dogs had been quarantined for two months before being set free in England. Plague from the liner could have scarcely been conveyed by them. If The Tower House had been situated in the East End, near to the docks, one would have deduced rats from some Eastern vessel. But here in the quiet, sanitary West of London, ten miles removed from the dock region, miles even from the river, the problem seemed baffling in the extreme. Yet it must be solved before the outbreak could be subdued.

Anstruther and his terriers and his marriageable daughters and his distress at being bundled out of his own house receded into the background as a human factor. Magnum now considered the household as only so many possible carriers of infection. They, and Mr. Henry Gedge, must be watched for any sign of symptoms. It was too late to inoculate them.

Magnum's first move next morning was to inquire at the office of the Australian line for the health conditions on board the vessel which had conveyed Mr. Anstruther to England. She was now on her return voyage to Australia. Ignoring underlings, he forced his way to a responsible official, and at the point of the bayonet, metaphorically speaking, demanded explicit information.

The result was reassuring, yet from the point of view of the problem to be solved, disappointing. There was not the slightest evidence of mysterious illness on board the vessel or traced from her. A cipher cable to Perth confirmed that.

Magnum then approached the Medical Officer of Health and the Sewers Department. It might be possible that rats had migrated from East to West via the sewers. He made his questions guardedly, not revealing his very special reason for inquiring. Here again the information was reassuring. Plague in London was *nil*. The last case was eight months back. Nor were there any mysteriously dead rats reported from the sewers.

He returned from the City westwards in a tube train, puzzled and unwontedly indecisive. Clearly, his duty was to stamp out the source of infection without alarming the sensitive nerves of London and ruining the Coronation season. But it would not be sufficient to disinfect The Tower House and leave it at that. The whole of Wensleydale Gardens might have to be emptied of its inhabitants, perhaps a whole district, unless one knew positively that the source of the infection was in The Tower House alone. Ought he to proceed quietly and circumspectly, or ought he to rouse and alarm before the focus of mischief spread?

The tube train approached the station nearest to Wensleydale Gardens, where Magnum would alight. He was not accustomed to traveling on this particular line, one strand in the complex network of London's underground burrows, and a series of joltings and swayings of the carriages, well-known to the habitués of the trains and passed by them as a matter of course, roused his quick ire. The fools of engineers who had constructed the line had made an S-curve instead of going straight from station to station. What could be the reason? There were no strata of rocks to avoid, since the "London Clay" underlay the district for miles around. Straight tunneling was a perfectly simple matter. The waste labor and the traveling discomfort of a sharp S-curve annoyed his scientific mind.

As he walked to the station from Wensleydale Gardens, a curious coincidence impressed itself upon him. The curve of the railway line, a hundred feet or more below the surface, would just about avoid The Tower House and the grounds flanking it.

In the late afternoon, with the westering sun full upon it, the little plot of grass and trees looked singularly pretty and peaceful. It carried his mind to a thought of olden days, when the district around was a country village to which Corinthian bucks or Stuart roysterers might have tooled a tandem or a shay, and taken wine and kisses at a village inn.

In the midst of that unwontedly fanciful train of thought, Magnum suddenly stopped dead, reversed his steps, and hurried back to the tube station. He was carried swiftly Citywards, a hundred feet or more below the surface, past the S-curve which he now reckoned for certain was avoiding The Tower House. He no longer thought of the stupidity of the engineers who had constructed the line—the idea had dawned upon him that they might have abundant reason on their side. It might be that the S-curve was the clue to the whole problem of his difficult case.

Magnum made for the British Museum. The great reading-room under the dome was now closing to the general public, but by dint of special representations Magnum received permission from the Director to make his research.

This lay with ancient maps of London and books two hundred years old.

On the following day, a couple of workmen from the department of the Medical Officer of Health, regular workers and inoculated against plague, were inconspicuously unloading disinfectant and cement for the cellars of The Tower House. Magnum, smoking a rank curved briar, was superintending with an air of casualness elaborately intended to rouse no curiosity on the part of neighbors.

Mr. Anstruther and his daughter, a tall, capable, managing young lady, came to demand of Magnum when he proposed to allow them to return to their home.

He took them into the study, and closed the door and windows before answering.

Said he: "The house is insanitary."

"What do you mean exactly?" questioned Miss Anstruther. "Is it drains—typhoid—or what?"

"The sewerage system is completely out of date," evaded Magnum.

"Will it mean a big expense to put it right?" asked Mr. Anstruther.

"Very heavy expense, and a long job."

"That will fall on the landlord, I trust?"

"No."

"You mean I must pay for it myself?"

"Not if you follow my advice."

"Well, sir?"

"I consider that this house has been let to you under false pretenses. If you leave the whole affair in my hands, I undertake to get your lease canceled and compensation paid to you for the fixtures you've put in. You can then take another house and move your furniture there."

"But it would be most inconvenient—"

"There are no *buts!*" interrupted Magnum curtly. "Health considerations are priceless. I warn you not to live here under any circumstances. Leave the affair entirely to me, and I will get you out without monetary loss."

Father and daughter consulted together while Magnum left them to resume his superintendance of the workmen. Finally they agreed to follow his advice.

The last episode of the case took place in a little den of a City office, where a wizened little old man, owner of Wensleydale Gardens, found himself confronted by Magnum and the Medical Officer of Health.

"Mr. Anstruther's lease is to be canceled, and The Tower House is to remain unlet for the future," ordered the public official.

"Why?" blustered the landlord.

"You know very well why. For the same reason that the engineers of the tube railway avoided running their line underneath. To let sleeping dogs lie."

"But it happened two hundred and fifty years ago!"

"The germs are still there," interposed Magnum. "Two terriers have died in the house from plague, and a dead rat has been found. The rats must have got at the heap of skeletons buried in the triangle of ground alongside The Tower House."

The little old man crumpled up and complained pitiably: "You want me to lose all the money I've spent on the house!"

"The Crown will buy it from you at a valuation. But understand clearly that this is dependent on your keeping the matter entirely to yourself. It's Coronation year!"

To this day The Tower House remains empty. Passers-by some-times wonder why such a desirable residence does not find a tenant. They do not know that it is now Crown property, nor do they know that the pretty and peaceful plot of grass and trees alongside was a burial-pit for the victims of the Great Plague of London in 1665.

DEAD LEAVES

"If it were not for wills," rasped Magnum in his brusque, intolerant-of-stupidity manner, "you lawyers would be dining off cold mutton. There's more idiocy over wills than over anything else—except perhaps marriage."

"Marriage is all right," said young Stacey, who happened to be well suited.

"If this client of yours lost his will, he had only to sit down at a desk and write a copy of it. Perfectly simple."

"He did something equally simple. He 'phoned to us to prepare another copy. And that very same day, last Tuesday, while our duplicate was in the post, he slipped on a greasy street and . . . A motor-'bus. . . . It was ghastly."

Magnum pulled heavily at his pipe.

"Well?" said he. "How am I to help in this matter?"

"I'd like you to find the will," answered Stacey simply. "Take it for granted that we've ransacked his house and his office—searched for secret drawers, pulled up the flooring; and all that."

"Why pull up the flooring?"

"It was Mr. Williamson's own idea that he had hidden it in a state of somnambulism. He said so when he spoke to us over the 'phone. He was annoyed about it because he had just got engaged, and somnambulism would be awkward for a married man. . . . The will was a temporary one for the period of engagement, leaving mostly everything to his fiancée. I remember, when he was drafting

199

it with us, he said he had a presentiment he might die before marriage. Queer how those presentiments turn out true."

"Occasional coincidences. . . . But isn't it possible for you to swear to the accuracy of the duplicate will and the signing of the original?"

"It might be if the document were not disputed. You see he was going to marry this girl in absolute opposition to the feelings of his family—two married sisters and their children. They were very sore over the affair—taken it for granted he would remain a bachelor forever. Based the boys' careers on it."

"The world is chocked with selfishness," remarked Magnum sententiously. He added: "Why come to me? I'm not a clairvoyant."

"Mr. Williamson was a scientist. Therefore you might be able to gauge his thoughts and deduce his actions. That was my idea."

"You imagine that all we scientists share a common set of thoughts?" queried Magnum ironically.

"Frankly, we're at our wits' end. If *you* can't help us, I don't suppose anybody in London can."

It was a shrewd appeal to Magnum's very human vanity. Stacey was very anxious to enlist his help, and added another shrewd touch: "She's a charming girl. Charming! And it would be a real kindness to—"

"I'm impervious," interjected Magnum.

But he was not.

Mr. Theodore Williamson had been a lecturer at the Royal College of Science on the subject of zoo-geography. There was not a professorship in that very specialized and out-of-the-ordinary field of knowledge, nor had he heeded the higher post, since he had a very fair private income of his own. He had traveled all over the world in the pursuit of his specialty, comparing the fauna of various countries, deducing from their distribution the past configuration of land and sea on the earth's surface, and forming acquaintanceships in remote parts of the world.

At his house in Sussex Place, South Kensington—a trim little house in a well-to-do neighborhood, with a shady garden and an aviary which was his special pride—maps hung on the study wall showing the results of his researches, and there were many mementoes of foreign travel. His official office at the Royal College of Science was a plain, rather formal room, chiefly filled with books and specimens relative to his subject. It gave the impression that he used it only in an official and not in a proprietary way.

So much Magnum learnt as he went with the young lawyer on a tour of survey. It was abundantly evident that East, East and Stacey had fine-combed the house and the office in search of the missing will. Nor had they neglected the garden and the aviary.

An old reprobate of a parrot cocked a knowing eye at Magnum, as though it knew volumes it was unwilling to divulge.

"Was that parrot allowed out?" asked Magnum.

"I'll ask the housekeeper," said Stacey.

The quiet and dignified lady who had attended to Mr. Williamson's household answered yes. The parrot had been his master's particular pet, had accompanied him on travels abroad, and was often allowed to wander about.

"I'm thinking of the historic example of the Jackdaw of Rheims," said Magnum.

"Very possible," agreed the housekeeper.

"That would mean searching the whole neighborhood," commented Stacey without enthusiasm.

"But I have never known him to steal any papers," amended the housekeeper. "Only nuts. He is very fond of nuts."

The parrot chuckled as though he quite understood the conversation.

"Couldn't he be hypnotized and questioned?" asked Stacey, who had very vague notions as to the practicalities of science.

Magnum ignored this layman's futile suggestion and returned to the study of the dead man. He sat himself down in the chair at the desk, with a photograph of Mr. Williamson in front of him and a photograph of his fiancée, and examined them intently. Miss Deans was indeed a charming girl, not very young, perhaps twenty-six, with a somewhat idealistic and wistful expression. It might have proved a very happy marriage. Yet who could prophesy for certainty?

The portrait of Mr. Williamson showed a man of forty, florid, inclined to stoutness, with straggly mustaches. He looked humdrum, as many scientists do. Apart from their special knowledge, they are often unimpressive and dull. Would it have been a happy marriage? Or had Fate wisely stepped in and closured it?

It was an unusual train of thought for Magnum—ordinarily occupied with matters of the most matter-of-fact. He examined the photographs for such a long period that Stacey moved impatiently and clicked the stem-winder of his watch.

"Somnambulism?" asked Magnum, coming out of his reverie.

"So he said."

"Ask the housekeeper."

Stacey went to fetch her. She explained that she usually retired early to bed and slept soundly. Mr. Williamson had once asked her if she had heard him moving about the house in his sleep late at night. She had not. He said something vague about consulting a doctor.

"Had he any peculiarities?" asked Magnum.

"A great many," answered the housekeeper with truth tinged with charity towards the dead. "But not what one might term objectionable."

"Fussy? Domineering?"

"Well—" She hesitated. "He was very absent-minded. He would mislay things and then blame me for them."

"Did he blame you for the loss of the will?"

"No. At that time I was away in the country. My brother was very ill, and I had to be with him for a whole week."

"Who was in charge of the house?"

"There was only the cook-general."

"And she would have her evenings out?"

"Yes—every Sunday."

"Then it's possible that there might have been some visitor here on a Sunday evening quite unknown to yourself or the servant."

"I suppose it would be possible."

"And it's not you that uses scent?"

"Oh dear no!" The suggestion was quite out of keeping with her character.

Stacey sniffed as he heard this question, but his powers of scenting were nowhere so keen and refined as Magnum's, and he could detect nothing.

The scientist's eyes had been roving around the room during this cross-examination, and he now rose from the desk-chair and picked up a crinkled hairpin lying near the hearthrug.

The housekeeper examined it. "No—I always use a straight hairpin."

"Please ask the cook if it is hers."

She left the room and returned presently with the information that it did not belong to the cook.

"That will do for the present," said Magnum, and sat down again at the desk.

Stacey, who had become wearied by Magnum's long inaction, now blazed into excitement. "A visitor here! A woman! That looks queer. Mr. Williamson's two sisters—one of them might have come here, and seeing the will lying about. . . ." His suggestion needed no further elaboration.

"Yes. Or some one else," returned Magnum cryptically.

"Miss Deans? Of course that's possible. Very natural. But what reason could *she* have for making away with the will?"

"Or some one else," continued Magnum imperturbably.

Stacey did not relish this throwing out of vague surmises. He retorted: "You've suggested four different lines of inquiry. The parrot; Mr. Williamson's sisters; his fiancée; and now some vague unknown. You sit there and do nothing. Am I to go out and scour the whole neighborhood for a place where the parrot might have hidden the will; and then chase the three women in order to match hairpins?"

Magnum answered with somewhat provoking calmness: "You haven't the scientific mind. Listen to my principles of work. When an unknown substance is sent to my laboratory for analysis, I first of all have it examined in the routine way by my assistants. That corresponds to the search of this house and the office. If nothing results, I have to invent a special method of attack out of dozens of possible ways. I don't waste energies chasing clues one after another just as they happen to suggest themselves. I sit and think— perhaps for hours—until I've decided on the quickest method. I sit and think."

He suited the action to the word. Stacey subsided into a chair.

Magnum continued presently. "That crinkled hairpin is of a very ordinary kind. Scores of millions are made and sold. If we matched it, say, with the kind used by a sister of Mr. Williamson's, it would settle nothing. It merely tells us that some woman visited these rooms." He held the pin close to his nostrils. "She used a peculiar scent on a basis of ambergris. Not pure ambergris. You recognize that, of course?"

Stacey took the hairpin and sniffed at it energetically. "There's some sort of odor," he replied, "but I wouldn't go into the witness-box and swear to identity. It might be any sort of hair-perfume."

The scientist pursued: "We now search the desk for possible letters from some feminine correspondent."

"He wasn't that kind of a man," said Stacey. "The firm knew him for years."

"Scientists can be human—at times," answered Magnum sententiously. "Mr. Williamson was human enough to become engaged."

He delved into the many drawers of the desk and the filing cabinet. Letters from Miss Deans had a locked drawer to themselves. A sense of delicacy restrained Magnum from reading them, but he sniffed closely at them in order to detect a possible resemblance to the peculiar perfume of the hairpin. There were other feminine letters, amongst the crowds of papers, but clearly they were social invitations of the most formal and unsentimental character. Nor could he match the perfume amongst them. There was also a heated letter from one of the two married sisters, reproaching her brother bitterly for what she described as his "perfectly heartless conduct." That referred, of course, to his engagement.

Magnum studied the letter for a long time, and then put it aside.

"Well?" asked Stacey.

"We must search further."

He came upon a check-book, three parts used, and examined the stubs of the checks torn out.

"Self, five hundred pounds," commented Magnum. "And dated the day before his death. Was that money amongst his possessions?"

"No."

"Ah!"

"You think she found it here and took it as well as the will?" asked Stacey eagerly.

"For an ambitious young lawyer," answered Magnum, who believed in subduing the younger generation at convenient intervals, "you are singularly forgetful of vital details."

"Of course! A slip of the tongue!" caught up Stacey, annoyed with himself at forgetting that the check dated Monday could not have been cashed on the Sunday.

"Nor need it be assumed that she—this unknown—took the will." He waited for Stacey to trip over this deduction as well, but the young lawyer, though not seeing the point, prudently made no comment.

"We must go to the bank," continued Magnum, rising briskly.

At Mr. Williamson's bank, they learned that he had cashed his check for five hundred pounds on the Monday afternoon, and had taken the money in bank notes of tens and twenties. The numbers of the notes were furnished.

"Now the pass-book," requested Magnum.

This was also shown to them.

"Did Mr. Williamson give any reason for wanting to take out such a large sum?" asked Magnum. "I see that it overdrew his current account by some three hundred pounds."

"That is so," confirmed the bank manager. "He gave us a lien on some railway shares in order to cover the overdraft. He mentioned that he needed the money for scientific apparatus."

When they were outside the bank, Magnum observed, with some satisfaction at his own perspicuity: "That settles the matter!"

"What settles what?"

"The excuse. No man would need five hundred pounds *in cash* to pay for scientific apparatus. A check would have answered the purpose."

"And the next move?" answered Stacey.

Though they had discovered no letter or memorandum relative to the unknown woman, and the only evidence of her existence up to the present was the scented hairpin, Magnum did not lose confidence in his ability to trace her.

Back at the study, he searched afresh for some possible clue. After a tedious and fruitless examination of letters and odd papers, he turned to the large sheet of moss-green blotting-paper on which the ink-well and pens rested. The paper was old and covered with a bewildering criss-cross of dried impressions.

"Like a pot-pourri of hieroglyphics," commented Stacey, looking over his shoulder.

"There's always a way to read hieroglyphics," answered Magnum.

"In this case?"

"I shall photograph, to get a reversal, and stereoscopically, to get perspective—one impression standing above the other—and examine under the microscope."

They hailed a taxi and drove to his laboratory in Upper Thames Street. Many hours were spent in the photographing and the microscopical scrutiny. As each word or group of words was deciphered, Magnum wrote them down on paper. Finally he had a long list of names, addresses, fragments of correspondence. Many of them he could correlate with the social invitations and other letters found in the desk.

Stacey looking over the list, uttered a sudden exclamation: "That's queer! Highgate, N!"

"Why?"

"I didn't tell you that he was run over by the motor-'bus outside the Tube station at Archway Road, Highgate."

Magnum pounded the table in anger. "No, you wouldn't tell me a vital matter like that! You lead me to believe that he was run over in town, where he might have been for any one of a hundred reasons. Highgate—why on earth should he have been out there unless he had some very special reason? Great heavens, to keep a clue like that secret!"

"I'm sorry," said Stacey contritely.

Magnum turned the brass screws of the microscope to shift the negative to the requisite position. "I can just get the bottom half of the words Archway Road," he observed presently. "And as I remember, no one of his letters came from that neighborhood."

The scientist's memory for detail was prodigious. Out of all that mass of desk-papers glanced over, he had forgotten no single name or address.

"Any number?" asked Stacey.

"Too faint to decipher."

"Then we're in a *cul-de-sac*. Archway Road is a very long street."

"A *cul-de-sac*? Rubbish! Here's the list of the bank-note numbers—all in tens and twenties. No five-pound notes. Unusual, and therefore easy to trace. We inquire at the shops and banks in Highgate. Come along at once!"

It was dusk when they reached the northern suburb which hangs steeply over London. Banks were closed. But the shops around the Tube station, where trains and 'buses meet profusely, and trading is brisk, were full of life and movement.

Magnum took in mind a large drapery shop, a provision merchant's and a footwear retailer's as his first sources of enquiry. It happened that his second shot was successful. In the counting-house of the provision-store, a cashier recalled the recent changing of a twenty-pound note in payment of a small bill. As the note was an unusually large one, he had asked for it to be endorsed with name and address. Magnum passed over his list of numbers, and the cashier compared it with his books.

"Yes, that's right, sir. Here it is."

"Do you remember the endorsement?"

"It was an Archway Road address, I can't recall what number in the road exactly it was. But the name . . . let me think. . . . Williamson."

"Mr. Theodore Williamson?" asked Stacey eagerly.

"No, Mrs. Williamson," answered the cashier.

Magnum looked as though no secret in the world were hidden from him. He maintained that attitude for some moments while Stacey stared in surprise.

"Your delivery department might know the exact address," suggested Magnum.

"I'll make inquiries, sir."

Presently he returned with a number, and they left the shop to walk up the slope of Archway Road. The way led them past a medley of small shops to a row of villas where Apartment signs indicated the nature of the houses.

"Mrs. Williamson in?" asked Magnum of a slatternly maid.

"Yes, sir," answered the maid, who was not accustomed to the conventions of society where a servant always "will see if her mistress is at home."

"What's your names?" she asked crudely.

"Friends."

They were shown into a front sitting-room communicating by folding-doors with a rear bed-room. Half-packed boxes around the apartment indicated that the occupant was on the point of leaving. Magnum sniffed at the air, and nodded sagely to the lawyer.

The folding-doors parted.

Magnum and Stacey had not exchanged their expectations of what this "Mrs. Williamson" would be like, but silently they had framed a portrait of some rather bold, hard-featured woman, powdered, enameled, with penciled eyebrows. The reality gave them the shock of a sudden cold plunge.

She was small, graceful, exotic, and so dark-complexioned that there must assuredly be native blood in her. She was neither painted nor powdered, but the peculiar scent that had clung to the hairpin was wafted in with her entry.

"Please explain," she said, in a voice that was soft and liquid and unmistakably foreign in its accent.

"Mrs. Williamson?" asked Magnum formally. "The wife of Mr. Theodore Williamson?"

"Yes, I will not deny that. I promised him that I would go back and never see him again, but I did not promise—"

"Go back to where?" interrupted Magnum.

"Tahiti. And my ship will sail tomorrow."

"He is dead," said Magnum abruptly, and with a purpose.

"Dead? Dead!" Her eyes opened wide in horror. "I did not know. When . . . when was it?"

"Tuesday afternoon last. Crossing at the bottom of Archway Road. A motor-'bus—"

"He had just left me! I had promised him and he had left me!" She dropped into a chair, and her eyes were full of thought and memories. There were no tears, but only an overflowing memory of the past that had been between them.

"You were at his house in Sussex Place on the Sunday evening before last?"

"Yes," she answered mechanically.

"And you found a will lying on his desk?"

"No, no!" She roused into sudden hostility. "I did not do that. He put it in an envelope to me by mistake."

"A foolscap envelope?" questioned Stacey suspiciously. "Why should he use that one size?"

"He was sending back many things in that envelope, and he put in the will by mistake."

"Where is it?"

"I burnt it. I was very angry when I read it, and so I burnt it."

Stacey took up the word, since legal questions were involved. "If you were really his wife, that was a criminal thing to do."

"I *was* his wife!"—defiantly. "He married me in Tahiti. I came to England to find him."

"Burning the will would have the effect of leaving him intestate, with two-thirds of his estate devolving on you."

She did not grasp this legal point of view. "I do not want more. He gave me money, and that is sufficient. I promised to go back."

"You must stay," replied Stacey curtly, for the burning of a will was an action that horrified his legal mind. "You swear to that in court."

Magnum interrupted. "I think," said he, "that Miss Deans should be consulted first. If she knew the circumstances, she might not wish to be Mr. Williamson's legatee."

"You think that?"

"I do. Having seen her portrait"—his hand unconsciously edged towards his pocket—"I judge she would want to make her own decision."

Stacey looked at the scientist with a keen scrutiny that suddenly revealed to him a hidden side of Magnum.

"Well, I'm— This is a legal matter."

"The decision must be hers," said Magnum firmly. "We have raked up the dead leaves of the past. She may wish to bury them."

THE THREE HENRY CLARKS

Out of the Bridge of Sighs archway of Scotland Yard, one sunny May morning, came Detective-Inspector Callaghan and Magnum, scientific consultant. In the Yard of which the name stands for the grim and black side of life, the scene was homely and inclined to the comic. A stout chauffeur with a bibulous nose, endeavoring to pass the tests for a licensed taxi-driver, was cutting figures which sent the onlookers into cackles of cockney laughter. These spectators were mostly friends of Bill the examinee, or nondescript loafers. Even the sparrows seemed to be chirping impudent laughter at the desperate and perspiring earnestness of Bill.

Magnum and the detective paused for a moment to watch the scene. A man touched the scientist on the arm of his rough tweed suit, asking: "Is this Scotland Yard?"

"Yes. Entrance over there," answered Magnum without turning his head.

"Thank you."

The inquirer, a powerfully-built, middle-aged man with a somewhat mastiff-like pendulousness of cheek, moved on a few yards with a curiously uneven gait, then muttered aloud and leaned against the wall under the archway of the Bridge of Sighs.

"Early in the morning for that kind of thing," remarked the detective lightly.

The man roused himself and lurched onwards.

"That man's not drunk," replied Magnum, whose powers of scent were abnormally keen and constantly noting impressions without conscious effort. "There was no smell of drink. He may be ill. We'd better—"

His words were cut short. The man lurched violently and fell sideways to the pavement. They rushed to raise him and carry him indoors. Before a doctor could arrive, the man was dead.

Callaghan searched the pockets for cards or letters which would enable them to communicate with the relatives. He could only find a half-sheet of paper with the address, "17 Nell Gwynne Walk, Chelsea," and a plain visiting-card marked "Henry Clark, Esq." As he read it, he remarked:

"Queer coincidence! There was a Henry Clark died suddenly only yesterday."

"A very ordinary name. Who was the other man?"

"A commercial traveler. Fell down dead while booking a customer's order. Heart failure."

The keen-scented scientist bent down to sniff at the lips of the dead man. When he arose, his face was grave.

"There was a reason for this case of heart-failure," he said.

"Poison?"

"Yes. I'd better go with you to the Chelsea address."

Passing through the Yard where a disconsolate Bill was being told officially that his standard of chauffeuring was insufficient for the satisfaction of the Commissioner, they hailed a cab and gave the address of Nell Gwynne Walk.

They knocked at No. 17. "This is Mr. Henry Clark's house?" asked Callaghan of the maid who opened the door.

"What name, sir?"

"Henry Clark."

"No, sir, he doesn't live here."

"Perhaps I'm making a mistake over the number. He lives in this street, doesn't he?"

"I've never heard the name, sir."

"Ask your mistress if we can see her for a moment," ordered Callaghan, and passed his card.

A little old lady, very fluttered and frightened at the card's mention of Scotland Yard, received them in a drawing-room, which was almost an exhibition room for old china, lace fans and marquetry. It was impossible to doubt her word when she told them she knew nothing of a Mr. Henry Clark. The house had been hers for fifty years, and had never even been let to strangers for that period.

Puzzled at this unexpected development, the detective and Magnum proceeded to every house in the street with their inquiry. The result was the same—blank.

They drove back to Scotland Yard, and examined the clothing of the dead man for further clues. The only markings on the linen were those of the laundry.

Magnum looked at his watch. "I'm busy to-day. I'd better leave you to chase the laundries for the man's identity. Send the internal organs to my laboratory for investigation."

"Very good," agreed Callaghan.

At this moment a police clerk in uniform came in and saluted. He gave his message: "News by telephone of the death of a third Henry Clark, sir."

"Good God!" the exclamation came involuntarily from the lips of the detective. Hardened as he was to every kind of crime, yet there was horror in his voice. He looked at Magnum for the explanation of this extraordinary occurrence.

"It may be another form of the 'Jack the Ripper' mania," suggested the scientist. "Some man with the insane idea of vengeance against the name of Clark."

"All the other Clarks in England may be in danger!"

"Quick action wanted."

"Will you help us, sir?"

"Decidedly." Magnum, in spite of his money-making proclivities, had a strong sense of public duty.

He 'phoned to Meredith, his chief assistant at the Upper Thames Street laboratories, giving him directions to carry out in regard to the ordinary analytical work on hand; and then hurried with

Callaghan to the address given in the news communicated to Scotland Yard. It took them to a working-man's district in South London—to a little shop that offered a service of tool-grinding. Tragedy in miniature met them. A wife and four children had had their bread-winner taken from them. He had died in his shop, behind the counter where he received or passed tools to his workmen customers.

His widow, broken-hearted, could offer no facts whatever to throw light on the tragedy. The existence of the household had been ordinary and commonplace in the extreme. She knew of no enemy who could go to the length of such a revenge. He had been a good husband and a good father except when he was worried about business matters.

Magnum surreptitiously passed a five-pound note into her hand to tide her over current expenses, but his thoughts were concentrated on this extraordinary mystery. Why and how? Callaghan searched the shop, household and the person of the dead man—Magnum watching—and no clue came to light.

Again they hurried into a taxi and made across London to the address of the first victim, the commercial traveler. He had been a single man living in lodgings in Camden Town, and according to his landlady's report, his reputation was that of a "good sort," making friends easily and earning fair commissions. She knew little of his life out-of-doors, and could offer no facts that seemed relevant.

"Blind alleys!" commented the detective. "We must get back to the man who dropped dead at the Yard."

But Magnum suggested a very necessary first move. They must spread a public warning of this danger. Every man of the name of Clark must be on his guard. The quickest and surest way was to communicate with the Central News Agency, which would disseminate the warning through every important newspaper in the United Kingdom. Callaghan agreed.

The tracing of the address of the second Henry Clark was tedious, commonplace detective work of a routine character, leading through laundries and tailoring establishments. Magnum, with his impatient temperament, left this part to Callaghan and betook himself to his laboratories to superintend the analysis for poison.

The results came almost simultaneously: the nature of the poison from Magnum's end, and an address in Chelsea once again from Callaghan's end. They communicated over the telephone.

"The case looks more complicated than ever," said Callaghan. "The man lived all alone in a small house, with only a scrub-woman to clean up for him occasionally."

"The more complicated the case, the easier to find the solution."

Callaghan's voice expressed distinct annoyance as he answered: "Perhaps you can explain why he carried a false address in his pocket, and how he got poisoned!"

"Search the house for papers."

"Mr. Magnum, we're not altogether fools in the service! The house has been fine-combed from cellar to attic."

"Then I'd better come myself and get the clue!" snapped Magnum.

He reached the Chelsea address in the frame of mind that it only needed the eye of a scientist to clear up the mystery within half an hour. The house was one of a terrace of two-storied houses, quiet and respectable, tenanted by people of limited means. It was within half a mile of Nell Gwynne Walk, where the chase had first led them.

The house was very sketchily furnished, only a kitchen and two rooms being in occupation. The rest had curtains and blinds and nothing else.

A waste-paper basket first held Magnum's attention. But it contained only a few circular letters, of the kind that are showered upon householders in sheaves by enterprising tradesmen and manufacturers. They offered him player-pianos, free samples of shaving-soap, shirts at bargain prices, and some marvelous new remedy for falling hair.

He then turned to the desk, and produced a revolver from one of the drawers.

"The man was afraid of somebody," said Magnum.

"I already know that, sir."

"He came to Scotland Yard to get protection."

"Of course."

"Then that's the track to follow."

"One moment. He was poisoned on the way. How?"

"Cyanide."

"Potassium cyanide acts at once, doesn't it?"

"Potassium cyanide, in sufficient quantity, is fatal inside of a few minutes."

"Then he must have swallowed it within a few minutes of our seeing him at the Yard."

Magnum deliberately seated himself. "Continue," said he with a tinge of irony in his voice.

"We can eliminate suicide. Then he must have taken the stuff without knowing it. Now you've searched through his clothes, I understand—did you find where the poison came from?"

"No."

"Any theory?"

"No."

"Well, that's your end, sir, and you don't seem to have settled a very simple problem," continued Callaghan with some complacence. "Within a few minutes of reaching the Yard, the man swallows prussic acid—"

Magnum interrupted: "He didn't."

"I thought you told me cyanide."

"A derivative," said Magnum calmly. "It would take an hour or two to have effect. Shall we go back to the main track?"

Callaghan, disconcerted, made no answer; and the scientist rose to resume his search, remarking: "He came to Scotland Yard, as I said, to get protection. He knew, or suspected, that his life was in danger. The matter that's immediate is to get on the track of the criminal, and stop any further crime."

The desk contained letter-paper, envelopes and the usual appurtenances of correspondence, but it was singularly free of "papers" in the ordinary sense of the word. Magnum examined the desk minutely for a secret drawer—the dead man's trunk and portmanteau, his wardrobe, the mattress of his bed, the chimneys, the underneath of the carpets, the overneath of the kitchen dresser.

Callaghan had regained some of his normal self-esteem during the scientist's fruitless search. "Well, sir," he asked, "have you found anything that I overlooked?"

"Henry Clark was an assumed name," answered Magnum, evading this inconvenient question.

"I know that already."

They were interrupted by a brisk postman's *tat-tat* at the front door. Going to the hall, they found on the mat underneath the letter-slit of the door a small package addressed to Henry Clark, Esq. The detective took it up eagerly, tore it open, and then laughed at his disappointment.

"Only a sample of shaving-soap," said he, and read out a letter wrapped round it—a "form letter" in imitation typewriting of a too obvious shamness—"'Dear Sir: In response to your esteemed inquiry, we have much pleasure in enclosing a sample stick of our—'"

He tossed it contemptuously into the waste-paper basket, and resumed: "What's to be the next move? We've drawn blank here, haven't we?"

"There might be some fresh news at headquarters. Will you 'phone and inquire?"

Callaghan went out to the nearest telephone box, made his inquiry, found that no fresh news had come in, and returned to the house of mystery. But Magnum was no longer there. He had left behind a brief penciled message: "Have found the clue. It is in this room. Communicate with you later."

Magnum had gone to the South London district where the unfortunate tool-grinder had carried on his trade. Here he obtained permission to search the rough, untidy business desk of the dead man, with such a speedy result that within five minutes he was out again and driving to a city address in Fenchurch Street.

A third-floor set of offices carried the sign: "Vincent Colnaghi and Co., Manufacturers' Agents." Inside a rather dingy public office he found a clerk and a flapper languidly typing addresses onto an interminable pile of envelopes. Around the walls were samples of the goods traded in by the firm, which ranged from Venetian beads and fancy blown glass to Roman shawls and Turin vermouth. The firm apparently acted as middleman for any sort of product which offered itself.

"Take my card to Mr. Colnaghi," said Magnum authoritatively.

"Not in, sir."

"This is important. Mr. Colnaghi will want to see me at once."

"He hasn't been here to-day, sir."

"Then take my card to the office manager."

The clerk showed Magnum into an inner room, furnished with more pretension to comfort, where a limp and highly undistinguished manager and a fluffy, pinkish typist seemed to be engaged on nothing in particular—unless flirtation.

"What can I do for you, sir?" asked the manager in shop-worn phrase.

"I have important business with Mr. Colnaghi. Where can I find him?"

The impressiveness of Magnum's tone commanded a truthful answer: "I really don't know."

"Don't know!" snapped Magnum.

"The fact is, sir, Mr. Colnaghi went away for a week-end, and we've heard nothing from him since."

The general air of do-nothing about the offices backed up this statement.

The scientist tried another line of inquiry: "You're selling shaving-soap by means of a free-sample scheme?"

The limp manager brisked up at this. "Yes. An excellent article— quite a new product. Perfumed slightly with oil of bergamot. Would you like to try a sample?"

"I would like," said Magnum authoritatively, "to make an examination of your offices on behalf of Scotland Yard."

Incredulity first, indignant protest later, greeted his cool request. But Magnum insisted on the manager's 'phoning to the

Commissioner of Police and verifying authority. Eventually he obtained his own way—a habit with him—and amidst the hushed awe of the staff, began to examine methodically the recent correspondence of the firm—in desks, in waste-paper baskets and even in the dust-bin. When he had gathered and pocketed some cast-away papers, Magnum shot out an abrupt question:

"Have you any business relationship with 17 Nell Gwynne Walk, Chelsea?"

"Why, that's Mr. Colnaghi's address."

"Not his house?"

"No—where he's been staying. An aunt of his. But I must ask you, sir, to tell me the meaning of all this questioning. It's most irregular, and if it hadn't been that the Commissioner of Police—"

Magnum interrupted brusquely: "I dare say you're innocent in the matter. But if you don't want to find yourself in the dock, stop that sample-soap-scheme immediately. Pack letters, envelopes, soap and everything pertaining to it inside cases, and seal them up."

The limp manager went white, and his weak hands trembled. "Yes, sir, certainly. It shall be done at once," he yammered.

An hour or so later, the scientist had made the requisite laboratory tests of his material, and sure now of his ground, 'phoned to Callaghan at Scotland Yard.

"I'm driving to 17 Nell Gwynne Walk, Chelsea," he remarked. "Meet me there."

"What have you found?" asked the detective with ill-concealed eagerness.

"The criminal and the method."

"Surely not that old lady?"

"A nephew of hers is the man we want."

"Ah, then you needn't trouble to go to Chelsea. Meet me at Liverpool Station, instead. Burnham platform."

"Why?" demanded Magnum.

"Six-ten train," added the detective, and pleased at having been able for once to surprise his collaborator, he rang off before any further questioning could be made.

Magnum, unwontedly disconcerted, obeyed the request. Securing a first-class compartment to themselves in the train for Burnham-on-Crouch, they exchanged the result of their day's work. It appeared that the old lady of Nell Gwynne Walk had visited Scotland Yard to make inquiries about her nephew, who had gone to Burnham for a week-end yachting holiday and had failed to return. She had become very anxious as to his whereabouts.

"He had his reasons for wanting to keep out of the way," answered Magnum, and showed an envelope he had rescued from the dust-bin of the Fenchurch Street building.

It was an envelope printed with the address of V. Colnaghi and Co., with an embossed penny stamp, and postmarked Chelsea. Callaghan examined it concentratedly, but could not grasp its relation to the case.

"Very simple," explained Magnum. "This was a return envelope enclosed with the circular about the shaving-soap. Henry Clark received it, like many others, and applied for a free sample. He licked the flap to close the envelope, and then—"

"Good God! Cyanide in the gum of the flap."

"Exactly. I've stopped any further sending out of the envelopes, by way of precaution, though the rest of them I have examined seem to be harmless. All we have to do now is to find Colnaghi."

"But why should he have sent poison to those other two unfortunate men?"

"We'll know when we find him," returned Magnum confidently.

Burnham is a tiny port on the estuary of the Crouch, subsistent on the East Coast yachtsmen who make it headquarters for their seafaring. It is easy to trace anyone in Burnham, and they quickly found track of Colnaghi. He had arrived alone on the Saturday afternoon, and had taken his bag on board his five-ton yacht, which he was accustomed to sail alone. Giving out his intention to cruise up the coast to Yarmouth and the Broads, he had left Burnham on the ebb tide. Since then, nothing had been heard of him. Better ask at Yarmouth, suggested the chronic loungers on the waterfront.

Callaghan wired to the most likely ports of call on the East Coast—Clacton, Harwich, Felixstowe, Aldeburgh and Yarmouth—and they retired to the "White Hart" to await replies.

The answers from the several harbor-masters were disconcerting. Colnaghi's yacht had not been heard of.

"Skipped over to the Continent," whispered the detective to Magnum. "Fair weather ever since Saturday. We'd better cable the Dutch and Belgian ports."

They left the inn in order to do so.

It was late at night now—but clear with the starlight and the riding-lights from the tangle of small yachts and oyster-dredgers in harbor. As they were turning away from the waterfront, a clatter of excitement recalled them. Up the steps of the waterfront men were bearing the burden of a dark shape, and in some magical way the news had spread until a small crowd were clotting around the bearers.

It was the body of Vincent Colnaghi. An oyster boat had found it drifting amongst the shallows of Foulness. Of his yacht there had been no trace, but to the experienced seamen of Burnham, the story was plain enough. In the night-time, perhaps on the Saturday night, perhaps on the Sunday, he had run aground on a sandbank on a falling tide. The East Coast is a maze of such shallows.

Doubtless he had tried to get his boat afloat—had signaled for help, had caught no friendly eye. Gradually, on the ebbing tide, his yacht had been sucked under, silently, ruthlessly. He had fastened a life-belt around him, and attempted to swim to shore. When they found the body, it was kept afloat by the life-belt—drifting for days to and fro in the waters of the North Sea.

Part of the solution to that strange problem was found by Magnum and Callaghan in the letters in his pocket-book; part of it they had to deduce.

There could be little doubt of the feud between Colnaghi and the man who had passed under the name of Henry Clark. It had been a case of the far-reaching hand of the Camorra. In fear of his life, Colnaghi must have made some violent threat which sent Clark to seek the protection of Scotland Yard—or perhaps, merely to seek useful information.

But Colnaghi's blow had landed first. He had prepared the poisoned envelopes for his enemy. No doubt he had intended to send one or more when he reached his office on the Monday.

Though he had not returned to Fenchurch Street, an office-girl, ignorant of their deadly nature, had sent the envelopes to the next names on her mailing-list. Four Henry Clarks had received them. One envelope had luckily been thrown away by the receiver; in the other three cases they had spread death to those who licked the poisoned flaps. The unfortunate tool-grinder and the commercial traveler, in no way concerned with the feud, had fallen victims.

It was strange to think that Vincent Colnaghi, floating a corpse on the North Sea, had yet been the posthumous instrument of death to his enemy.

CLEANSING FIRE

Sometimes a private wrong may be a public right. The individual has to suffer for the good of the many. Nice questions of ethics arise for which no rule-and-rote solution is ready.

These philosophic reflections are not set down idly. They have a direct bearing on one of the strangest cases in which Magnum, scientific consultant, became involved. In legal prose it was entitled, "Morkel versus the Imperial Fire, Life and Accident Insurance Co., Ltd." The consultant had been retained on behalf of the Company to resist the payment of an insurance policy, and to prove that the plaintiff in person, or by deputy, or by fraudulent connivance, had been guilty of participation in the burning down of his own factory.

On the external face of it, the case was a simple one. This is how it was spread before Magnum by Sir George Herries, a director on the board of the Imperial.

"We want to make an example of this man Morkel," said Sir George in his best Kitchener manner. A newspaper writer had once referred to him with casual irresponsibility as "the Kitchener of the insurance world," and Sir George had ever since cultivated a cavalry mustache and a decisive military manner.

He pursued: "An example, which will put the fear of God into these shifty-eyed little manufacturers. When one of these petty swindlers finds his business on the down-grade, he insures it far beyond its real value, installs safety appliances to reduce his premium to a minimum, arranges that they become out of order, and has the place set fire to while he himself is ostensibly on a holiday. Nothing is more difficult to prove than arson, and they know it. We want absolute scientific proof to lay before the Court. That is why I have called on your services. First, we resist this civil action; and then we see to it that the Crown institutes criminal proceedings."

Magnum, business man as well as scientist, underlined one of Sir George's statements. "As you say, nothing is more difficult to prove than arson. The case will probably take up a large amount of my time. My fee will have to be based on the eventual expenditure of time."

Some discussion ensued, but Magnum, very conscious of his own value, adopted a take-it-or-leave-it attitude which usually effected his purpose.

Sir George, a trifle subdued, resumed the thread of his explanation: "We have taken particular care to have the ruins of the factory left exactly in *statu quo*. A squad of our own watchmen have been guarding the place day and night. I don't trust the police force in a case such as this."

"Why not?"

"It is always possible that a constable might be bribed to turn a blind eye towards a man who entered the ruins to remove evidence of arson."

"Very improbable with the London force," commented Magnum.

"No man is beyond bribery," answered Sir George sententiously. "However, the point is that your investigation will deal with virgin material."

"Your own assessors?" interjected Magnum pointedly.

"Of course, our own assessors have made their routine examination."

"And found no evidence of arson?"

"Not definitely, or I should not have called on your services."

"Nor disturbed the remains of the building?"

"No." Sir George cleared his throat preparatory to delivering a dictum. "I have no doubt whatever in my own mind that it was arson," he stated, pressing a desk-bell which would summon his secretary. "Your work is to prove it."

Magnum did not openly contradict this statement, but he did not agree with it. Though he was retained by the Company at a substantial monetary figure, he did not regard himself in their service as a special pleader. His duty as a consulting analyst was much broader. It stood towards the public in general. His work was to lay bare technical *facts* which might otherwise be hidden. Hence his rather judicial, impersonal attitude towards the case.

The secretary, appearing to the summons of the bell, was directed to accompany Magnum and assist him with any detailed information he might need. This young fellow, by name Channing, was pleasantly blond in appearance and frankly unaffected in manner. Magnum liked him at sight.

"What's your opinion of the case?" asked the consultant as they drove eastward in a taxi.

"Mine? It doesn't count, you know," replied the young fellow unassumingly.

"Still—"

"Well, strictly between ourselves, sir, I think Sir George is barking up the wrong tree."

"Why?"

"One thing and another. In the first place, our chaps could find no evidence of criminal intent. I mean, nothing to clinch the point definitely. And then again, this man Morkel looks to me rather genuine. You should have heard him in the office when the Company refused to meet his claim! No actor—I don't care who he is, not even Beerbohm Tree—could have put up such a show. Of course, he has that foreign hysterical way with him—"

"Nationality?" interjected Magnum.

"Russian. Fur business, you know. Imported skins from Siberia and places like that, and had them furriered in his factory by a crowd of his fellow-countrymen. I gather that he treated his workpeople pretty decently."

"And his financial standing?"

"That's always a difficult matter to be sure about. You can't rely much on the reports of the trade agencies."

Magnum nodded agreement. He knew well that in England the organization of confidential trade reports is very unsatisfactory.

The taxi wormed through the rabbit-warren of the City of London, and emerged into the comparative breadth and open-airedness of the Whitechapel Road. The names on the shop-fronts began to epitomize Central and Eastern Europe; the odors drifting from side-streets added the testimony of a Slavic menu. It was from this neighborhood that Morkel had recruited his work-people.

Left to himself, the chauffeur of the taxi would have floundered rather hopelessly in the by-ways of the unknown East End, but guided by Channing, he brought them eventually to the heap of ruins which stood for Morkel's factory. It was like a battlefield skeleton in the sightlessness of its windows and the starkness of its broken limbs. What little woodwork that was left standing was charred and twisted like used kindling-wood. The stock of pelts and the accessories of the furrier's trade were now dust upon the winds. And where the fire had spared, the water from the hoses had rounded off the work of destruction.

The thought which first registered itself amongst Magnum's impressions was the completeness of the ruination. He had seen gutted premises before this, but none so utterly eviscerated. That fact was peculiar and noteworthy, because the building was, apparently, an easy target for a fire brigade. The factory was detached—yards and outbuildings separated it from factory neighbors on either side, while to the rear it looked over a canal, across which hose-jets might have easily been thrown, Nor was it a large and complex building, being merely two-storied and squarely squat on its own little plot of ground.

"The fire brigade must have been very late in arriving on the scene," was Magnum's first comment to Channing.

"Yes, sir, and that's a point of mystery. Morkel had a patent safety device with a wire leading to the fire station. I don't know if you've seen the system—the idea is that when the temperature of a room rises over a certain point, it makes an electrical connection and rings a bell at the brigade station."

"Yes, yes," nodded Magnum.

"The system failed to work."

"Show me the lead."

Channing directed a path amongst the ruins to which an electric wire protruded from a pipe in the basement, its free end melted to an unsightly blob of metal. "Sir George believes that the wire was cut inside the building."

"Was that the only precaution against fire in the factory?"

"No." Channing went into technical details of the equipment. "It was so complete that it made a substantial reduction on Morkel's fire premium."

"Then he seems to have spent a good amount on protecting himself against fire."

"Yes and no. The firm that makes these appliances puts them in on the installment system. 'Pay us out of your premium reductions,' is what they advertise."

"Of course there was a night watchman as well?"

"Yes. He was asleep—drunk asleep—when the fire broke out. It ought to be a criminal offense, but it seems that one can't punish the man except by dismissing him."

"Nationality?"

"A Pole, and a senseless kind of animal."

Magnum trod cautiously among the rubble of ruin, searching with his eyes, sniffing with his ultra-keen sense of smell, reconstructing with his brain, from tiny indications, the course the fire must have pursued. The search was long and minute, yet it had led to no conclusions of value. Ruination had been so complete that it was small wonder the Company officials could find no definite proof of arson. The scientist began to experience an uncomfortable feeling—proceeding upwards from the region of the midriff—that his own efforts would be equally fruitless, and that the case would merely damage his carefully-built reputation for uncanny shrewdness.

However, he gave no hint of that to Channing. On the contrary, he staged a little comedy of portentous frowns followed by sage noddings of the head, hinting of puzzles solved by master-strokes of deduction. He took samples of rubble for analysis from a dozen places, though he had small hopes of proving the presence of incendiary material. He even went to the length of lying flat on the ground in places, as though nosing out something imperceptible to grosser senses.

The search, in brief, was inconclusive. The one solid fact was the fire. Whether it had been started by accident, or whether it was the result of deliberate intent, was still in doubt. Leaving his samples of rubble for analysis in his laboratories by Meredith, his right-hand man and a genius in patience, the scientist proceeded to interview Morkel, the focus of the case.

Morkel was not difficult of access. Full of his grievance, he was eager to seize an opportunity of denouncing the rascally insurance company. Broad-built, black-bearded, with the high cheek-bones and the narrow eyes of his Russian origin, but sufficiently Englished by his long residence in London to have a plentiful command of the English language, he poured out a stream of explanation, vituperation, angry threats. It was as Channing had phrased it: "No actor could have put in such a show." Magnum came to the judicial conclusion that the fur importer was probably genuine.

Another possibility remained: that the fire had been started by some one with a grievance against Morkel—one of his work-people, perhaps—some man sweated to desperation, some woman insulted and revengeful. Channing had said that "he treated his work-people pretty decently," but this must be submitted to analysis. The motley crowd of hands drawn from the slums of Whitechapel ought to be interviewed discreetly. A mere shadow of a hint might serve as a clue, and with that foundation to work upon, Magnum should be able to build up a complete and scientifically impressive report for the benefit of the Company and the welfare of his own reputation.

Accordingly he made his way to Bow Street to obtain the services of a police-court interpreter familiar with the Slavic languages.

In the very doorway he met with Callaghan, detective-inspector and a collaborator in many former cases. Magnum mentioned that he was seeking an interpreter.

"Very good, sir. I'll get you the right man."

"Some one who knows Russian, Polish, Czech and those kinds of languages."

Callaghan, by way of polite interest more than active curiosity, inquired the purpose.

"In connection with a fire insurance down in Whitechapel," responded Magnum. "I'm retained to investigate for the Imperial versus Morkel."

Callaghan suddenly stopped dead short. He seemed to be wrestling with qualms of conscience. Then he whispered earnestly: "I would strongly advise you, sir, not to touch that case."

"Why? Good heavens, why?" demanded an astounded Magnum.

"I suppose I oughtn't to have said even that," murmured Callaghan, obviously ill at ease and divided between the claims of friendship and the obligations of official position. "But I mustn't tell you anything further. My advice to you is, leave the case to the Company's own assessors."

To escape further questioning, he hurried off.

Magnum was more than astonished: he was highly annoyed.

To be kept in the dark and treated as a child! He, Magnum! It was approaching an outrage. Interested in the case up to now as a professional problem, he became keenly anxious to solve the mystery from the angle of personal pride and self-esteem.

Deliberately brushing aside the inspector's advice, which might be well-meant but was certainly humiliating, Magnum engaged his interpreter and proceeded to Whitechapel to cross-examine Morkel's work-people.

It was tedious work and very trying to Magnum's irascible temper. These aliens were highly suspicious of him. A man who might have stolen a chicken in Poland in his childhood's days regarded Magnum as some mysterious emissary of Nemesis. Even when suspicion was overcome, there resulted an irrelevant jumble of family histories, misfortunes, illnesses, deaths—a welter of "hard-luck stories" garnished with appeals for help.

A whole two days of investigation left Magnum some ten pounds poorer in charitable contributions, and apparently no nearer to his object. There was no vindictive feeling towards Morkel as an employer of labor, so far as the interpreter could gather. Their general feeling was regret that the factory had been burnt down, throwing them out of immediate employment.

Returning to his laboratories in decided ill-humor, Magnum was greeted with an unexpected piece of news from Meredith, who had been toiling over the analysis of the samples of rubble.

"There are traces of petrol—combustion products," explained young Meredith with his mild and modest sureness, and gave technical details.

Magnum's ill-humor had vanished. "That's fine!" he exclaimed. "You never fail me. But you look tired to death." The boy had in fact been working almost continuously for forty-eight hours. "Come along with me to dinner and a music-hall!"

Traces of petrol were an indication that the factory had been deliberately set on fire. That fitted in with Sir George Herries' view. The completeness of the ruin, the late call on the fire brigade, the drunken watchman—all these pointed to arson rather than accident.

Who could be the criminal?

The watchman?

Magnum had not hitherto been able to find the man at his East End home. While he sat snugly in a stall at the music-hall performance, he resolved to visit the suspect to-morrow, and force a confession out of him, by threats if necessary.

But why the warning from Callaghan? It seemed entirely out of the picture.

Had Callaghan's hint to do with Magnum's personal safety? An Anarchist focus, dangerous to meddle with?

The scientist had a fair share of healthy prudence, but he resolved to go on with his investigation.

The next morning he again enlisted the services of the interpreter, and proceeded in a taxi to the Whitechapel slum-street where Worschek, the watchman, made his one-room sketch of a home. Inquiry brought out from the landlady that the Pole was still away.

"Where?" demanded Magnum.

"In the country somewhere. They do not know where," translated the interpreter.

"Why is he away?"

"They say that he has a sick sister. They think that he has gone to see her."

"Offer them a sovereign for the address."

But even the lure of the gold coin failed to secure the information. It seemed as if the landlady and the neighbors genuinely did not know. Magnum was turning away disgustedly when a postman came striding briskly down the alley, and made for the door of the dwelling-house. With a sudden inspiration, Magnum waited for him and coolly asked: "Anything for Worschek?"

"Yes, sir, one letter."

"That's right," said Magnum authoritatively, and reached out his hand for the letter. "Worschek asked me to take it for him."

The postman very properly hesitated, surveying the letter in his bundle and Magnum alternately. Then he refused the request, on the plea of postal regulations, and learning from the landlady that the Pole was away, went on with his rounds.

But Magnum had had opportunities to see the writing on the envelope. It was in firm, educated English lettering; the stamp was English, and in the top corner was a printed address of the sender: "St. Mary's Home, Claythorpe."

At a venture, Magnum repaired to a newspaper shop, looked up Claythorpe in a railway guide, found it to be a village in Essex, and ordered his taxi to drive there. He might have taken a train, but that would have meant some delay. A taxi was likely to be quicker.

The drive, after the clearing of frowsy Whitechapel and the pinched, huddled suburbs of the northeast, led pleasantly through glades of Epping Forest and into peaceful rural flats, orderly with centuries of patient nurture, as sleekly comfortable as the grazing cattle. They passed through villages which no self-centered Londoner has ever heard of—communities that pursue the simple round of seed-time and harvest, marrying and begetting, remote from the complexities of a great city, a world apart.

Claythorpe, reached at lunch-time, might have been a thousand miles from London. At its one inn, they refreshed themselves and Magnum inquired the way to St. Mary's Home. A curious look of suspicion met the inquiry. The direction was given reluctantly.

Two miles on, the taxi stopped at a gate in a stone wall fencing in an estate of some size. A porter guarded the entrance. It suggested an asylum. Magnum asked to see the superintendent, mentioning the name of Worschek. A long wait ensued. The solid gate hid any view of what might be inside. At length the superintendent himself came to parley—a middle-aged man of authority with the stamp of the doctor about him.

Magnum, offering importantly the credential of his card, asked to see the watchman.

The reply was that Worschek was not there.

"If I could see his sister?" suggested Magnum.

"Impossible," answered the superintendent politely, but decisively.

"Will she be confined here for long?" fished Magnum.

"What is the object of these questions?"

The scientist had perforce to explain. His words were listened to impassively. "I am sorry that I cannot help you," was the answer, given with a hint of impatience.

"Is this an asylum for the insane?" demanded Magnum.

"No,"—curtly. "I will now bid you good-day." And the superintendent retired inside his solid gate.

Magnum returned to the village and began further questioning—which was met with rather sullen protestations of ignorance. When he pressed his inquiries, the attitude of Claythorpe became distinctly hostile. The mystery of it all pricked him to internal anger. What lay behind that stone wall? What bearing had it on the case of Morkel versus the Imperial? By now he felt very sure that some connection there must be. He resolved to send the interpreter and the taxi back to town and to wait himself around the neighborhood until the evening. Then he would find means to climb the stone wall and solve at least one aspect of this series of mysteries. If a criminal lunatic were confined inside—which was his thought at present—then there would open out a reasonable solution of the fire at Morkel's factory.

The September evening came early with a fine mist drifting over from seawards. That made a big help in this rather burglarious enterprise. Magnum had bought a rope in another village and a convenient iron hook from a blacksmith. He knotted the rope into a simple form of a scaling ladder, and covered by the mist, made an easy entrance into the walled grounds.

It was park-land inside, trees and sward. Presently he came to a small house of a mid-Victorian pattern—stucco front, pillared portico, low windows like well-fed paunches. It suggested a middle-class country residence rather than an asylum. Magnum made his way round the side. Through a lighted window, unprotected by blind, he noted what was clearly a laboratory adapted for pathological work—microscopes, staining reagents, some anatomical specimens in spirit.

Magnum moved on until he had made a complete round of the house. It was very silent. There were no sounds of lunatic patients. Indeed, the house was so small that it was difficult to imagine that many patients could be accommodated there.

Perhaps there were other buildings inside the grounds. The scientist, walking pussy-footed, made onwards in the rear of the house. And presently he came to a wooden fence with a row of huts behind it looming vaguely through the fine, clinging mist. It was a simple matter to scale the fence. Magnum came to the end hut. A light showed inside. The window was only curtained with thin muslin.

Magnum approached cautiously and peeped inside.

One look was sufficient to send him recoiling in sheer horror, almost gasping for breath.

What he had seen inside was something he had never suspected in England, something that few men outside the circles of public health officials would ever dream of. It was a reality that threw a flood of light on this mystery of the drunken watchman, his invalid sister, the hostile silence of Claythorpe, the fire at Morkel's factory, the strange warning given by Callaghan.

Magnum retreated hastily, scaled the wall to the wholesome outside air with a feeling of intense relief, made his way to a railway station, and so back to London.

He was very sure now as to who would know the inner history of Morkel's fire. That man would be the Chief Officer of Health for London.

It was a curious interview on the following day. The Officer of Health knew Magnum, knew that he was to be trusted with information of public import, and under a seal of secrecy confirmed the suspicions which had crowded upon the scientist.

"It was the third case which had arisen in Morkel's factory," said the Officer of Health gravely. "There was only one course open to us in the public interest—to burn down the place. Whether infection had come from the imported furs or was inherent in the building is a point one could not determine. We had to make a clean sweep of it. Now as a matter of public policy, we could not condemn the building openly. We got the watchman out of the way— poor devil, thinking of his sister, he was willing enough to fall in with orders—and we then set the place thoroughly on fire. The brigade was warned not to hurry. They were merely to isolate the fire and prevent its spreading to any neighboring building. As you have seen, we thoroughly gutted the place."

Magnum considered thoughtfully. "It is a curious point of ethics as to whom the loss should fall on," he commented.

"Yes. One could scarcely say that it was Morkel's fault. The loss ought not to be his. On the other hand, for reasons of public policy, we must not let it be known that we took action. On the whole, the department feels that the loss must be borne by the insurance company. They are a rich company, and can easily afford it. Now, if you will be kind enough to withdraw from the case, that is what will happen."

"Yes," admitted Magnum, "public interests are paramount."

And with the horror deep in his mind of that isolated leper colony at Claythorpe, unknown to the general public, unsuspected by them, he reported to Sir George Herries that in his opinion the fire at Morkel's factory was of accidental origin—cause unknown.

RED HERRINGS

Sedately along Piccadilly plodded an open dray bearing large, fat glass jars carefully packed in straw and held together by chains. They were carboys of some chemical liquid. The wagon hugged the pavement, in obedience to police regulations for slow traffic, while faster vehicles impatiently sped past it.

"In any civilised city," remarked Magnum, who hated anything unsystematic, "no dray would be allowed on a main artery of traffic between eight a.m. and midnight."

He was seated in the sunny bay window of a Piccadilly club. The hour was ten o'clock. It was unusual for Magnum to be at the club, especially of a morning, because he had no political convictions, and despised idle lounging. However, he had a reason for this occasion. The man he was with was high in political circles, and Magnum wanted certain War Office consultant business. In a select and exclusive London club one is not supposed to discuss, solicit, or even breathe the word "business," but it *is* done, indirectly. Impecunious scions of the aristocracy sell motor-cars, yachts, shares, pictures and antiques inside the sacred precincts of old-established clubs. Magnum had no scruples about infringing etiquette. Moreover, he belonged to two political clubs, one Liberal and one Conservative, and used them according to which ever party happened to be in power.

The politician, following the offending dray with his eyes, observed:

"That's curious! Look."

Magnum looked. A most extraordinary phenomenon was taking place in gay Piccadilly. The passers-by were *weeping*. Hand-
kerchiefs fluttered. Tears were streaming. No royal funeral could
have produced such a lachrymose effect as the passage of that lum-
bering dray.

"Whatever is the matter?" thought the politician aloud, and
opened the window to help solve the mystery.

He quickly closed it, and reached for his own handkerchief.

"Formaldehyde," explained Magnum. "Popularly called formalin. Carboy leaking. Disgraceful! Call this a civilised city!"

All along Piccadilly, the trail of the chipping formalin was
smearing the air with pungent vapor, invisible but highly odorous
and tear-compelling. No concentrated essence of onion could have
produced a more ridiculous effect. A whole streetful of people were
weeping, and since they were a good-humored London crowd, also
laughing.

Eventually a policeman on point duty ordered the dray to "Clear
out," up some side street. He did not take the driver's name and
address, because the accident was unprecedented and outside the
realm of existing police regulations. He said "Clear out," and returned to his exacting point duties.

Half-an-hour later Magnum left the club and walked along
Piccadilly. The odour of the formalin still lingered. He covered his
nostrils with a handkerchief, screwed his eyes tight, and impatiently hailed a taxi.

> HOME
> SECRETARY
> VANISHES!

yelled the placards of a late edition of a halfpenny evening paper.

Magnum had no confidence in newspapers, especially halfpenny evening papers. He resisted the appeal of four contents bills,

until a fifth, issued by a sober penny paper and announcing "Alleged Disappearance of Mr. Holsworthy," induced him to buy and read as he went to his motor-launch. This was his customary mode of conveyance between his Upper Thames Street laboratories and his home out by Plumstead Marshes.

The newspaper dealt with the affair soberly and guardedly. The Home Secretary had left his house in South Audley Street, Mayfair, that morning in a taxicab at ten o'clock, on his way to Whitehall. He had not arrived at his offices, and nothing had since been heard of him. There was a rumor of a Suffragette kidnapping. Mr. Holsworthy was to be starved until death or votes for women arrived. The newspaper rather smiled at these rumors, pointing out the absurdity of a public man's disappearance in broad daylight, in well-policed, law-abiding London. No doubt there was some simple explanation, which would be found in the morning papers. They disapproved of sensationalism, and were insistent on the word "alleged."

The cautiousness of the newspaper affected Magnum more than any glaring headlines or emphatic statements would have done. His temperament was to oppose other people's opinions. He disbelieved the "alleged," and as his launch cut swiftly down the Thames he reflected on the possibilities of the story being genuine.

To the north side of the river he saw docks, warehouses, and a huge area of underground cellars; to the south side were factories, some in being, some closed and deserted, awaiting fresh tenants. What finer area could be imagined for the concealment of a kidnapped man? And then, one dark night, he could be slipped on board a barge or tramp steamer, and smuggled out of the country. Even in dusk, as at this moment, the procedure was quite possible.

"Stop!" hailed a voice. A police-launch shot out of the gloom.

Magnum threw off power and reversed with a flail of spray and soap-suds of angry water.

"What's this?" he demanded.

"Orders to search," answered a sergeant briefly.

"Looking for Mr. Holsworthy?" deduced Magnum.

"That's it, sir."

They quickly satisfied themselves that no concealed body was aboard, and backed away with apologies. Magnum proceeded homewards. His thoughts underwent a radical change. If the police were combing the docks and water-front, it was five to one that the quarry were elsewhere. He began to place himself in the shoes of the kidnappers, and imagine how a thoroughly successful affair could be carried out. They had taken their man in broad daylight, and apparently in the heart of London traffic. That argued unusual cleverness and resourcefulness. Therefore it might be assumed that they would pass over the obvious hiding-place of the docks and the deserted factories, and the obvious smuggling out by river. Something newer, more up-to-date, more criminally scientific must be looked for.

On the following day the newspapers were full of the story. They had interviewed the head of a militant organization, who was enjoying a week's holiday from prison in a house overlooking Buckingham Palace. The leader disclaimed any credit for the affair. She admitted that she would have liked to have planned the kidnapping. She would have greatly enjoyed starving or forcibly-feeding Mr. Holsworthy. Unfortunately, however, she had not thought of the plan.

The evening papers seized on the humorous side of the situation. Mr. Holsworthy was fair game for jesting. He was titular head of the police forces, and yet he had allowed himself to be taken in a ridiculously easy fashion.

But the next day public feeling, as expressed in print, changed. A telephonic demand for ransom had been made. Fifty thousand pounds was the sum asked, to be increased by ten thousand pounds a day. The police seemed to be helpless. They could find no trace of Mr. Holsworthy from the moment he left South Audley Street at ten a.m. in the taxi. He had vanished utterly. Every taxi-driver in London had been questioned and cross-examined. Every one of them was ready to account for his movements on the morning in question, going from one cab rank to another.

As the days went on, and the telephonic demands for ransom increased, the nation became roused to indignation. They might afford to sacrifice Mr. Holsworthy, but they were not going to pay blackmail. It would be establishing a precedent, of all things most to be avoided.

Then came a letter from the unfortunate man, reproduced by photography in the newspapers. He begged pitifully that the ransom should be paid, otherwise he would inevitably die. If the public could only realize the daring and resourcefulness of those who had kidnapped him!

A newspaper asked tentatively in what form the ransom was demanded. Quickly came the reply, through the too-convenient telephone. It was not wanted in banknotes, in sovereigns, or in bullion. It was wanted in radium. A hundred thousand pounds' worth of radium could be comfortably carried in a waistcoat pocket, and could be disposed of in driblets in any part of the civilised world.

The plan was essentially up-to-date. And, further, the manner in which it was to be delivered was carefully specified. The material was to be guaranteed as to amount and radio-activity by two public analysts mentioned by name. Magnum was one of them. He was at once indignant at the coolness of the kidnappers and flattered by the advertisement they were giving him.

Again, the certified radium was to be attached to four carrier pigeons which were forwarded to the office of a leading newspaper, and were to be released in a flock of fifty others. The innocent little birds suggested no clue to identity. Thousands of people trained and raced pigeons in England, France, and Belgium. And being released with a flock of others, the movements of the birds would be practically untraceable. It was a plan the ingenuity of which took one's breath away.

Three more days were given for decision. After that, Mr. Holsworthy would be quietly disposed of, and they would proceed to kidnap some other prominent man.

The point which most roused indignation was the demand for the ransom to be paid in radium. Gold could be spared, or bank-notes, but radium would have to be collected from hospitals and medical men. Sufferers must be sacrificed for the releasing of the Cabinet Minister. It was atrocious! Even if Mr. Holsworthy's family managed to collect the necessary hundred thousand pounds from friends and sympathizers, public opinion would actively resent the payment in precious radium.

There seemed nothing to be done but to sacrifice Mr. Holsworthy.

Magnum went to call at the house of mourning in South Audley Street. Relations and friends were there, despondent and despairing. He was gladly ushered into the family council. They clutched at any straw of hope.

"I have been investigating this case on my own account," announced Magnum.

"If you can only get him back," cried the red-eyed Mrs. Holsworthy eagerly, "there is nothing that we wouldn't do to repay you!"

"I don't need monetary payment," said Magnum. He was looking, indeed, to the War Office consultant business for his recompense. That would be sure to follow.

"What have you discovered?"

"Merely a direction for inquiry, as yet. But I have hopes. Now let me suggest this—you will announce through the newspapers that you cannot pay the ransom in radium. On the other hand, you are ready to pay double the amount in gold. You will send the sum to a deserted island—or to any place they like to name. You pledge your honor not to attempt to watch that gold. In other words, you must let those men think they are winning easily."

The family council would have agreed to any proposal. Immediately they set to work to draft out an announcement for the newspapers, the medium of communication between the blackmailers and the blackmailed.

When Magnum stated that he had been "investigating," that somewhat overshot the facts. He had been pondering very deeply over the peculiar problem; had kept himself in touch with the activities of Scotland Yard (where he was *persona grata* through his assistance in former cases); and had thought out a new line of attack.

This he now proceeded to put into action, and his first move was to compile from directories a list of London firms handling formaldehyde in bulk; to telephone for appointments, and to call on them in rotation. He wanted to trace a consignment of that chemical lorried through Piccadilly on the morning when the Home Secretary had disappeared with such magic swiftness and ease.

Since Magnum's name and status were well known to dealers in chemical products, he had no difficulty in obtaining the information he asked for. Formaldehyde is not an article of popular consumption in its pure state. The form in which it is retailed to the public, for the annihilation of flies and other objectionable insects, is a forty per cent. solution in water. A carboy of concentrated formaldehyde would only be sold to manufacturers in very specialized lines, and its sale and conveyance would be easily traceable.

After some elimination of obviously genuine purchases about the date in question, Magnum unearthed the fact that three carboys of acids, one of ammonia, and one of formaldehyde, had been sold to a man who sent his own wagon to cart them away. He had stated that he needed them for some industrial research work in aniline dyes, and since he offered spot cash payment, the firm had not troubled to verify his status or ask for trade references. They had sold him the chemicals, and there the matter had ended. What became of them afterwards was not their affair. Yes, they had certainly read in the newspapers an amusing paragraph about the leakage of a carboy of pungent chemical in Piccadilly. They had expected that the purchaser would have sent for another carboy to replace it. However, he had not done so. Perhaps he had bought it elsewhere.

"And now," said Magnum to the head of the firm, "I want a description of the man who ordered and the driver who carted it away. A close description."

"Any special reason for asking, Mr. Magnum?"

"A very special reason. In fact, if your employees can give me sufficiently accurate portraits, here's a fiver to distribute amongst them."

He passed over a banknote, which the business man placed smilingly in a box marked "Staff Christmas Fund," and answered:

"We'll do all we can for you." How few people can describe human beings! How few people observe and register observations! The staff could tell nothing about the driver of the dray except that he looked a driver and spoke with a hoarse voice. Of the man who had ordered and paid for the chemicals, the summary of several defective memories was that: he was tall and looked "a gentleman." He either had a dark moustache or he didn't have a moustache—opinions differed. He had a rather prominent nose, aquiline. He wore a dark suit of some kind.

But one bright little office-girl did manage to convey an impression. She said: "He looked like a straight line."

"How?" asked Magnum, delighted to find someone with a sense of description.

"He parted his hair in the middle, sir, and it came down on his forehead in the middle—"

"A little bald towards the temples?"

"Yes, sir. And then the line went down over his nose and chin."

"Pointed chin?"

"Yes, sir. And then the line went down his tie and chest."

"Pigeon-chested?"

"Not quite that, sir, but he looked to me just like a straight line."

"How would you describe myself?" asked the consultant, to test her accuracy of description.

"All reddish bristles," answered the girl promptly.

Magnum laughed at the truthful portrait, patted her on the shoulder, and turned to the head of the firm.

"This girl will be a fine little business woman some day," he said. "Keep an eye on her."

He proceeded to Scotland Yard, and interviewed Detective-Inspector Callaghan, with whom he had collaborated on many former cases.

"I have a description of the man who arranged for the kidnapping of Holsworthy," announced Magnum, and repeated the details given him by the observant office-girl.

Callaghan ran over a mental portrait-gallery for some moments.

"That sounds like Charlie de Vinne, who ran a *chemi* den we raided last year," he said. "There's a touch of Mephistopheles about him. He looks like a straight line, as you say."

"Where does he live? What does he do now?"

Callaghan conferred with other officials of the department. The impression was that he lived by racecourse punting, or perhaps amateur bookmaking. He had not come in contact with the law since the raiding of his Belgravia *chemin-de-fer* resort, and on that occasion he had been let off with a fine. He would probably be found around Piccadilly or Leicester Square.

"Find him at once," suggested Magnum. "Trace him home. But for Heaven's sake don't let him suspect he's being shadowed."

"Trust us for that," returned the detective.

Magnum went home. Shadowing was not in his line. He awaited developments.

They came speedily. Mr. Charlie de Vinne had been recognized in a certain bar, engaged on the quite lawful business of discussing winners. He had been followed to other sporting resorts, and finally home to his chambers. They were situated above an aristocratic cigar-shop in Piccadilly, and were on the-top, the fourth floor.

"The intervening floors?" asked Magnum.

"All chambers. 'Piccadilly Johnnies' live in those parts."

"The kind of people who wake up about midday and get out of bed about two," commented Magnum. "I'll see the chambers for myself."

"If your suspicion is right," warned the detective, "you'd better be very careful. Charlie de Vinne is not a man I should care to tackle myself without a revolver and a police whistle."

"If I'm not back within two hours, you'll know where to find me."

But Magnum had no intention of foolhardiness. He merely wished to examine the lay-out of the building. He found the usual narrow side-entrance, marked Cadogan Chambers; and inside the hall, an automatic lift, the kind one works oneself by pressing a button. The porter was not visible. He lived with his wife in a cubby-hole of a basement, and was available on ringing.

Magnum rang for him and asked: "Any chambers to let here?"

"Third floor. Furnished. Thirty guineas a month, sir."

"Show me over."

The flats at Cadogan Chambers were ridiculously small. Magnum complained of it.

"Look at the locality!" retorted the porter. "Thirty guineas a month is really dirt cheap."

"Haven't you anything larger on the top floor?"

"No, sir; the top floor's occupied. It's a double flat."

"Who lives there?"

"Mr. de Vinne and Mr. Bellingham."

Magnum grumbled a little further, but agreed to take the vacant flat and move in at once. He offered the thirty guineas in cash, and references, and received a key in return. At Cadogan Chambers they were not particular about the status of tenants so long as they paid in advance.

Late that same night, the third-floor flat held Magnum, Callaghan, and several police officers in the dress of ordinary citizens. The scientist had also brought a couple of large portmanteaus, which he proceeded to unpack. The one held chemicals for raising fire and abundant smoke; the other held fire-extinguishers. They watched at the keyhole of the door until both de Vinne and Bellingham and a man who looked like a valet were inside the top flat. They waited a further two hours to allow slumber to settle down upon the chambers.

Then they proceeded to clear all the furniture and carpets out of one room, and raise an alarm of fire. For a scientist, it was a simple matter to create an abundance of smoke and steam without much danger of actual conflagration. Leaving one man to handle the extinguishers, Magnum and the police officers rushed out on the landing in night-attire and shouted "Fire" at the tops of their voices.

The sleeping chambers roused like an ant-hill. Men and women scurried out of rooms and down to the hall, clutching jewel-cases, pet dogs and other valuables. Magnum himself pounded at the door of de Vinne's flat, yelling "Fire! Fire!"

The maneuver answered perfectly. The pyjama-clad de Vinne and his partner and the man who looked like a valet all came out, scared and half-asleep, and completely at a disadvantage. Before they realized what was happening, they were in the custody of the police. Magnum strode into the empty top flat, scoured around, threw open the door of a box-room, and found the Home Secretary trussed and gagged and looking remarkably like a stoutish, ruffled hen.

"Don't kill me!" implored Mr. Holsworthy through the muffle of his gag.

Magnum ripped the bonds with a stout knife.

"What are you going to do to me?" cowered the Home Secretary. He had been scared out of his senses by the events of the past week of terror.

"Put you at the head of the police force again," answered Magnum, with more than a tinge of irony.

"It was extremely neat, extremely simple," explained Magnum to the home circle at South Audley Street, at the romantic hour of four o'clock in the morning.

"The gang ran a leaking carboy of formaldehyde along Piccadilly," he went on. "That had a four-fold purpose. The first was to cause Mr. Holsworthy to pull up the windows of his taxi. Then the chauffeur stopped, and Mr. Holsworthy called to him through the speaking-tube to go on. On that, the chauffeur discharged concentrated ammonia through the tube full into your husband's face. The tube was arranged for it. You will note that they didn't use chloroform. They were too up-to-date for that. Chloroform acts slowly. A man would have time and senses to call out and raise an alarm. But ammonia, concentrated, paralyses instantly. It suffocates. The chauffeur drove on, and at the entrance to Cadogan Chambers de Vinne and Bellingham were waiting to open the taxi-door and carry the unconscious Mr. Holsworthy inside.

"Second reason for the formaldehyde: to have a whole streetful of people bathing their eyes and entirely concerned with their own troubles.

"Third reason: to overpower the smell of the ammonia.

"Fourth reason: to combine chemically with the ammonia vapor inside the taxi and so remove the traces of it. The chauffeur drove his empty cab about for a little to clear it, and then returned to a Piccadilly cab-rank. It was the safest place for him. The smell of the formaldehyde persisted for at least half-an-hour. No other smell could live against it.

"Who would have thought of searching for a kidnapped man in the heart of the busiest street in London? Who would have thought of searching for that taxi right in Piccadilly?"

Magnum pursued the monologue to which the circle was listening in awed silence: "There was only one contingency they failed to guard against."

"And that was—"

"Myself," answered the scientist, with entire complacency.

COACHWHIP PUBLICATIONS

COACHWHIPBOOKS.COM

LOUIS F. BOOTH

THE BANK VAULT MYSTERY

BROKERS' END

ISBN 978-1-61646-332-5

DETECTIVES 2

The Chronicles of Addington Peace
B. Fletcher Robinson

Luther Trant, Psychological Detective
Edwin Balmer & William B. MacHarg

ISBN 978-1-61646-097-6

COACHWHIP PUBLICATIONS

COACHWHIPBOOKS.COM

DETECTIVES
2

ASTRO, THE MASTER OF MYSTERIES
GELETT BURGESS

DR. XAVIER WYCHERLEY, THE MIND-READER
MAX RITTENBERG

ISBN 978-1-61646-103-4

MURDER

IN A WALLED TOWN

KATHERINE WOODS

ISBN 978-1-61646-326-7

COACHWHIP PUBLICATIONS

COACHWHIPBOOKS.COM

ANITA BOUTELL

DEATH BRINGS
A STORKE

CRADLED
IN FEAR

ISBN 978-1-61646-334-2

www.ingramcontent.com/pod-product-compliance
Lightning Source LLC
Chambersburg PA
CBHW020550020726
47494CB00006B/2006